ASHER'S SHOT

Acclaim for *Asher's Fault*, book one of The Asher Trilogy

ALA Foreword finalist for YA Book of the Year

IWPA and NFPW first-place winner of Young Adult Creative Fiction

"The search for identity and a place in life is never simple, and Wheeler strikes just the right balance in this debut, respecting loss and challenge while giving readers hope for a better tomorrow."
—Kenneth Kidd, Professor and Chair of English at the University of Florida, and Associate Director of the Center for Children's Literature & Culture

"*Asher's Fault* gives voice to the internal struggle of a young gay man whose isolation takes him to a place of self-doubt until he discovers through a camera lens that everything is not as it appears. What Elizabeth Wheeler achieves in *Asher's Shot* is the through-line of hope, which gives Asher—via the lens of his camera and the lens of those who know better—an assurance that God loves everyone, no matter what."—Rev. Lois McCullen Parr, Broadway United Methodist Church, Chicago and Co-Founder of Chicago LGBT Asylum Support Program

By the Author

Asher's Fault

Asher's Shot

Visit us at www.boldstrokesbooks.com

Asher's Shot

by

Elizabeth Wheeler

A Division of Bold Strokes Books

2014

This Trade Paperback Original Is Published By
Bold Strokes Books, Inc.
P.O. Box 249
Valley Falls, NY 12185

First Edition: December 2014

CREDITS
EDITORS: LYNDA SANDOVAL AND RUTH STERNGLANTZ
PRODUCTION DESIGN:
COVER DESIGN BY SHERI (GRAPHICARTIST2020@HOTMAIL.COM)

Acknowledgments

With gratitude to my family, friends, students, colleagues, and mentors for supporting my writing, along with my countless other passions. I'm overwhelmed by the response from critics, librarians, and teachers who have endorsed and recommended Asher's story, but my heart is with the readers with whom Asher has resonated. You are why I write. Continue to seek your truth.

Thank you to Reja Jager, Patricia Roth, Vicki Hill, and Mary Wheeler for affirming Asher's journey, and the McCoy family's Canon A-1 for the ability to see through Asher's lens. Also, my eternal thanks to Lynda Sandoval, Ruth Sternglantz, and the glorious BSB team for the opportunity to share this story.

For knowing exactly what to do when a manuscript disappears, I am grateful to Matthew. For editing alongside me, I am indebted to Dewey. For loving me through everything, I thank Ross.

Lastly, thank you, Ophie, for reminding me to ask for help when needed, and Lois Parr at Broadway United Methodist Church for her faith in an all-knowing and loving God.

Dedicated to the shots we miss and all the reasons why.

CHAPTER ONE

I never intended for Mom to see the photograph. After all, some secrets are bigger than others. Like when *you* know your mom had an affair with your best friend's dad, but *she* doesn't know you know. Or when you discover your little brother is only your half brother. But none of it matters—Dad left, my brother's dead, and Levi and I know the truth, so the only person left to get hurt was Mom. She'd done her best to keep her secrets, which just goes to show how weird secrets are. While Mom was hiding what she did from me, I hid what I knew from her. Like if either one of us said it out loud, we'd shatter to pieces. We're already plenty broken.

I didn't want Mom to see the photograph our batty old neighbor, Pearl, had taken seven years ago of Levi and me in our backyard. In the background of the photo, anyone could see the evidence: Levi's dad and my mom sitting close, leaning in, Mom's hand on his arm. Everything clicked in place. And one visit to Levi's house with the photo confirmed it—Levi's dad had already told *him* the truth.

It explained everything—Dad leaving, Mom crying, even Levi fighting—and I thought about showing her the photograph just to see what she'd do. But I knew exactly what she would do. If she broke into a million pieces, it would be my fault. Instead we acted like life was normal, or as normal as it can be when everyone leaves or dies.

That's why I was surprised when Mom announced we wouldn't be celebrating Thanksgiving at home.

"Seriously? A homeless shelter?" I asked as I rinsed a dinner plate and handed it to her.

She dried the plate and stacked it in the cabinet. "Asher, I can't stand the idea of making a turkey here."

I understood that. This would be our first Thanksgiving without Travis, but she hadn't faced a single holiday at home without him. Mom had scheduled herself to work on Halloween to avoid that holiday, while I'd been left at home alone to dodge the trick-or-treaters. What did she know about suffering through holidays?

"So volunteering at a homeless shelter is supposed to make us feel better," I said.

"Helping other people. Yes."

I raised my eyebrows. I didn't have anything against helping people. We did it all the time in youth group.

"So we can feel good about ourselves," I said. "So we can see how bad things are for them."

"When you put it that way, it sounds awful."

"But that's why," I said as I turned off the faucet.

Mom threw the towel onto the counter. "I'm sorry if helping others is so offensive to you."

Great. She stood still for a moment, and then picked up and smoothed out the towel. She carefully folded it into thirds and neatly tucked it over the oven-door handle. As she left the kitchen, I pictured Thanksgiving here—the turkey, sausage stuffing, and mashed potatoes. Last year had been tough. Dad's empty place had been hard enough to swallow. I tried to picture this year with two empty places at the table, just Mom and me sitting there without Travis excavating tunnels in his mashed potatoes.

I followed her out to the living room where she'd curled up on the couch. She had just reached for the grieving book John from church had brought to her.

"Mom."

She laid the book in her lap and turned an impatient gaze to me. "What."

"It's fine. It's a good idea."

She shook her head and started flipping through the pages of the book. "Don't placate me," she muttered.

"I'm not."

The book fell into her lap again as Mom turned her head to me. "Why do you do that?"

"What?"

"Question everything I do. Everything I say," she said.

I couldn't help it; the photograph of Mom with Levi's dad sprung into my mind. I pursed my lips.

Mom waited for me to say something, but I stayed silent. Finally she turned her attention back to the book. I went to my bedroom.

As I entered, I glanced at the wall above my bed where the black-and-white photograph of the twisted pine tree hung. It was from the first roll I'd ever taken with my Minolta camera. I kept the ruined camera on the shelf inside my closet, sort of like the ashes of my dead brother sat in Mom's closet. I had two other cameras now: a digital my dad and stepmom bought me (which shows you how little they know about me—I don't do digital), and a cool Canon my neighbor, Pearl, let me use (although if I broke it, she'd put a bullet in me). Neither compared to the Minolta, but the Canon came close. It's not possible to just replace something that matters so much, so I'd honored the Minolta by retiring my use of black-and-white film after it broke. Instead I switched to color film with the Canon.

That wasn't the only change. I used to only take photographs of inanimate objects—stuff I observed around me, like Mom's keys in the freezer, Travis's footprint in a fire-ant hill, and the numbers peeling off Pearl's mailbox. But when Travis was alive, he'd asked me to take his picture, and I'd refused. I'd tried to fix it by taking a photo of his hands folded across his chest in the casket, but it got me thinking. I still couldn't bring myself to take photos of people posing for the camera, but I did take photographs of people. They just didn't realize they were being photographed.

I reached into my book bag and pulled out the picture, the one with my mom and Levi's dad in the background. I hadn't taken this one. My neighbor, Pearl, took it years ago. In the foreground, Levi and I played. In the background, my mom is leaning into Levi's dad. Oblivious. If she'd known the photo was being taken, she would have guarded her expression. She would never have sat so close to him. Instead it was obvious to anyone looking at the photo that something was going on between my mom and Levi's dad. Which explained everything.

Travis's dark hair and eyes, his bulldog nature (so much like Levi), Dad's leaving, Garrett—*I can't think about Garrett, push it down*—everything.

I didn't want to hate my mom. I didn't mean to. I tried to understand. But the only shot we had at happiness meant I had to keep her secret.

❖

Levi shifted gears, and the Jeep lurched. I grabbed the strap above the door and braced myself against the console. He was driving with one foot—his other one was still messed up from our encounter.

He yelled over the wind, "Why don't you just tell her you're going to your dad's?"

I imagined my mom's reaction—the hyperventilating, the nervous breakdown. "Yeah, that's a great idea."

"What?"

"I don't mind volunteering!" I hollered.

"Man, that sucks!"

I smiled. It was sixty-five degrees—a perfect November morning in Florida—and a blow-off day since we had the homecoming game tonight. Levi had taken the top off his Jeep Wrangler. When he'd initially called and asked me if I needed a ride to school, I'd hesitated. I thought he might want to assault me for screwing up his leg. Now I figured it had something to do with our sharing a brother. We'd only talked about Travis once, but right after that Levi offered me rides to school. It beat the bus.

"Are you going to your uncle's?" I asked as we pulled off the main road into a residential street.

Levi decreased the speed. "Hell, yes."

"So your mom's not cooking a turkey at your house?"

"I don't know what she's doing, but I'm going to my uncle's."

Levi's uncle, an accountant, usually hosted Thanksgiving because Levi's senile grandma lived with them. It was easier to drag everyone there than to haul the old lady. I couldn't believe she was still alive—she had to be in her nineties. Every year, they pulled the *this could be her last one* card. She drank scotch and took her oxygen off to smoke her cigarettes. Back in fifth grade, I'd gone with his family to his uncle's for the holiday. His grandma kept calling me Thomas and reminding me about the time this happened and that happened. I nodded politely, which Levi found hilarious. I hadn't been back since.

Levi loved Thanksgiving. Everyone in his extended family brought their specialty—homemade key-lime and pecan pie, deep-fried and traditional roasted turkey, sweet potato casserole loaded with brown sugar and marshmallow—and he just showed up and ate. Last year, Levi's mom decided to host Thanksgiving dinner herself. I'd heard all about the dry turkey, the lousy store-bought pie, and the crappy healthy veggies from Levi.

"It took me two hours to clean the damn dishes," he said. "At my uncle's, the women clean up. Like it should be."

"Don't let Jennifer hear you talking like that."

"Hey, I dragged my ass to that musical of hers. I can talk however I want."

Godspell. "Yeah, how was that anyway?"

Levi shrugged. "She wore this coconut-bra thing. That was hot."

"What did you think of the show?"

"Come on, Ash. You know theater stuff isn't really my thing."

He pulled into the school parking lot and nodded at Josh, one of the guys on the football team with him. Josh nodded back, like they shared a secret society nod.

"You probably would have liked it. They were at this beach. And Jesus was the lifeguard or something," he said.

Garrett.

"So"—I cleared my throat—"how did Garrett do?" I'd already heard he was amazing, but I wanted to see what Levi thought.

"The kid can sing," Levi said, which is high praise from him seeing as how Levi rarely compliments anyone.

He shot me a look, and I felt my face grow warm. I'd told him where I'd been when Travis died. He knew I'd been with Garrett, but not like everyone thought. Still, he didn't *know.*

"It's not really my thing, Asher," he said as he parked the Jeep.

On my way to first hour, I spotted purplish-haired Kayla taking down a poster of *Godspell.* I'd hoped they were going to get around to that. A couple of idiots had defaced posters the week before the show.

"Hey," I said.

Kayla put the poster on top of a tall stack. "You want one?" she asked.

I shook my head. "I wasn't in it."

She shrugged. "You were supposed to be."

Initially I'd been cast as ensemble, but I'd decided to do crew instead. Then my mom grounded me, and I'd had to bail on the whole production. I thought Kayla, the assistant director, was going to throttle me, but she hadn't.

It didn't feel right, getting a poster when I hadn't really earned it, but Kayla rolled it up and shoved it into my book bag before I could react.

"There. One less I've got to carry to the Dumpster. You want to come with?"

"Sure."

We walked together down the hall and out the back door where she hid to smoke cigarettes during lunch.

"So you're riding with Levi. I guess cracking his leg got you some respect."

Before I'd figured out the connection with Travis, Levi and I'd exchanged a few whacks at my bus stop. I sort of messed his leg up a bit, and the only person other than Levi and me who knew the truth was Kayla.

"We worked it out," I said.

"Guys are so weird. You get over things fast. Girls…not so much."

"Haven't worked things out with Jennifer?" I guessed.

"What's to work out?"

Jennifer and Kayla had been best friends until high school. Jennifer thought the distance was because she'd made cheerleading and Kayla hadn't. She honestly thought Kayla's jealousy had turned her goth. I knew the truth, and it didn't have anything to do with Jennifer.

"You know she's seeing Levi," I said.

"I heard something about that. Maybe she'll lighten up a bit," she said as she tossed the stack of posters into the Dumpster. Kayla brushed her hands off and faced me. "She could have been yours."

I didn't know what to say. Sure, Jennifer had been interested in me, I guess. We'd groped a bit in the backseat of my mom's car Halloween night. I should have felt flattered—a cheerleader. But she wanted to talk about Travis and her dead grandmother.

"Levi really likes her," I said. "He's been after her forever."

"Right. Is that why you guys are chummy now? You finally backed off the girl he likes?"

I hadn't even thought of that.

"Kind of ruthless to go after a girl your best friend likes," Kayla said.

"I didn't go after Jennifer."

"So what, you aren't into the cheerleader types?"

I dug my hands into my pockets. What was I supposed to say? The only time I'd kissed Jennifer, she'd been wearing sticky black lipstick and a studded black collar. Everything about it had been awkward.

"I don't know that I have a type."

Kayla turned and looked out toward the parking lot. Trucks and cars lined the rows. A few students meandered across the black asphalt to the sidewalk. The lot was almost full. I spotted Garrett's sister's blue car.

"Types," she said. "We like to pretend like we don't have types, don't we? It's what we're supposed to say. Makes us sound so open-minded. Like we can choose who we like." Kayla kicked at an empty Styrofoam cup with her combat boots. "Like my brain would ever have chosen Josh," she said. "What a load of crap."

I heard the faint sound of the first bell. "I still need to go to my locker."

"Right."

We started moving back toward the school. I watched Kayla in my peripheral vision. She crossed her arms protectively across her body.

"He can't hurt you anymore," I said.

"He doesn't even know he did."

I stopped walking. "Wait." I lowered my voice even though no one else was around. "You didn't tell him when you—you know."

Kayla wrapped an arm around mine and pulled me toward the school. "I told you, Asher. Aside from the clinic and my mom, you're the only one who knows."

❖

Greasy-haired Iggy slouched like a bendy straw against the wall next to the entrance to my English class. The classroom door was wedged open with one of those scrap pieces of wood from the shop class. I planned to walk past Iggy and Garrett undetected, but Iggy called me over. I ambled over and avoided looking at Garrett.

"Garrett's looking for a place to race his bike," he said slowly. Iggy spoke like he was in thick liquid. "What about those paths out at your dad's?"

My dad's house was tucked back into the woods.

"The trails? Those aren't on our property."

"Yeah, but someone could ride out there." Iggy's voice oozed. "I mean, they're perfect, right?"

I shrugged. "The sand is pretty loose. I've run into people riding horses and three-wheeling on the trails, but not bikes," I said.

"It's okay," Garrett said to Iggy, touching his arm. "What about that other place you were talking about?"

"By the pool?" Iggy asked.

Pool. I swallowed and rushed into the classroom before I could see Garrett's reaction. I didn't want to exchange an awkward glance with him. I didn't want to see his face.

Another secret.

I slid into my desk and tried to convince myself how good it was Garrett was involved with someone, even if it was nasty Iggy. Jennifer bounced into class decked out in red, white, and black. Ribbons curled from her high ponytail. Even her lips were bright red, and I wondered if they were as sticky as that black stuff she'd worn on Halloween. I couldn't figure out how the cheerleading skirts were code when everything else had to cover to right above the knee. Jennifer wore black boots with her uniform, which I thought was weird until Shelly came in with boots, too. I found out later that to honor our mascot— the Cowboys—the cheerleaders all wore black boots that day. At least Shelly's dad owned acres of sugarcane out in Clewiston. Her boots looked worn from use. Jennifer's shiny new ones were about as noncountry as a person could be.

Everything about Jennifer was noncountry. Except for dating Levi.

She tossed her stuff onto a desk and pulled a folder from the stack. Jennifer handed half the papers in the folder to Shelly, and the two of them distributed them to everyone in class. I glanced at the heading at the top: *Homecoming Happenings*. It went on to list important information, such as the time of tomorrow's dance, which was posted on every wall in the school, and the cheers for the crowd.

"You guys, look these over. We're going to practice them at the pep rally. Seriously!" Jennifer said, handing one to our eccentric teacher, Ms. Hughes. "This includes you, too."

Ms. Hughes might have been the director of our theatre program, but she didn't bother acting enthused.

Shelly stood in front of the classroom and said, "Okay, last day for tallies! Seniors are in the lead. Stand up if you're wearing red."

I tried to make myself a little smaller in my chair since my favorite gray hoodie and white T-shirt wouldn't win any points for the sophomore class. Josh and Manny, who were both juniors, stood tall in their jerseys. Jennifer helped Shelly tally the classes. When she got to me, Jennifer put her hands on her hips and tilted her head.

"Asher!" she said, like you might to your dog when it poops on the floor. "Do you want us to lose?"

I didn't answer right away since it might have been a rhetorical question. When she didn't move on to the next person, I readjusted in my chair and said, "Uh…I forgot."

She rolled her eyes and walked over to a pink gym bag. She rummaged through it, pulled out two red shirts, and tossed one to me and one to the other sophomore kid who sleeps in the back row. I was feeling pretty decent about catching the shirt until I held it up in front of me. It would have fit Travis. Jennifer motioned for me to hurry up and put it on.

I shook my head.

"Asher, come on. You're going to lose us points," Jennifer pleaded. "Just wear it for the class photo."

Photo? I glanced at the kid in the back. He put his over his head and wore it like a scarf.

Just then the intercom announced for all students to report to their class hallways, and the cheerleaders ushered us out of the classroom. Ms. Hughes remained at her desk, jotting down notes on a paper. She looked up and removed her glasses. "Aren't you going?" she asked.

"Right," I said, and I hurried out of the room toward the sophomore hall.

Even though I tread lightly, my Converse made noise in the

empty hallway. All the other kids in the school were huddled in tight groups posing for pictures. The digital images would be posted online by lunch, and everyone would crowd around the computer screens, craning necks to see their own faces. The girls would complain about their hair and praise everyone else. The guys would grunt and nudge. Someone would have cleverly given bunny ears to some unsuspecting sap. No one would notice me missing, which was fine by me.

I hid out in the bathroom and waited until the crowds clamored past me. Then I fell into step behind them, a straggler on the way back to class.

CHAPTER TWO

Normally I'd rather take a punch to the throat than attend a social gathering, which was why I'd never been to one of our homecoming football games before. Way back in junior high, I counted on Levi to hang out with me. Now that we were in high school, he sat on the bench with the football players. I used to worry about whether or not anyone would talk to me, yet I'd be just as anxious about the pressure to keep a conversation going in the event someone approached me. Armed with a camera, I had a reason to roam the crowd, and I wasn't obligated to talk to anyone.

If you watched closely, people always revealed the truth—particularly at halftime. The scoreboard blinked seven to fourteen. Our marching band played this rock-anthem mix. I spotted blond, chipper Jennifer among the cheerleaders dancing a routine that involved simultaneous punching in a bunch of directions and angles, like they were boxing flies. I scanned the band for Iggy. His stringy black hair and skinny frame would make it easy to spot him, but I'd heard he'd quit to pursue his music career, code for smoke pot and strum his guitar. Whatever. Since he wasn't on the field with the band, he must be with Garrett. The thought of the two of them together filled my stomach with something like bile.

The bleachers were packed with people. The entire town turned out for the game, but I'd dodged most of the school activities my freshman year, so I didn't know if this was typical. Even Evan Llowell, former high school football star and current repo man, had traveled into town from Miami for homecoming weekend. He chatted with another thick-necked alum. Evan's wife hung on his arm like an accessory. She wore six-inch heels and was one breeze from being topless. Despite the attraction she made, the most bizarre part of the whole thing was that both my parents were sitting in the bleachers.

Not together, of course. My mom sat with her friend from work, Cheryl. Cheryl's son was the assistant coach for the football team, and she'd convinced my mom to get out of the house. Dad and Helen, my skinny stepmom, nestled together up toward the top, holding hands like two high school kids. I wondered if Mom knew Dad was there, too, but she was talking to my youth director, John, from church. She seemed so excited to be eating stale popcorn that she probably didn't notice. I'd taken a picture of both of them: my mom smiling at John, my dad huddled with Helen.

Meanwhile I wandered the crowd with the Canon A-1. I'd already gotten a cool shot of Jennifer looking at Levi sitting on the bench in his dirt-free football gear, his screwed-up foot propped up on a cooler. From the angle, you can tell she's into him. I'd also taken a picture of a crowd of girls scrutinizing Evan's wife from a safe distance. I decided to keep the object of their disdain out of the picture. Instead the group looked like an antibullying ad. One girl leaned in, a nasty expression on her face. Another looked like she wanted to vomit. The other two contorted their faces into legitimate sneers. Sure, Evan's wife wouldn't have gotten as much attention if she were wearing a neon sign and blaring a foghorn, but the hate the girls generated was still intense. I'd gotten it on camera.

I'd actually managed to get a photo of all three of the Llowell brothers. I snared one of Josh Llowell, a junior and the biggest jerk at the school, right after he'd fumbled the ball. He glared down at his own hands like he wanted to pummel them for not following directions. The best part was his much cooler little brother, Vince, was in the shot, too, entirely oblivious to the game and chowing down a corn dog. I couldn't wait to see how that one turned out.

Then I saw them: Garrett and Iggy. Halfway up the bleachers, they sat with a bunch of kids I recognized from the musical. I lifted the camera up to my face and framed the group, but I centered on Garrett and Iggy. I waited for the right moment, even though I risked being observed. If any of them noticed me taking the shot, it would be ruined by pointing or poses. Oblivious to me, Iggy smirked, as usual, but I waited until Garrett's head tilted back laughing to press the button. It felt like a kick to the gut, watching them together, but it was honest.

Over the intercom, I heard, "Ladies and gentlemen, we will now announce this year's homecoming court."

Levi and Jennifer represented our sophomore class on the court. Big surprise. The jock and the cheerleader. I took a picture of Levi limping out onto the field, his uniform uncharacteristically clean. Jennifer hurried over to tuck her shoulder under his arm for support. Some guys might have shrugged off the help to show how manly they were, but Levi ditched his crutch next to the bench. He likely saw it as an opportunity to wrap an arm around her. He wore his black hair a tad longer than usual, and Jennifer fussed over him in preparation for the photo. A swarm of parents, yearbook students, and our local reporter held cameras ready to capture the posed pictures. I preferred photographing people awkwardly trying to figure out where and how to stand. I'd already gotten what I wanted, so while this year's royalty positioned themselves for the newspaper reporter, I moved off into the crowd.

That's when I noticed Kayla leaning over the chain-link fence, wearing her black trench coat. Her hair covered half her face. To the casual observer, she probably looked mildly bored, but her jaw clenched as she studied the homecoming lineup.

Of course. She was watching Jennifer, her former best friend. I lifted the Canon up to get the shot of Kayla shooting daggers at Jennifer, but I hesitated. There was something a little too vulnerable about the moment. I gave myself a mental slap. That's what photography was about, finding those honest moments, so I got Kayla's profile, and I still managed to get a fuzzy cheerleader lineup in the distance. I sort of hoped the weird mix of longing and hate in Kayla's face wouldn't be as visible on film.

Kayla kicked the fence with her black combat boot and started to dig around in the inside pockets of her trench coat.

"Hey," I said as I approached her.

She didn't smile when she saw me. I didn't take it personally. Kayla rarely smiled. "Oh, hey," she said. "This sucks, right?"

This.

She might have been talking about the homecoming court. Of

course, she might be talking generically, sort of implying everything sucked. I asked, "Did you go to last year's homecoming game?"

Kayla gave me a withering look, like she'd hoped for more from me than an asinine question. She tugged at my arm. "I want a smoke. Come with me."

"They won't let you back in if you leave," I said.

Kayla linked her arm through mine. "We're not leaving."

Most people crowded around the fence and bleachers to catch the halftime show, so we didn't have to shuffle around groups as she led me under the stadium bleachers. Bunches of sandspurs littered the ground. I'd have to dig them out of the shoelaces of my Converse later, but it wouldn't be the first time. A couple of stoner types had already claimed a section at the end. I checked to see if Iggy had ditched Garrett to hang with his friends, but I couldn't tell in the shadows. Once we got to the middle section, Kayla reached inside her trench coat, pulled out a cigarette and lighter, and cupped her hand around her face to block the breeze. Her face illuminated briefly in the flame. The black trench coat and lipstick combined with the flame made me think of jack-o'-lanterns. She inhaled, slid the lighter back into her pocket, and billowed smoke out of her nostrils. Kayla's taut face visibly relaxed.

How could something lethal, like smoking, calm a person? "You know, that's really bad for you," I said.

Kayla leaned against the metal frame and held the cigarette between her fingers. I held my breath since the smoke sort of lingered in the air between us. "Really?" Kayla widened her eyes like she was astonished. She took another drag and exhaled. "Wow, thanks for the public service announcement."

She made me feel like an idiot.

"What brings you out to the game?" she asked. "You thinking of joining the team?"

I could have asked her the same question, but I was already pushing it with Kayla. I tapped the camera.

"Always the artist," she said. "It makes for a good excuse to watch people, right?"

I forgot she was like me, always watching. It made me wonder who else might have noticed me trying to slip through the crowds.

She inhaled again. "I saw you watching Jennifer," she said as she exhaled smoke. Her eyes narrowed at me. I wasn't sure if she was squinting at the smoke or judging me. "I thought you didn't like her."

"I don't."

"You took her picture."

"Because she was looking at Levi."

She actually cackled like that witch from *The Wizard of Oz.* Seriously. And then she abruptly stopped. "Okay," she said.

"I don't like Jennifer," I said, and then I got mad, because why was I defending myself?

"Hmm," Kayla said. "I thought maybe you got jealous when you found out Jennifer and Levi were going to homecoming together."

"Uh, no," I said. "I don't dance."

"Levi won't be doing much dancing with that leg of his," she said. "They'll get the picture, and Jennifer gets to wear a princess dress, so that's all that matters." Kayla leaned into me like she was sharing a secret. "What do you want to bet it's pink?"

I shrugged.

"So, Asher doesn't dance or lie."

Lie. I wasn't sure about that anymore. Turns out lies were more complicated than I realized. People lied for a lot of reasons, and I knew I would lie if it meant protecting someone.

The marching band piped up again. I tried to place the song, but before I could, the stoners started singing. Some 80s rock ballad.

Kayla flipped her hair back in a manner reminiscent of her pre-goth days. She wasn't a hair flipper anymore. She shoved her free hand into her trench coat pocket. "Do you like me?" Kayla asked.

Whoa. I went through a mental list of the things I could have done to make her think I liked her. Sure, we'd shared some hefty stuff with one another. She knew I took the picture of Travis in his coffin, and I knew her transformation from a prep to a goth had nothing to do with not making the cheerleading squad. But this was something else.

"Uh…"

"It's not a difficult question. Christ, Asher, don't overthink it."

"Like. You mean *like* like, as in…?"

She punched my arm. Sort of hard. "As in picturing what I'd look like naked," Kayla said.

I rubbed my arm, but I couldn't help smiling. The image made it easier. "No," I said. "I've never thought about you that way." I braced myself in case she punched me again.

"You're absolutely sure?" she asked.

"Yes. I'm sure."

"Good," she said.

I stood stock-still in the dark and watched her smoke her cigarette. She was glad I didn't like her, so I'd answered right. And it had been the truth, too. I mean, I liked her. I really liked Kayla, but not like that. I didn't like anyone like that.

Almost anyone.

I tried to focus on Kayla. She tapped her cigarette, and a chunk of ash fell off the end and landed on the dry leaves that had been blown under the bleachers. The edge of the ash still glowed orange, and I nudged some sand on top of it. I didn't want to add *fire starter* to the list of complaints my mom had about me.

"I don't even know why I'm here," Kayla muttered. She leaned against the metal support and stuck out her chin defiantly.

I thought about last year, and how my dad had left and my mom went nuts. Last year I turned down every invitation Levi had extended for me to join the football team and hang out with the guys. Granted they were idiots, but at least he'd tried. I was the one who pulled away. If Travis hadn't died, we probably wouldn't be friends at all anymore. I studied the smoke curling out of Kayla's nostrils.

"Does that burn your nose?" I asked.

"What?"

"When you breathe out like that, does it, you know"—I tapped my nose—"burn?"

She held the cigarette out to me. "You want to try?"

I shook my head.

She grinned all Cheshire cat–like. "Oh, Asher. I love you. Do you know that? I really do." Kayla snorted. "And that's something, because I hate most people."

Love?

I cleared my throat. "You're not alone. Not like you think you are."

It was quiet for a minute.

"Neither are you." It was a whisper, but the edge was still there.

Kayla flicked her cigarette away and stepped toward me. She wound her arms around my middle. I started to tense up, but then she whispered, "If you try to kiss me, I'll kick you in the nuts."

The camera wedged between us, keeping us a good four inches apart. She reached for it, like she was going to take it off me, but I stopped her. No way was I putting Pearl's camera on the ground to get stomped on. Kayla bit her lower lip like she was considering my death, and then she settled on nudging the camera aside with her body. I rested my chin on the top of her head. She smelled like soap. We sort of swayed back and forth, shifting our weight from one foot to the other. She mumbled something into my shirt.

"What?" I asked.

She pulled back and smiled at me. *Smiled.* "I said, *You're dancing.*"

I stopped moving. "Oh."

Kayla pulled away and straightened her trench coat. "Okay," she said. "You can take me to homecoming."

"What?" I stepped back.

"The homecoming dance."

"Uh, that's tomorrow."

"I know. I bought tickets."

"*You* bought tickets to the dance?"

"Jesus, Asher."

"I just didn't think you were into that sort of thing." My head sort of spun. Images of social hell—standing by a punch bowl trying to look busy—swirled in my imagination. "I'm not sure about this. Dancing. I don't know." I avoided large groups of people. If it wasn't for the camera, I wouldn't be at the football game at all. The idea of sitting in the stands—or worse, mingling in the crowd—caused my stomach to roll. No one questions a guy with a camera. But homecoming?

Kayla tilted her chin up and stood rigid, like she was holding her breath. Then her shoulders slumped.

"Please," Kayla said, and I could tell how much it cost her just to ask.

I didn't normally think about Kayla, but I tried to picture her as if I hadn't known her most of my life. Her hair had an edge, cut at angles. And even though she definitely had a dark thing going on, her skin was sort of perfect and creamy, like something out of a commercial.

A disgusted glance from her could make anyone wither, but when she let her guard down, like now, it was like when a moody cat bestows a gentle nudge. I felt honored by her lack of loathing.

"I have to ask my mom," I said.

"What are you, like, seven?"

It was a random comment, but that was the age my little brother, Travis, was when he died.

"I need to ask her," I insisted.

Because sometimes people leave without permission, and I wasn't one of those people.

Chapter Three

I'd just reached in to adjust the temperature on the shower when Mom knocked on the door. "What?"

"Open up," she demanded.

"I'm about to get in the shower."

"So?"

"I'm naked."

"I need to hang your suit up."

My suit? I secured a towel around my waist and cracked open the door. Mom brushed past me carrying the dark gray suit I wore to Travis's funeral. She hung it on the towel rack.

"What are you doing?" I asked.

"The steam from the shower might get the wrinkles out," she said, running her hands across the jacket front. "If I'd known you were going to the dance, I would have had it dry-cleaned."

"Mom, I didn't know—"

"I know. We'll see if this works." She rushed back out of the bathroom, slamming the door behind her.

I had owned two suits in my life. The one from when I was little had been buried with Travis. The other, this one, had only been worn once. After the funeral, I'd dumped it in a corner of my closet. I ran my hand across the creases. It wasn't too bad, considering I'd left it in a heap.

Mom rapped on the door again. "Did you get a corsage?" she called through the door.

"A what?"

"Flowers."

"Why would I get flowers?"

I heard an exasperated groan from outside the door. "Do you know what color her dress is?"

Color? How would I know that?

I thought for a second. "Maybe black. Look, I'm getting in the shower."

I pulled the shower curtain back and stepped inside the tub. The hot water ran over my body. I tilted my head from side to side, letting the water fill my ears. The gurgling was a welcome reprieve from my mom's badgering. Ever since I'd told her Kayla had asked me to the dance, Mom freaked. She scheduled a haircut for me, forced me to trim my nails, and started the inquisition.

How were we going to get to the dance? I didn't know. I mean, wouldn't I just meet Kayla there? When I suggested Mom drop me off at the school, she said that wasn't how it was done. She insisted we had to pick Kayla up. I told her I'd try to get a ride with Levi. She handed me the phone—*Call him now*—even though I knew he wouldn't be out of bed before ten. Before I'd even finished dialing his number, she wanted to know where I was taking Kayla to dinner. Why would I take her out to dinner? We were going to a dance. No one said anything about dinner, and even if we did go to dinner, I thought Kayla might want to pay, since she had asked me. Mom said she thought she'd raised me better than that. So instead of using my savings for more film or developing, I would have to buy Kayla food.

Whatever.

I finally gave in and called Levi. At first he said he and Jennifer already had plans to go with a group—code for football players and cheerleaders—but then he called back about ten minutes later to say he arranged to pick me up first, then Jennifer, and finally Kayla. We planned to eat at this fancy Italian place I'd gone to once with Dad and Helen. Then we would go to the dance.

When I called Kayla to tell her the plans, she was ticked. I'd forgotten she wasn't talking to Jennifer, but it was too late to back out now. Kayla asked, "Why couldn't we just meet at the school?"

When I got out of the shower, I found a note on the counter from Mom. She'd gone to the store for flowers.

❖

If I'd known they would want me to get my picture taken, I would have told Kayla no. I had carefully dodged having my photograph taken since middle school. When Levi arrived, they discussed the best place to use as a backdrop while sweat dripped from my underarm to my waist. Levi suggested we use the dead bush out front or perhaps the rusty Windstar. Mom swatted at him. I couldn't look at them without thinking about Levi's dad and my mom. How could Levi play it off like no big deal?

"What do you think, Asher?" she asked me. "You're the photographer."

"No."

"You're not getting out of this."

"Mom...I..."

"No posed pictures. Right," she said. "How about the backyard?"

The backyard.

I risked a glance at Levi to see if he was thinking about the other photograph, too, but his expression didn't change as they headed past me to the sliding glass door. I watched Levi and my mom dodge the fire-ant hills in back, stopping where the orange grove butted up against our yard. I wondered what would happen if I just stayed inside the house. It seemed sort of juvenile, so I reluctantly followed.

It wasn't until I got outside that I noticed Mom was using the digital camera Dad had bought for me. I'd never used it. Everyone knew I didn't take digital photographs. It figured Mom would use it to take pictures of Levi and me. I shifted my weight back and forth.

I lowered my voice. "Mom. Please." I got up close to her, even though I knew Levi could hear me. "I don't want to do this."

She ignored me. Levi gently took my arm and limped me over in front of the grove. We stood stiffly beside each other, a couple feet separating us, as Mom lined up the picture. I couldn't get the other picture out of my head. I could hear the faint buzz of a mosquito near my ear and swatted at it. I chewed on the inside of my mouth and waited for her to go ahead and do it, but she didn't.

"You need help with that?" Levi asked her.

She nodded, so Levi limped over to her, took the camera, and pressed a few buttons. I looked down at my tight black dress shoes. They'd fit when I'd worn them to Travis's funeral four months ago.

"Just push there," Levi said, showing her buttons. "And you can get a close-up with this."

He seemed so comfortable next to her, like she hadn't slept with his dad. Like none of that ever happened. And as he stood there next to her, I couldn't believe I had never noticed how much Travis resembled him. He'd slicked back his short dark hair, and when he grinned back at me, I pictured an older Travis. I swallowed down the thought about the dances Travis would never attend. Levi hobbled back over beside me.

Mom looked at us through the camera. A deep thudding started in my temple, and I felt my breath starting to come fast, but she didn't take the picture.

"Asher, you aren't planning on taking that thing to the dance, are you?" she asked.

She meant the Canon A-1 hanging around my neck. "What's wrong with it?"

"It could get broken. Or stolen. It's not even yours." When I didn't answer her, she said, "Well, at least take it off for the pictures."

"How about we skip the pictures?" I said, but my voice felt tight in my throat.

She folded her arms in front of her and shot me a stony stare, so I pulled the strap from around my neck and placed it on top of our dilapidated grill.

"Okay. Now act like you're friends," Mom joked, but it wasn't exactly funny considering the past six months.

Levi slung an arm over my shoulder, and I tried to disappear. Mom held the camera out in front of her but didn't take the photo.

"Come on, Mom," Levi said. "We've gotta go get the girls."

He called her *Mom*, just like he used to.

Mom poked her face above the camera. "Can you at least try to smile, Asher?"

I showed some teeth, but the corners of my mouth refused to budge.

Mom shook her head slightly from side to side, clearly frustrated with me. "You'd think you were being tortured," she muttered.

"What, were you hoping for model poses?" Levi asked. "Ash. Think Abercrombie."

Right. Like that would happen. Levi leaned his back to me, and I pressed my back against him. My God, the air felt thick, like water.

Mom stared hard at the image in the viewfinder. I watched her swallow and her face flushed. I recognized the pained expression—it was what she did when she was about to have a meltdown. I wondered if Levi reminded her of Travis, too. I couldn't take this. I covered my face with my hands and walked right out of the sightline.

"Asher." Mom's voice sounded defeated, tired, and I felt awful.

"You're doing it all wrong," I heard a voice cackle. Our cranky neighbor, Pearl, was standing in her screened-in porch watching us. She squeaked open the screen door and waddled over to my mom. "Okay, you need to get closer to him."

Levi eyed me for guidance, but I had none to give. Mom and Pearl shuffled forward.

"All right. Now you," Pearl said to Levi. "Tell me. You going stag or did you hire a prostitute to pretend she likes you?"

Levi's mouth opened for a retort, but nothing came.

"What are you waiting for?" Pearl said to my mom. "Take the damn picture!" She glanced over Mom's shoulder at the image on the screen and hooted. "Now that's a keeper right there!"

Mom grinned, too, but her hands shook and her eyes looked all watery. Levi ambled over to check out the image, so I figured we were done and rushed over to the grill to get the Canon A-1.

"Asher, no," Mom said, wiping at her teary eyes with the back of her hand. "I'm getting a picture of you."

I braced myself for an argument, but before I could say a word, Pearl demanded, "Where did you get that?"

I turned to her to see what she was talking about and found her staring at the camera around my neck. "This?"

"It looks like mine," she said.

"It is yours."

Pearl worked her jaw, like she was chewing tobacco or something. I wondered if she wore dentures and maybe they'd come loose. "What the hell are you doing with it?"

Mom's tears evaporated as she looked from Pearl to me, and back again.

"You gave it to me to use. When I told you I broke my Minolta," I reminded her.

Pearl had made a big deal about how it wasn't her nice camera when I'd hesitated to take it. She'd threatened to hurt me if I broke this one.

"Don't you think I'd remember giving you my camera?" Pearl's wrinkles deepened as she regarded me with disgust.

Mom's eyebrows knit. The shirt she wore hung off her small frame—she'd lost a lot of weight in the last few months—but she managed to look fierce. "Give it to her," Mom insisted. "Give it to Pearl now."

Give it to her? My heart started racing. How could Pearl not remember? All the images on the roll of film flipped through my memory—the homecoming game, Kayla, Mom sleeping—and I wanted to argue, but Mom eyed me like I was a hardened criminal. Levi stared at Pearl.

"But I have film in it," I explained, trying to keep the panic out of my voice.

Pearl shifted her slippered feet back and forth. She squinted at me, like some villain from one of those spaghetti Westerns poised over a holster, ready to fire off a round at me. "That's it," she said, her voice steady as death. "I'm calling the cops." Pearl turned and slowly waddled back toward her house.

"Wait, Pearl," Mom said, but Pearl ignored her and kept moving. Mom ran up beside her, which didn't take long since Pearl wasn't exactly a fast mover.

"You put one hand on me and I'll have *you* arrested, too!" Pearl threatened.

Arrested? Mom held her hands up and backed away from our whack-job neighbor. She spun on me as Pearl slammed her screen door behind her. This couldn't be happening. Pearl had told me my photos were crap. She'd promised to help me make them better. I held the Canon in my hands like a peace offering.

"I swear, she told me I could use it. I'm not making it up. I wouldn't…"

"Give me the camera now," Mom said.

I lifted the camera off my chest and placed it in her grasp. Mom's hands trembled as she took it from me. "Is your mother working tonight?" she asked Levi.

Levi's mom worked as a police officer.

"No, she's home if you want to call her."

I pictured that, Mom calling the wife of the man with whom she'd had an affair. Levi must have been thinking the same thing, because he said, "You know what, I need to call her anyway. I'll fill her in."

Mom ran a shaky hand through her hair. "Don't forget the corsage. It's in the fridge," she said.

She'd forgotten to take my picture.

❖

"Damn," Levi said when Jennifer appeared in the stairwell.

Jennifer's dad, a sandy-haired guy in khakis and a polo, seemed friendly when we first arrived, but judging his head-snap toward Levi's *damn,* the nice-guy routine was over.

"Sorry," Levi said. Then he motioned toward Jennifer. "But seriously. Look at her."

Jennifer's mom tucked a strand of blond hair behind Jennifer's ear. Her locks were pulled back in complicated braids, and she wore a tight-fitting, short blue dress. Her boobs spilled over the top, defying gravity. It looked like she was one step from a wardrobe malfunction, but what do I know.

Frankly, I was distracted by the idea of incarceration. My eyes kept shifting to the front window, expecting a squad car to pull up next to the palm trees that lined Jennifer's front yard. Levi insisted Pearl wouldn't call the cops, and even if she did, his mom knew everyone on the force. No one would believe saintly Asher Price would steal from an old lady. Since Levi's mom wasn't working, this brought me zero comfort.

I tugged on the sleeves of my dress shirt and wondered what the prisoners would think of my suit while Jennifer's family discussed where to take pictures. Seemed to me just about anywhere would do. Their immaculate two-story house looked like something out of a decorating magazine. It was situated right on the Caloosahatchee River, so the whole back was a series of french doors overlooking the murky water. And that's exactly where they wanted to take photos of Levi and Jennifer.

While everyone else took photos of Levi and Jennifer posed, I couldn't help but think about the moments I would have taken pictures. I would have gotten a few of Jennifer's plastic mom fussing—it looked like she had spent almost as much time getting ready as her daughter—and a couple of the dad's lethal looks at Levi. They attempted to coerce me into a photo with Levi and Jennifer, but I managed to avoid it by claiming we were late picking up Kayla.

"Make sure Kayla's folks take pictures of the two of you," Jennifer's mom said.

"Yeah, I'll make sure," Jennifer said, picking up a tiny sparkly purse that matched her spiky heels. They looked treacherous.

We headed out to Levi's mom's shiny sedan. I climbed in back so Jennifer could sit next to Levi. Jennifer smiled and waved to her parents as we backed out of the driveway, but the second we pulled away, she slumped in the seat.

"Mel is pissed," Jennifer said. "I told her we'd help pay for the limo."

"Fine, I'll give them money," Levi said.

"What did Josh say?"

"I sent him a text. It's cool."

"I've been on the phone all day. Shelly's bringing that guy, and she was counting on us to sit with them at dinner. So she's freaking out. I tried to—"

"Okay," Levi murmured.

"It's okay for you."

"Stop," he snapped.

Jennifer crossed her arms in front of her and stopped talking. Great. I'd ruined everything. I drummed my fingers against my legs and stared out the window. Expansive ranch houses zipped past as we drove out of Jennifer's gated subdivision.

"Hey," Levi said, and at first I thought he was talking to Jennifer, but he said, "Hey," again and his eyes met mine in the rearview mirror. "It's cool." He held a hand out to Jennifer. She hesitated, but then she uncrossed her arms and placed her hand in his. He squeezed it. It wasn't fine. "Shelly will get over it. And if she doesn't, who gives a shit? This is better. We'll have more fun just us," he said. He pulled up to a stop sign, but he didn't drive through the intersection. Instead, he gently turned her face toward him.

She sighed. "What?"

"You look beautiful."

Jennifer stuck out her bottom lip.

"Even when you're pouty." Levi kissed her hand, and she sideways smiled. "Really."

We turned onto the main road and headed toward the other side of town. When we passed the grocery store, my gaze lingered on Wild Bill gathering carts out front, probably hoping for a tip. Now that I officially understood the term *third wheel*, the drive to Kayla's across town seemed sort of terminal. Still, I dreaded arriving. Kayla's dad owned and operated an auto shop in town. He looked like a guy in a motorcycle gang. I felt my hands grow clammy as I pictured the clumsy introductions. I was trying to figure out a way to avoid more pictures when we pulled into the empty driveway to her ranch-style stucco home. Jennifer and Levi started to pile out of the car, but before I could even climb out of the back, Kayla rushed out the front door. She paused at the entrance to her house and adjusted a strap on her shoe before ambling down the driveway to us.

"Hey," she said as she slid into the backseat. "You guys ready?"

"Do your parents want pictures?" Jennifer asked stiffly, still standing beside the car.

"They aren't home."

Jennifer blinked at Kayla through the car. "Where are they?"

"Out."

Jennifer, Levi, and I exchanged confused glances over the roof of the car and climbed back in. Kayla smoothed down her dress. It was dark green and made out of something velvety with little sleeves that rested on her shoulders. Kayla had stacked her hair up into a messy nest on top of her head, but wisps of hair fell and framed her face. The ring on her eyebrow had this green stone in it that matched her outfit.

"You clean up nice," Kayla told me as Levi pulled out of the driveway.

"You, too."

"Thanks."

She smelled like something sweet. I tried to place it. At first I'd thought it was vanilla, but it wasn't that kind of sweet. Honeysuckle?

"It's not like your parents to not want pictures of you," Jennifer said.

"They don't know I'm going."

Jennifer turned around in her seat. Her eyelids were lined in black, sort of catlike. "You didn't tell them you were going to homecoming?"

Kayla grinned wickedly. "Nope. Frankly the whole thing would make my mom far too happy. So when I found out they were going out of town tonight, the dance sounded appealing."

Jennifer faced forward again in her seat. She sat in silence, staring out the window. "They're going to find out," she finally said. "My mom knows. She wants pictures of us."

"I *thought* I was just going to meet Asher at the dance."

I shrunk in my seat. "I…my mom…"

Levi reached a hand back to swat at me.

"Hey!" I said, dodging him.

He swatted a few more times.

"What are you doing?"

"I'll stop hitting you when you stop apologizing," he said, and I noticed him grinning at me in the rearview mirror. "This is perfect. We're all right where we're supposed to be."

When picking a restaurant for a fancy occasion, I recommend anything but Italian. I ended up with red sauce on my pressed white shirt. Kayla dabbed at it with her cloth napkin dipped in ice water, but that just made it spread.

We weren't the only people from our high school at the Italian place either. Iggy's little sister perched on a chair by the window with this guy from my history class.

"She looks adorable!" Jennifer said. "Like a fairy."

She wore her hair short, like a flapper from the 1920s, and her dress had an iridescent quality to it. It was floaty.

"I've got to go tell her," Jennifer said, and she ditched us to go chat with them.

"Jesus," Kayla said.

"What?" I said.

"Maybe Rose doesn't want company, you know? I mean, they're on a date."

I watched Rose light up as Jennifer approached and knew Kayla was wrong, but I kept my mouth shut.

"Twenty bucks for a plate of spaghetti?" Levi said as he studied the menu. "What a rip-off."

When Jennifer returned, she reported that no one planned to show up at the dance until a half hour after it started. Also the group of people who'd been planning on driving to the beach after were staying local instead and throwing a party after the dance.

"Where is it?" Levi asked.

"The party? I didn't ask."

"Go ask her. Maybe she can get hold of Iggy. He'd know."

"I'm not going to ask her for details to a party we aren't invited to," Jennifer said. "Been there, done that. Remember the summer before high school?" She leaned into Kayla. "The time I almost got arrested over your crush on Josh Llowell?"

Kayla stabbed a meatball on her plate and bit off a chunk of it. "Vaguely," Kayla said. "It seems so long ago."

"Don't feel bad," Levi said. "Asher almost got arrested, too. Didn't Evan plant drugs on you or something?"

"Something like that," I said.

"Oh, that's right!" Jennifer said. "Oh my gosh, I'd forgotten all about that. I was so worried about Kayla, and Evan handed you"—she lowered her voice—"a joint, right? What did you do with it?"

"I flushed it down the toilet."

Levi and Jennifer laughed, but Kayla just studied the meatball on her fork.

"We were so stupid," Jennifer said, tossing her head even though her hair wasn't hanging loose.

"Yep," Kayla said, and she stuck the rest of the meat in her mouth.

"That's the day I got my camera," I said.

"And the night your dad moved out," Levi added.

I couldn't take my eyes off Kayla and her masked face. She managed to look bored. That night Evan Llowell had lost his smoke, Jennifer lost Kayla, and I lost my dad. But I was the only one at the table who knew what Kayla had lost.

"So what do you say we get out of here?" Kayla asked.

A few minutes later the waiter brought us the bill, and even though I tried to pay for Kayla's meal, she wouldn't let me. As we maneuvered through the restaurant toward the front door, I saw my youth pastor, John, sitting at a table. I started to wave at him, but then I realized he was with some lady I didn't know. They were holding hands.

CHAPTER FOUR

The homecoming theme was Vegas, so the gym was decorated in black, red, and white with giant dice and white Christmas lights. A makeshift dance floor protected the gym from the pointy-heeled shoes, but by the time we walked in, most of the girls had kicked their sparkly heels off in a corner. I'd wanted to just go inside when we arrived, but Levi and Jennifer made us wait in the car until a decent amount of people had arrived so they weren't the first ones.

Pointless, if you asked me.

The music thumped, and although Levi limped on his lame leg, he bobbed his head to the beat. Jennifer's preppy friends gathered and fussed over each other's dresses. One of Jennifer's cheerleader friends, Shelly, brought her date over to where Levi, Kayla, and I were standing by the wall.

"Hey!" she yelled over the music. "This is Thad. Thad, this is Levi and Asher."

Thad wore skinny black pants and a matching jacket with the sleeves rolled up. His turquoise shirt matched Shelly's dress, and a thin black tie hung loosely around his neck. He extended a hand to us.

"Hey," he said. He was slightly shorter than Shelly with blue eyes and strikingly tan skin for November, even in Florida. He also looked familiar. "Do I know you?" he asked me.

"I was just thinking the same thing about you," I admitted.

He snapped his fingers. "Missions! Last year."

That was it. Thad and I had both worked on this local mission to send goods to people in Haiti. We hadn't been assigned to the same group. I couldn't place him before, but now that he'd mentioned it, I'd remembered seeing him there.

"How do you know Shelly?" Levi asked.

"Her grandmother goes to my church."

Levi snorted. "Shelly goes to church? Are you sure?"

Shelly jabbed him. "Shut up, Levi," she said as she hoisted up her strapless dress. "I'm a good girl."

"Yeah, I'll bet," he said, and she punched his arm.

A slow song came on, and Shelly grabbed Thad's hand to lead him out on the dance floor. I wondered if Kayla was going to make me dance with her, but when I turned to check, she wasn't positioned beside me. Jennifer found Levi and carefully steered him out to dance, too. I strolled over to the refreshments and ladled some punch into a plastic cup. A few minutes later, Kayla sidled up beside me.

"It's weird, isn't it?" she said, studying our classmates on the dance floor.

"How so?"

"I used to be friends with Shelly, too, but now it's like I'm invisible. She didn't even introduce me to her boyfriend."

I hadn't noticed, but she was right.

"It's bullshit."

I rocked back and forth in my too-tight shoes. "You want some punch?" I asked, lifting my cup toward her.

"I know some people I'd like to punch," she said. "Does that count?"

Kayla nudged me, took the clear plastic cup out of my hand, and placed it on the table. She wrapped her arm around mine and ushered me out onto the dance floor. We stood the same way we had under the bleachers—sort of hugging—and rocked back and forth. Her hair tickled my nose, so I patted it down a little. I scanned the crowd of people. A large group of jocks sat at a nearby table, leaning in like they were playing poker. I spotted Josh among them. He saw us, too. I was so busy watching him that I didn't notice when someone took a picture. My feet stopped moving.

"Hey," I called to the girl with the digital camera.

"It's for the yearbook!" she said and disappeared into the crowd.

Seriously? I shook my head in disgust. "Can you believe that?" I asked Kayla.

"You realize you do the same thing to people all the time, right?" Kayla cocked her head to the side and arched her pierced eyebrow. For a moment I didn't like her very much, and I opened my mouth to argue that what I did was different, but closed it. She was right. Sort of. I resumed our slow dance, but I felt this stupid urge to cry.

I felt a tap on my shoulder and pivoted, prepared for the digital demon to reappear. It wasn't much comfort to look at Josh Llowell's smug face. The black suit fit snuggly, like it had been tailored to him. His dad probably paid big bucks to have it made. He peered back and forth between Kayla and me, like we were a fascinating science experiment. "Aren't you guys cute."

I angled us away from him, headed toward the crowd.

"Hold up," Josh said, following us. "Can I cut in?"

Kayla gripped my hand. "No, thanks." She turned her head away from him, so I wet my lips and tried to ignore him, too. I could feel him still standing next to us. We continued to sway back and forth. Why didn't he go away?

"You look nice," Josh said, his face close to Kayla.

"Look Josh—" I started, but Kayla spun on him.

"Don't you have something better to do?" Kayla demanded, her hand tight in mine. "You know, a football to throw? Something? Anything?"

"Hey, what could be better than this? You guys make such a cute couple."

Kayla yanked me past him. "Screw you," she muttered.

"Save me a dance!" he called to Kayla.

She didn't let go of my arm until we reached the other side of the gym. Kayla plopped down on the bleachers and adjusted her dress, sputtering expletives. I touched her bare shoulder, and she flinched. "Don't touch me," she huffed, and then added, "I'm sorry."

I sat there like a useless lump trying to figure out if there was some guideline for what to do when someone is a jerk at homecoming. Was I obligated to restore Kayla's honor by fighting Josh? Because Josh was built like a Mack truck. Would Kayla have a better time in the waiting room at the hospital? I clenched my fist. Not terribly intimidating. Kayla sat next to me with her legs extended, her shoes dangling from her toes. I nudged her, and one fell off.

She gave me an evil stare, tilted her head toward her shoe. "Well, don't just sit there," she said, then she wiggled her shoeless toes. "Put it back."

I saw a hint of a smile, so I bent over, picked up her shoe, and propped it back on her toes.

I kept surveillance on Josh. He returned to his group of thick-necks across the gym. I intended to spend the rest of the night protecting Kayla from him, but then I spotted Garrett dancing in the middle of a crowd of drama club people. I only caught glimpses of him as the crowd moved. He wore black pants and a vest over a pink shirt. *Pink.* And a pink bow tie. Even from the sidelines, his energy surged. He danced with absolute abandon, like no one else was in the room. How did he do that?

"He's something, right?" Kayla said.

I jumped. She'd caught me looking at him.

"Come on," she said and tugged me toward the circle of people.

"I don't dance, remember?"

"Just bounce up and down. No one else knows what they're doing either," she said.

Except for him. I followed her to the outside of the circle. When Garrett spotted us, a nervous jolt spread through my body.

"Asher!" he hollered.

He rushed through the crowd of people with abandon, and he lunged toward Kayla and me. Just before he reached us, he paused and did some ridiculous archaic move from the 70s or something. Then he broke into laughter and clapped his hands together. I couldn't help but grin, too. My pulse pounded. Something about Garrett's easy nature panicked me, so I tugged Kayla slightly in front of me. If I had to protect her from Josh, this was only fair.

"Kayla!" he shouted, oblivious to my efforts to dodge him. He wrapped his arms around her and swung her in a circle. She didn't flinch when he reached for her. He winked at me over her shoulder, then led Kayla through the swarm of people into the middle. She didn't resist, and I watched as Garrett mirrored every move Kayla did before fading into the circle to give her the moment. She spun around with her arms stretched high. Then Kayla moved with the thumping of the music, and a grin spread across her face. *A grin.* A few strands of her purple hair flew loose, and she glowed in the lights.

I wondered if this was who Kayla might have been if she'd never hooked up with Josh. Instead of working crew in the shadows, maybe she would have been front and center on the stage. She could definitely move, but unlike most people, she wasn't dancing with the idea of being watched. It was like we'd all disappeared.

It was the happiest I'd seen her. Maybe ever.

A chant erupted, "Go Kayla!" I joined in, my fist raised high in the air. They cheered her name, a litany, and I yearned for my camera so I could capture this moment. Instead I flashed through the crowd, securing this in my memory. Everyone focused on Kayla. I would put her in the upper-right-hand corner of the frame, like one of the pictures kids draw with the sun in the corner, the source of light for their green-stemmed stick flowers and rectangular houses with square window frames. Then I spotted Garrett on the other side, directly across from me in the circle. People danced around him, but he stood stoic with a look so filled with longing that it about knocked the air out of me. Was he staring at me?

Just then Iggy brushed past me. Not me. Iggy. I saw Garrett wave him over, and it mirrored how he motioned me over that day at the pool. A last cheer rose up as the circle closed in, forming smaller groups. Kayla joined one, her hair tumbling loose. I thought she might abandon the dancing and return to me, but she gravitated toward the drama kids. Suddenly it was too awkward, standing there at the edge, and all that anxiety of social gatherings welled up in me. I scanned the crowd for Josh, but I didn't see him anywhere nearby. My mind raced for answers to how I was supposed to be right now. What was normal behavior? Not standing at the edge, like I'm poised at the pool trying to decide if I should ease into the water or jump in. I turned to head off the dance floor. I'd barely made it halfway across the room when a pair of hands covered my eyes.

"Guess who?" a playful voice asked.

Even his hands smelled like coconut. I'd recognize his voice anywhere. My whole body launched into a code red. Everything about me wanted to respond, to laugh, but I forced a controlled smile.

"Hi Garrett," I said and turned to face him.

"How did you know it was me?"

I smelled you didn't seem like a great response, so I said, "Who else would cover my eyes?" Fortunately the low lights hid the blush I felt creeping from my neck to my face. I willed the floor to open up and swallow me. I should have just told him I smelled him.

"I didn't know you were coming to the dance," he said. He stood there so easily, and I wondered what it must be like to be Garret, so comfortable in his own skin.

"It was a last-minute thing."

"I'm glad you're here," Garrett said. "Did you come alone?"

"With Kayla. Just as friends," I added, and then I felt stupid for clarifying. What did he care?

"I love Kayla."

Love. The way people threw that word around, so easily, generally bothered me. When Garrett said it, it occurred to me that maybe he had plenty to spare. But if you love everyone, no one's special.

"Kayla's great," I agreed.

"I came alone," he said, and I thought of Iggy. "You know, just to see what it's all about. The guys from *Godspell* threatened to beat me and drag me here, so I figured I should avoid that."

It would have been funnier if Levi hadn't punched him the first day of school. Now he was joking, underplaying the fact that everyone wanted him here. He'd made friends and gained fans through *Godspell*. That's how he'd gotten to know Iggy. You couldn't help but like Garrett with his easy smile and humility. I wasn't the only one affected by his warmth; Travis had instantly liked Garrett. And an hour later, Travis died.

I spied Iggy hunched in the corner with a couple people.

"I heard the show went great," I said.

"Jennifer said you were grounded or something?"

"Yeah."

"I missed you."

I nodded. I never knew what to say when he said things like that. He had a way of making me feel special, but I was pretty sure he said things like that to everybody. I cleared my throat. "Yeah."

Over Garrett's shoulder I saw Iggy's little sister, Rose, skipping toward us. A delighted grin spread across her face as she broke into a reckless run toward Garrett. Before I could warn him, she jumped on his back. Of course they'd be close—he probably hung out at Iggy's house all the time.

"Why aren't you dancing?" she hollered.

"I don't know!" he yelled back. Garrett spun her around, then she soared off and back toward the crowd. He moved to follow but turned back to me. "You coming?"

I opened my mouth to say something, but closed it again.

He tilted his head to the side. "All the cool kids are doing it," he joked.

I dug my hands into my pockets and shook my head.

"Garrett!" Rose called. "Come on!"

As he held my gaze, his smile faded. I was remembering the day at the pool, following Garrett into the bathroom, slipping on the tile, and my own voice *I'm not...gay*, right before we'd kissed. It was like he could see it playing out on my face.

I said, "No thanks. You go ahead."

❖

Aside from the chaperones, we were the last ones to leave the dance. Jennifer helped to clean up as part of student council, and Levi kept checking his phone for updates on where everyone was going. So far there wasn't any word on the relocation of the beach party. Kayla and I opted to get dropped off before Jennifer and Levi hit the late-night scene.

As we pulled onto Kayla's street, Levi whistled and said, "Someone's having a party."

Cars and trucks lined both sides of Kayla's street.

"That's Nick's truck," Jennifer said. "And look, Shelly's here, too."

Kayla unbuckled her seat belt and leaned forward between Levi and Jennifer. She hit her fist into the back of the seat.

"There are cars parked in my driveway," Kayla said.

Sure enough, lights and music blared through the windows of her house. We paused in the middle of the street in front of her house. There wasn't anywhere to park.

"Oh my God," Kayla whispered.

"Did your parents come home?" Levi asked.

"Those aren't our cars. People are inside my house!" Kayla yelled. I thought she was going to launch out of the car. Levi parked behind the cars in the driveway, blocking them in.

"Shit," Levi said, and he flung the gearshift into park. Kayla bolted.

"Hold on, Kayla," Jennifer said as Kayla started out of the back.

"Wait." But Kayla darted up the driveway between the cars to her front door. Jennifer unlatched her seat belt and scrambled out of the vehicle.

"I'm going with her," Jennifer said to us and slammed the door.

Levi hit the steering wheel. "Damn Josh."

"Josh?"

Levi grabbed his keys, opened his car door, and turned to face me in the backseat. "We weren't going to a party," he said. "Josh asked me if I was, and I told him I was planning on having time alone with Jennifer since Kayla's folks were out of town."

No one had said anything about hanging out at Kayla's after the dance, but apparently Levi had made his own plans.

I sprinted to Kayla's house, leaving Levi to hobble after us. A ton of people from the dance had shown up, still dressed in their formals. I'd never been inside Kayla's house before. It was an older ranch style, kind of like my dad's, only not updated. Wood paneling covered the walls. Kayla positioned herself in the center of the room studying the scene. Jennifer stood beside her. Someone must have picked up some alcohol, because kids kicked back beer in plastic cups identical to those at the punch table at the dance. Synthesized dance music blared. A cluster of people gyrated in the center of Kayla's living room. Kayla marched over to the black lacquer entertainment center and pressed a button. The music died, and a loud protest erupted from the dancers.

"Screw you very much, but you can all go home now," Kayla announced.

Josh sauntered up to her. Before I took the time to figure out if it was a good idea, I stepped out of the crowd to defend Kayla.

"Hey, guys! Our host is here!" Josh hollered, cozying up to her.

Kayla recoiled from him as the crowd cheered and returned to their drinking and dancing.

"Come on, Kayla," I heard Josh say as he reached over to massage her shoulder. "No big deal. Everyone will clean up after."

I shoved his hand away, lunged in between them, and mustered the courage to say, "Just tell everyone to go, Josh. There's no party here."

A few people nearby reacted briefly, but then continued with their conversations. Josh took a swig from a beer bottle and motioned toward the room of people. "Uh, there's definitely a party here."

Kayla glared, but her voice sounded smaller than I'd ever heard it. "How did you get inside my house?"

"We shimmied the sliding glass door."

"By *we* you mean…?"

"Me and Manny. Look, Levi told me you had the house to yourself and…"

Great. Levi had just joined us. He flinched a little, and I could tell his leg was bothering him.

Jennifer piped up. "Levi? Levi did this?"

"Wait," Levi said. He didn't bother to address Josh at all. Instead he spoke directly to Jennifer, locking eyes with her. "I did not tell them to do this."

Josh stepped between them.

"Excuse me," Levi said, giving Josh a gentle shove.

Josh ignored him and inched his face close to Jennifer before he whispered, "Levi told me he was looking forward to some alone time with you."

Jennifer's face flushed.

If Josh hadn't stepped away right then, Levi might have killed him.

"Hey, I'm not judging," Josh continued. "If the four of you were looking forward to some time by yourselves, there *are* bedrooms. We know how that goes, don't we Kayla?"

That was it. I launched myself at Josh, shoving him hard. He stumbled back, surprised, but caught his balance. "You want to pick a fight with me?" He shoved me back. "Is that right, smasher?"

Smasher. The name he'd called me in seventh grade right before he'd knock me into a wall. Josh had already taken his suit jacket and tie off, but now he undid the top button on his shirt. The crowd around us expanded to make room for what might be a legitimate altercation. I'd had more brushes with possible arrest in the last five hours than I'd had in my entire life. A smile tugged at the sides of Josh's mouth, like he welcomed the chance to slug me. I caught sight of scrawny Iggy from the corner of my eye. Did that mean Garrett was here? The crowd silently waited.

"Hey," Levi stepped in between us. "Josh, come on. You said there was a party somewhere else. What's up?"

His eyes didn't budge from me. He didn't respond to Levi. Everyone waited to see what Josh would do.

Kayla pulled her cell out and said, "I'm calling the cops."

That got Josh's attention. He spun on her. "You've got to be kidding me."

But when Kayla started dialing the phone, he grabbed it out of her hands.

"Give it to me!" she yelled as she scrambled for him. She lunged for his hands, but he held the phone beyond her reach, far above his head. Levi plucked the phone from Josh's hand.

"Josh, it's not cool," he said, his voice just this side of menacing. "You guys have to go somewhere else."

But before Josh could respond, Kayla started shrieking, her hands covering her head. "Get out of my house! Get out! Get out!" She paced the floor like something wild and caged, and people from school backed away from her like they were genuinely frightened. Even Josh put his hands up to shield himself in case she turned on him. I didn't move. Jennifer rushed forward and wrapped her arms around Kayla. They sank onto the floor together.

Kneeling next to Kayla, all entwined in purple hair, green velvet, and porcelain skin, Jennifer laid a steely gaze onto Josh. She said one word. "Leave."

"Jesus. Fine," Josh said, his face red like when he came off the field after fumbling the ball. "What a freak."

Kayla angled her face up to him. "I hate you," she hissed.

"Oh, you injure me, Kayla. Really." Josh turned back to the crowd and meandered over to consult with Iggy. They huddled in the corner, an unlikely combination of jock and goth. Finally Josh asked, "Who's bringing the keg?"

A few people stopped to apologize to Kayla, but Jennifer brushed them away. Most just made a hurried exit. Jennifer and Kayla disappeared into the back of the house while the remaining people scattered. Levi and I helped Manny load the keg into the back of someone's truck. I found a trash bag under the sink in the kitchen and started collecting the plastic cups that littered the surfaces. When Levi came back inside, we got the sliding glass door back on track. Once we'd picked up, Levi and I headed down the hall. He knocked on the closed door.

"What?" Kayla called.

"It's me," Levi said. He tried the handle. It was locked. "Hey, open up."

Levi leaned into the door, trying to hear the content of the urgent whispers. Finally, the door swung ajar. Even though Kayla only opened the door a crack, I could see Jennifer sitting cross-legged on a purple comforter.

"You need to go," Kayla muttered.

Jennifer's mascara was smeared. I was confused. I thought Kayla was the one who was upset.

"Uh, we just picked up the entire house," Levi pointed out.

"What, you want a prize?" Jennifer called, scrambling off the bed to the door. "You told Josh we were all headed back here for a *good time*. What is that all about?"

"You aren't seriously listening to anything Josh—"

Jennifer rushed past him and yelled, "Go home, Levi!"

Levi hesitated. *What the hell?* he mouthed to me. "Jennifer," he called, using the same tone he once used with Travis when his temper flared, then he followed her down the hall. I stood in the hallway, trying to decide if I should go talk to Kayla. That's when I noticed the pictures.

I recognized the blue background in the framed photograph hanging on the corridor wall leading to the back of Kayla's house. They'd used the same backdrop for all of our school photos that year. Kayla's feet, out of the picture, were lined up on the T mark the old guy had taped to the floor. Systematically, we stood in lines clutching our envelopes, smoothing cowlicks, delusional enough to think we'd look like the kids in the promotional materials. With her long blond hair and practiced smile, Kayla had nailed it. Anyone looking at her photo would have predicted a stellar high-school experience filled with all the trappings of the top rung in the social ladder.

"Hey, Ash," Levi called. He moseyed down the hall toward me and leaned in close. "You ready? If I don't get Jennifer home by midnight her dad will have my ass."

"Is it that late?"

"No, we've got another hour, but I want some alone time." He nudged me, and I was thinking he was a lost cause when his expression shifted sheepishly back down the hall toward Jennifer. "You won't tell Jennifer I said that, right?"

I pictured my one encounter with Jennifer in the backseat of my mom's car. It rated among the top ten most awkward moments of my life, and I'd had some pretty awkward moments. No way would I ever tell Levi about that.

"Cool," Levi said, even though I hadn't answered him, one way or the other.

"I'm just going to let Kayla know we're headed out," I said, pointing down the hall.

"Oh, right." Then he noticed the photograph I'd been looking at of Kayla. "Damn, when was that? Seventh grade?" he said.

"Sixth."

He took a step back from it. "I'd kill my mom if she put mine up from that year. You remember how fat I was?"

No one would accuse Levi of that now. Hours spent slamming himself into people and sprinting across the field had resulted in his stocky bulldog build. Still, he was too solid to be thin.

"People change." I traced the glass surface of the frame, then shoved my hand in my pocket. Levi's gaze shifted back down the hall.

"Makes you wonder, doesn't it?" He pulled his phone out of the pocket of his pants, glanced at it, and slid it back.

I motioned down the hall toward her bedroom. "I'll tell her we're taking off."

But she wasn't in her bedroom. I followed the matted beige carpet farther back. A thin line of light appeared through the doorway of a room. Through the open crack of the door I saw Kayla standing at the sink, an orange container in her right hand, dishing a small white pill into her palm.

"What are you doing?" I said, even though it was obvious.

She startled, saw me in the reflection of the mirror, and kicked the door closed. It was dark in the hallway. I stood outside, momentarily indecisive, and then knocked on the door.

"Go away," Kayla called, her voice hollow.

I turned the doorknob and pushed the door open. "What is that?" I asked.

Kayla scooped her hand to her mouth, tossed the contents in, and mumbled, "Meds." She swallowed without water.

"How many did you take?" I asked as I picked the bottle up and read the side: Valium. My mom took those. Kayla's name was typed neatly at the top. She snatched the plastic container from my hand.

"Kayla," I pleaded.

"They're mine. And I'm taking the right dosage." She opened the medicine chest and placed it carefully on the second shelf next to an assortment of other meds. "Don't screw with me, Asher. It's been a tough night."

"Why are you taking those?"

Kayla leaned against the countertop and leveled her gaze at me in the reflection. Her hair fell loosely around her pale face. Only a tiny trace of mascara was smudged under her right eye, otherwise she looked normal. I thought about Jennifer's raccoon eyes when she cried; Kayla's eyes were red, but dry. The counter was covered with little jars, pencils, plastic eye-shadow boxes, and contraptions. My mom didn't own this much makeup.

"I'm not going to hurt myself," she said steadily. She slowly rotated toward me. Kayla rested her soft hand against my face. "I promise, Ash. I'm okay. They're for anxiety. Panic attacks."

"You have panic attacks?"

"Not if I take the meds." She lowered her hand to rest on my shoulder. "You okay?"

I nodded and shifted my focus to the items on the counter. Cover-up, lip liner, waterproof mascara. She was comforting me, making me feel better. "Levi said we need to go," I told her. "Are you going to be okay?"

"I'm always okay," Kayla said.

She said it like she believed it, but I was pretty sure her I'd remember her shrieking voice for the rest of my life.

Chapter Five

The handle on the paneled office door looked like the one to my own bedroom, which was weird, since no one lived here. A tall lamp stood in the far corner. A brown leather sofa butted against the wall across from the door, and a wing-backed chair was tucked in the corner to my right. A vanilla-scented candle burned softly on the second shelf of a desk. An open laptop sat on top of the desk, the screensaver a picture of two grinning girls, one with gapped teeth, the other with nubs of baby teeth. I read the titles of the books on the shelves: *Family Dynamics*, *Surviving the Suffering*, and *The Lost Boys: America's Males At Risk*. Above the sofa, a framed poster read: *Nothing in this world worth having comes easy*.

I watched the second hand tick on the clock above her head. We'd been sitting here for fifteen minutes. I noticed my left leg bobbing up and down, so I shifted against the stiff sofa and planted my foot solidly against the floor. She wrote something down on a yellow legal pad. I wanted to ask her what she was noting, but I didn't want to seem paranoid.

She seemed nice enough.

I focused on the flame of the candle on her neat desk. It wasn't a desk, really. It was more like a bookshelf and computer table—an entertainment center—only you could sit at it. Levi had one in his room. His shelves held trophies. One of them hid a crumpled five-dollar bill underneath it. I read more of the titles of the books on her shelf: *Family Dynamics*, *Grief: A Teenager's Guide to Acceptance*, *Unleashing the Inner Child*. At school, the guidance counselor's office walls used thumbtacks to put up posters. Here, the posters were framed.

I recognized the frames. She'd gotten them at Target. Cheap black frames that looked nice, but didn't hold up well over time. I bought them to display my black-and-white photographs. If anyone looked at the backing, they'd see the duct tape I used to hold them together, but no one sees the backs of picture frames that hang on the wall.

Everything looks nice from the front.

People don't pay attention to the back. Like my mom's hair. When she took the time to do it, which she didn't very often, she'd puff it out in the front and frame her face, but she took all the hair from the back to get that effect. The back looked stringy. Her hair looked best when she didn't do it at all—not that I'd ever tell her that.

The lady sitting across from me in the black pants and crisp blue button-up shirt had nice hair. When I'd followed her down the hall to the office, I'd noticed her hair looked okay from the back. She didn't do anything fussy with it. It was brown, cut above her shoulder, and all the same length. She'd told me her name, but I couldn't remember what it was. Something that ended with an *ee* sound. Chrissy? Debbie?

"I graduated from your high school," she said.

"Oh."

"Of course, that was almost twenty years ago. Do they still have the Duke painted on the wall outside the gym?"

She was talking about the giant mural of a cowboy riding a horse. Everyone called the cowboy *Duke*.

"Yeah."

"I helped paint that," she said.

"That's cool."

"I wasn't much of an athlete, but I liked drawing."

She waited for me to say something. I felt bad for her. She was really trying, so I took a deep breath. "I'm not much of an athlete either."

"Are you an artist?"

I thought about Garrett and the anime drawings that covered his walls. "No."

"Are you involved in any clubs or activities at school?"

Levi had tried to convince me to go out for football, but bashing myself into people wasn't my idea of a good time. Catching a ball wasn't in my skill set. Mostly though the guys on the team made me nervous. "No."

"Why not?"

Even though I had been all set to do tech with the school play, Mom had grounded me two days before the show opened. That didn't count. I glanced back up at the clock. "I don't know."

"Is there anything you'd like to be involved in?" she pressed.

Maybe drama again, but that didn't start up until after Christmas. If I said it, she might latch onto it, like Mom, so I said, "Not really."

"What do you do outside of school?" She waited a long time, but I was still thinking. "Do you hang out with friends? Or do you prefer to do things on your own?"

I adjusted my weight on the sofa. "On my own, mostly."

"What types of things do you do?" She waited a long time again. "Do you play video games? Are you a computer guy?"

I shook my head. "Pictures"—I cleared my throat—"I take pictures."

"Pictures?"

"Photographs."

"Oh, I have a nephew who's really into Photoshop. He does amazing things with—"

"No. Not digital," I said. "I used to use a Minolta, but it broke. Then a Canon A-1. Film. I don't like digital."

"Why?"

"People can change the image digitally, make it into something else. So I use film."

"Does it bother you when people do that? Change things?"

I shrugged and fidgeted in the chair.

She scribbled something on the legal pad. I wondered what she was writing. "Tell me more about your photographs."

"Uh."

"Where did you get your camera? You mentioned a Canon A-1, that's not a new camera. Did someone give it to you?"

I leaned back onto the cushions. The couch wasn't very comfortable considering it was supposed to make people feel at ease. "My neighbor, Pearl, she let me use it."

"That's nice of her. She must really trust you, to let you use her camera." I tried to read her expression. She sat there with this pleasant look on her face. Nothing about her gave any indication she was trying to get me to talk about stealing Pearl's camera. When the appointment was made, didn't anyone explain? "Tell me about Pearl." Maybe she knew more than she was letting on.

"She's old. She smells like, you know, old."

"Do you like her?"

I thought about Pearl and her old flowery robes and how cheap she was when it came to paying me to mow her yard. "Yes."

"Why?"

I shrugged.

"Why do you think she let you use her camera?"

"She didn't give me her nice one."

"But she gave you a camera to use. *Her* camera. That says something. What do you think that is?"

I had no idea why she let me use her camera. Particularly if she intended to accuse me of stealing it. "She says my photographs are crap."

"Really?"

"Yeah."

"And you like her?"

I shrugged.

"Do you agree with her? Are your photographs crap?"

"No."

"So she's wrong."

"I mean, I have stuff to learn. I can get better."

"So she's right."

"She thinks she's right."

"Do you trust her judgment?"

"I don't know."

She jotted something else down on the pad, and I wiped my sweaty hands against my jeans. This lady stressed me out.

"It looks like we're done for today," she said. "Let's go see your dad."

I followed her down the hallway, and she held the door open. Dad looked up as I walked into the waiting room. She waved at him and said, "Next week?"

"Same time," Dad said. "Ready, sport?"

Sport. Stupid nickname. "Yeah."

He folded the local newspaper and set it on top of a stack of magazines on the table. I opened the door leading out to the parking lot. The crisp air cooled my skin. I sniffed, clearing my nose of the scent of vanilla from the candle in her office. I smelled like Dairy Queen. Dad tossed his keys into the air and caught them as we headed down the sidewalk to the side of the building. Plenty of parking spaces had been available right in front of the counseling center, but they were visible from the road. If there wasn't anything wrong with going to therapy, why did he feel the need to hide his Land Rover?

❖

In English class, Ms. Hughes took us to the computer lab to do research on careers. I wrote *photographer* on the blank at the top of the form she gave us and filled in *salary range* and *job description*. We had two computer lab days—plenty of time to get it all done—so I spent most of my time looking for deals on Canon A-1s on eBay. I didn't bother to look at Minoltas.

In all honesty, the Minolta had started to irk me long before my dad made me take a photo of him and his new wife and I'd chucked it in the pool. I know, pretty stupid, but it made sense at the time. It did this autofocus thing, so if I wanted to focus on an object in the distance, the Minolta would never let me do that. Whatever object was closest, the camera zoomed in on, like it thought for me. The Canon allowed me to choose from five different AE modes. It put me in the driver's seat. I could do what I wanted.

"You haven't gotten very far, Asher."

Great. Ms. Hughes reached down in front of me and picked up my career form. I minimized the Canon A-1 tab and the career website popped up on the screen.

"Sorry, it's just I know a lot of this already," I said.

"Photographer," she read from the top of my form. I'd written it in black ink, all caps. "What are the educational requirements?"

I scrolled down the career page and showed her the section on education. "It's all right here, but it really doesn't apply to me. Most programs do a lot with art and digital photography. I don't do digital."

Ms. Hughes put the form down in front of me again. "So your specific job title would be, what?" she asked. "Are you going to work in marketing? Be self-employed? A freelance photographer?"

I opened my mouth, but then I closed it. I sort of saw my photos in a gallery or something.

"And what's the job outlook?"

I stared blankly at the screen. I didn't even know what she was talking about, but sure enough there was a blank on the paper that asked about it.

"Think about the kind of lifestyle you want. How are you going to pay your bills?"

Bills? The only bills I had were for buying film and developing it. It's like she was trying to talk me out of my career.

"It's what I want to do," I said defensively.

"Good. That makes you way ahead of most people your age. Now educate yourself. You need to know what you're up against or you'll never be successful." Ms. Hughes glided down the row. I scrolled down to the types of photography: portrait, commercial, aerial, scientific, news, fine arts… I stopped.

Fine-arts photographers must be highly skilled in the technical elements of camera use and lighting and are generally classified as creative artists who market their work in galleries. They typically work with film, not with digital media.

I thought of my photographs as art. I never used digital cameras. It never occurred to me that a title beyond *photographer* might exist for what I do. A tingling sensation raced through me. I returned to the word photographer at the top of the page and added *fine arts* above it in capital letters.

❖

Most of the lunch tables were full when I walked in, but I spied an empty one toward the back just in case no one offered me a seat. I got my usual burger and Tater Tots, then meandered into the seating area. Levi sprawled out at the jock table with Manny, Josh, and a bunch of other thick-necks. He'd propped his leg up on an open seat. I knew he'd begrudgingly move his foot for me, but considering I'd narrowly escaped a beating from Josh at the party, I walked past them. Kayla and Jennifer sat at the drama table with Iggy and Garrett.

My stomach lurched at the sight of them.

"Asher!" Jennifer called and motioned to me. It wasn't an invitation. It was an order. Typical Jennifer. She met me halfway, grabbed my arm, and led me over to the drama table. She nudged me into a seat and sat down beside me. Iggy was in midsentence, but Jennifer launched in as though no one had been talking.

"So, I have this great idea," Jennifer announced. "I was thinking Asher could do head shots for the actors. If anyone wants one."

I wasn't the only one who stared blankly at her.

"Head shots?" It sounded violent.

"Yeah, brilliant, right?" Jennifer said, flipping her hair.

Kayla frowned. "The play is over."

"Duh," Jennifer said. "So we have time to do this."

"But it's pointless," Kayla argued.

"It's not *pointless*. For the people who are serious about having a career, they have to have a head shot. If you knew anything about acting you would know—"

"Uh, what are head shots?" I asked.

"Head shots are photos actors use to get work," Jennifer explained to me. "They send their photographs to casting directors to get roles."

"Oh," I said. I suspected Jennifer's career project was on acting.

"Asher doesn't take pictures of people," Garrett said. His eyes locked with mine. I couldn't look directly at him without feeling my face start to burn.

I thought about that day at the pool, Garrett slinging his arm over Levi's shoulder, and asking me to take his picture. Levi told him then: *Asher doesn't take pictures of people.* Garrett remembered. I cleared my throat. "Actually, I do," I said. "Not posed photos or anything. I've been looking into candid shots."

"Candid?" Jennifer asked.

Iggy scoffed. "It means he creeps up on people and takes their picture without them knowing." His stringy black hair hung over his beady eyes. He slumped in his chair, his back curved like a gargoyle latched onto the side of a Gothic castle.

"What made you change your mind?" Garrett asked.

I shrugged. "I didn't like photos of people because they were always posing. Sort of fake."

"Is that legal?" Iggy asked. "Taking pictures of people without them knowing?"

I'd never thought of that.

Garrett rested a hand on Iggy's shoulder. "It's cool," Garrett said, and he let his hand drift down Iggy's shoulder before resting it on the table in front of him. It was a casual move, but definitely *not* a typical guy-friend nudge.

Iggy sat stock still, but his eyes skittered around the table and lunchroom to see if anyone had noticed the gesture. No one else but me seemed to be paying attention. Iggy frowned at me, shook his hair back into his eyes, and slumped hunchback style in his chair.

"I don't know how that would work," Jennifer said as she tapped a perfectly manicured pink fingernail against the table. "We'd have to know we're getting our pictures taken, you know?"

"Jennifer, Asher already has a picture of you," Kayla said. "Right, Asher?"

The football game.

"Uh…"

"You do?" Jennifer asked, leaning forward.

"Yeah, that's normal," Iggy said.

My face felt hot. Garrett was staring at me. I tried to smile like it was no big deal. "Uh, yeah," I stammered. "I was just taking pictures at the football game. You know, sort of testing out the camera."

Jennifer rested her chin on her hands, fascinated. "What was I doing?"

My hands fidgeted in front of me. "You're sort of looking at Levi. He's in the background, sitting on the bench. It's not a big deal."

Jennifer put her hand over her mouth and squealed, "Oh my gosh, it sounds perfect! I have to see this. Do you have the pictures? I want to see!"

"I don't have them anymore. I don't even have a camera."

"Asher, you have to do the head shots," Jennifer said. "The whole purpose is to try to capture a person's real expression. Seriously."

"But they know they're getting their picture taken," I said, clenching my fist. She had no clue. "Plus, I mean, it costs a lot of money to buy film and get it developed."

"How much?"

"What, you mean, like a roll of film? Or to have it developed?"

"Yes," she said. I started adding things up in my head, but Jennifer didn't wait for a response. "I'll pay you for your film, developing, and your time. Deal?"

"Jennifer, I don't have a camera," I repeated.

"My dad has a digital. It's nice."

I chewed on my bottom lip. Digital? No way. And taking photos of people *posed*? Absolutely not. But there weren't many opportunities to mow the neighbors' grass for cash in the winter months.

"Just try it," Jennifer urged. "Please? If I'm going to be an actor, I need this."

Kayla snorted.

Jennifer turned toward her. "What?"

"It's all about how it benefits you," Kayla said.

"This would benefit everyone. Especially Asher. He'll get paid to be a photographer." Jennifer turned back to me. "So do you want me to put together a schedule for you?"

Even though I didn't answer her, Jennifer showed up at my locker with a list of potential dates for me to do the head shots. She was the only one on the schedule.

Chapter Six

I found a note from my mom on the kitchen counter. John was coming over after dinner. Probably something to do with the grieving class he started at the church. Since my dad attended the sessions they held in the choir room, Mom refused to go. In fact, we hadn't been to church since then, but John deserved an award for trying to convince us to return. She instructed me to put the clean clothes away, empty the dishwasher, and pull the weeds in our driveway before she got home at five. I know, weeds in our driveway.

As I started yanking the tangled green cropping up in our cracked driveway, I noticed our neighbor Pearl's yard. Old bat. Some weeds had grown up around the shrubs in the front of her house, too. Her car sat in the driveway, so I knew she was home. Probably sitting in a flowered zip-up robe watching one of her game shows. I thought about that counseling session, and the photo I'd taken from her portfolio, so I went ahead and pulled those weeds, too.

Mom came home while I was in the shower. As soon as I turned off the water, she thumped on the door. "I thought I told you to put the clothes away," she said.

I grabbed a towel. "Did you see the yard?" I asked.

"Yes." A pause. "But you still need to put your clothes away."

I made a point of wrapping my towel around my still dripping body to trudge out to retrieve my stack of clean clothes.

"You're getting water all over everything," Mom said as she pulled her nice jeans from the pile of clothes fresh from the dryer.

"You told me to get my clothes."

"Asher," she warned.

I trudged to my room and closed the door. Hector, my hermit crab, skittered across his tank. He'd eaten the lettuce I'd put in there this afternoon. I placed a hand against the clear plastic wall of his cage, and Hector tucked himself inside his shell. It must be nice having a place you can hide when everyone's ticking you off. I didn't mean to be a jerk, but every time I looked at Mom, I felt angry.

You lied.

You cheated on Dad.

Travis died.

It's all your fault.

But I knew she wasn't entirely to blame. I was wrapped up in there, too. Still, she lied, and I knew the truth. I couldn't figure out how to get over it when both of us were invested in the other not knowing. I knew why she lied to me—fear that I would hate her, blame her. So I protected her from knowing that I knew, but a part of me hated her and blamed her anyway.

I heard music start up from the other room, some Beatles tune. *Music?* Mom usually kept the TV on as background noise. She hardly ever listened to music. I got dressed and headed into the kitchen to unload the dishwasher but discovered it was empty. She must have unloaded it while I was in the shower. I found her standing at the bathroom sink applying mascara and humming along to a song about a blackbird. *Weird.* Mom never wore makeup.

"I was going to unload the dishwasher," I said. "I just hadn't gotten to it yet."

"It's okay," she said. She studied her reflection in the mirror, blinked a few times, and then turned to me. "Really, it's okay. Thank you for your help."

"When is John coming over?" I asked.

She looked at the clock on the bathroom wall. "In an hour. Do you want to make the pasta? I was thinking spaghetti."

"Sure."

"You need to start it now. I don't want us to be in the middle of eating when he gets here."

I hated when she talked to me like I was an idiot. I headed back to the kitchen, filled a pot with water, and put it on the stove to boil. The phone rang. I expected Mom to get it, but when it rang four times I went ahead and picked it up.

"I didn't ask you to pull weeds," said an old, scratchy voice. Pearl. "I know."

"I'm not paying you for it."

"Okay."

Silence.

"What are you up to?" she asked. "You trying to pull something?"

"Yeah, pulling *weeds*. I was working on our yard and noticed you had weeds, too. No big deal."

"Oh. Okay, then." She hung up the phone. Crazy old lady.

I remembered I still had her photograph. The photo revealed the truth, but I needed to return it before Pearl discovered I'd borrowed it from her portfolio. It's not stealing if I had every intention of giving it back.

I opened the fridge to get the leftover jar of sauce and discovered a package of assorted cheesecakes. A chill ran through me, and it wasn't because the fridge was open. Mom only bought food like that for special occasions. The only person who was coming by was John, and that was just to go through the grief book with her. John's wife died the same day Travis did, but unlike Travis, her death was the result of a long illness. Still, it had only been a few months. And I had seen him at the Italian restaurant holding hands with some woman. I gripped the fridge handle and reached past the cheesecake for the sauce.

"Mom?" I called.

I found her looking at herself in the mirror. Again. She'd changed into a pair of jeans and a soft blue button-up shirt. I felt sick. "Who was on the phone?" she asked.

"Pearl."

Mom stood up straight and met my eyes in the mirror. "Oh? What did she want?"

"I pulled her weeds. She thought it was some sort of hostile act." It felt good to see Mom smile. She did it so rarely these days. But I went ahead and asked, "So what's with the cheesecake?"

"There's a thing at work tomorrow," she said. "Joanie is retiring, and we're all supposed to bring something in."

Okay. The cheesecake wasn't for John.

"Did you put the pasta on?" she asked. She pulled a brush through her hair.

"I'm waiting for the water to boil."

She inspected herself closely in the mirror, and then she flipped off the light switch.

We'd just finished dinner when the house phone rang again. This time Mom answered it. All she said was hello, and then she listened, turned toward me, and hung up the phone.

"O-kay," Mom said, drawing it out.

"What?"

"Pearl wants you to go pick up your photos."

"What photos?"

"I have no idea."

And then it came to me. She'd had my film from the Canon A-1 developed.

The doorbell rang.

"That's John," Mom said, and she started for the door.

"Can I go to Pearl's?"

"Asher, seriously, I think the woman is going senile or something. I don't think it's a good idea." She hesitated at the door.

"Mom, please."

She nodded reluctantly, so I retrieved the photograph from my room and slid out the back sliding glass door as I heard her say, "John!" Her breathy voice reminded me of Jennifer.

It took Pearl a long time to answer the door. I put my left hand in my back pocket to check for the photo, but clasped my hands behind me when I heard the lock turn. Sure enough, she was wearing a flowered robe and blue slippers.

"Took you long enough," Pearl said, holding the door in front of her like a shield.

For a second I thought she was just going to slam the door, like maybe the photos were only available if I responded within a certain time frame.

"Come in." She left the door open, so I followed her into her living room. As soon as I stepped inside the door, a stench hit me so hard I struggled to keep from throwing up. Pearl didn't seem to notice.

She said, "They weren't too bad this round. The one with the girl, the one who looks like she's hiding an AK-47 under her coat, she's got an interesting look. Rest are dribble, mostly."

More unsolicited criticism. I would have been offended if I wasn't trying so hard not to vomit. She brought a regular envelope over to me. I held it. "What the hell are you waiting for? Open it."

I jumped and reached inside for the photos. There they were. I flipped through the stack. She was right: the one with Kayla was the best. She nestled up next to me, and I was glad she wasn't the stench.

"This one here," she said, pulling the one of my mom resting in Travis's room. She jutted her chin out and nodded.

"Where did you get these developed?" I asked.

She ignored me. "So, what are you working on now?"

I remembered Jennifer's harassment from lunch. "Head shots, maybe."

"Actors are the worst. What have you done so far?"

Was she serious? I walked past her into her living room. "Uh, nothing."

"Nothing? Why nothing?"

I stared at her, unblinking. Lately it felt like everyone was screwing with me. Nope, she honestly didn't know why I wasn't working on photography.

"Maybe it's because I don't have a camera," I said, and I spread my arms wide to illustrate my point.

"You *lost* my camera?" Pearl demanded, lifting a bony finger and pointing it at me. "Don't you tell me you lost my camera."

I studied her. She was serious. "You don't remember?" I should have told her then. It was the perfect time, but Pearl's expression changed. She looked confused, worried. The bony hand she pointed at me shook. I should tell her she accused me of stealing her camera. Sweet justice. But I suddenly felt exhausted and terrible.

"I didn't lose your camera," I said.

"Well then, where is it?"

I motioned to her house. "I'm pretty sure you have it here somewhere. That's where you got the film." Her eyes scanned the room, but she was searching in her head. "Remember?"

Her expression troubled me, but then it was as though someone had turned on a light. "Yes, yes," she said. "Of course. I'll be right back."

Pearl motioned for me to sit on the sofa and hobbled into another room. I heard a door squeak open and the sound of papers shifting and falling. The smell was worse the farther into the house I got. Did she have a dead body behind the sofa? I needed to get out of there or I was going to vomit. I tried to breathe through my mouth. I reached back into my pocket again, pulled the photo out, and slid it partially under the sofa. She waddled back a few minutes later, carrying the Canon A-1. I stood up.

"Pearl, I really appreciate your letting me use the camera, but I think it might be better if you keep it," I said.

"You have another camera?" she pressed.

"No. But I—"

She shoved it toward me. "Then use it. I'm not using it. You aren't interested in photography anymore?"

"No, it's not that, I just don't want to have anything happen to it."

"Take it."

And that's when I noticed the brown grocery bag leaning against the wall. It was discolored at the bottom, like something had leaked. Great.

"What have you got there?" I asked.

"What?"

I pointed. "In the bag."

"What bag? Oh shit." Pearl ambled over toward it. "Damn cashier packs those bags so heavy. I was going to put it in the fridge to defrost."

"How long ago did you go shopping?"

"This morning," she said.

It didn't smell like this morning.

"Maybe yesterday. I'm sure it'll be fine." She lifted the bag by the top and a mess of gooey, rancid turkey and assorted other items spilled out the bottom.

It was everything I could do not to vomit. Instead, I pinched my nose and asked, "You got plastic bags?"

"Under the kitchen sink."

I hurried into the kitchen. A rack in the sink contained dishes stacked upside down like we do when we set them out to dry, but the silverware still had food stuck to it. I reached under the sink, grabbed a couple of plastic bags, and rushed back to the hall. Pearl was sifting through the nastiness. She had a box of instant stuffing in her hand, oblivious to the foul turkey juices dripping off it. I took the box from her and stuffed it into the plastic bag.

"That was fine," she snipped.

I ignored her, held my breath, and scooped as much of the mess as I could into the bag. Using the dry part of the paper bag, I picked up all the groceries, even the cans, and tossed them. Pearl protested, but I was keeping a list in my head of what all had been in the bag. I'd replace it if I had to. There was no way I was going to rinse off those nasty cans and save them. I went back to the kitchen for paper towels and cleaner to wipe up the last of it. It was the most disgusting thing I'd ever cleaned in my life. The turkey must have been there for at least five days. How Pearl hadn't smelled it was beyond me.

"I'll put this in our trash bin," I said, and then I turned to look at Pearl. She was sitting in the chair in the living room. Her pale eyes were rimmed red.

"There wasn't a damn thing wrong with the cans," she said. "And I need the cream of mushroom for the casserole, you know."

I wiped my hands on my jeans and tried to remember what all we had in our cabinet at home. "I'm pretty sure we have some. I can bring it over," I said.

"I don't want your cream of mushroom soup. Pull mine out of there!"

"What? You want me to dig it out of the trash?" I asked. "Jeez."

"You're an asshole," she said.

I pointed down at the floor. "I just cleaned up your rotten turkey!" It had been everything I could do not to puke all over her floor.

"That turkey was fine. Just been sitting there since this morning."

"Are you kidding me?"

"No one asked you to!"

Right. I could have left it there. I could have walked out the door and let it stink. Or I could have let Pearl cook it up and eat it and die. "I'm going home," I said, but I didn't move. More than anything, I wanted to take a shower. I reeked. But Pearl sitting in her chair all huffy made me feel bad. Maybe she'd spend Thanksgiving all alone. "What are you doing for Thanksgiving anyway?" I asked.

"None of your damn business."

"Look," I said, "my mom wants to volunteer at the shelter for Thanksgiving, otherwise we'd invite—"

"I've got plans," she said.

Maybe her brother, Mitford, was coming into town.

"Well, let me know when you're going to the grocery store. I can carry bags in for you, if you want. Maybe I—"

"I thought you were going home."

I glanced at the photograph resting faceup on the floor as I moved toward the door.

"Don't forget your photos," she said. "And will you please just take the damn camera?"

I felt so awful about the whole thing, I did.

CHAPTER SEVEN

The food pantry was located next door to the community swimming pool. The last time I'd been to the pool, my brother had drowned. I remembered Levi's voice echoing in the bathroom, *It's Travis.* I pictured Jennifer's face lined with tears I hadn't cried, and the imprints of the tiles on the bathroom floor on Garrett's skin. The last time I'd been to the pool, my brother had drowned. The black asphalt on the parking lot had turned the soles of my feet black. I noted how Mom's eyes stayed glued to the road as she pulled into the next driveway. I wondered if she was thinking about Travis, too.

People huddled up outside, waiting for the front doors to open. It was fifty degrees—cold for Florida—but I hadn't bothered with a jacket since it would probably warm up to the low seventies by noon. The condensation on the windows dripped in rivulets. I stifled a yawn. Mom parked the car in the back parking lot, held on to her keys, and tucked her purse under a beach towel in the backseat.

"Can you hold these? I don't have pockets," she said, holding her keys out to me.

I stepped out of the car and buried the keys in the back pocket of my jeans. The scrawniest calico cat I'd ever seen limped along the side of the building and stopped, alert, as it spied us making our way across the asphalt. Its back paw dangled a few inches off the ground. I thought about catching it to check out its leg, but it was like the animal sensed my intentions. The cat inched downward, pressed its ears back, and darted across the parking lot. It didn't have any problem running, that was for sure. We headed for the back entrance, but before we made it up the concrete steps, the door swung open.

"Happy Thanksgiving!" John said, holding the door for us.

John was here?

When Mom smiled, I noticed her glossy lips. She was wearing makeup. Again.

"Happy Thanksgiving, John. How long have you been here?"

"Just a few minutes. There's coffee in the kitchen. Are you a coffee drinker, Asher?"

I wasn't, but I figured it was as good a time as any to become one. "I'll have a cup."

Mom didn't comment on my change of beverage selection. Instead she walked beside John as he led us down a hallway into a room with stainless-steel everything. A room off to the side contained an industrial-sized fridge and three giant cylinders marked *regular, decaf,* and *hot water.* I watched Mom fill a Styrofoam cup with the regular and did the same.

"You're probably going to want cream and sugar," she whispered to me as I joined her at a side table loaded with creamers and sugar.

Mom poured a splash of milk into her coffee and joined John at a table. I did the same but added a spoonful of sugar as well. I stirred it up and took a cautious sip. *Nasty.* I tried not to make a face and added another three heaps of sugar. Still nasty, but I could tolerate it. I concentrated on not spilling as I headed to the table.

"So, you'll serve up the pie," John told Mom. "We have pumpkin and cherry. Whipped topping, too. I'll show you where the gloves and all are. But really you're just manning the station. If we get low on pie, we have runners to get more from the back fridge."

Mom nodded. "Do you work Thanksgiving every year?" she asked.

"When Meredith was healthy, we volunteered together," he said.

I'd never known the healthy Meredith. My memories of her were of a skeletal, frail person in a wheelchair. For a long time, I thought Meredith was John's mom; she looked that old. I sipped the bitter coffee.

John cleared his throat. "What do you say, Asher? You up to doing dishes?"

Great. That meant scraping nasty trays of turkey fat and mashed potatoes into a giant rubber trash can. Mom would be up front wearing plastic gloves and a smile while my hands turned to prunes in dank dishwater. "Sure."

It turned out to be a good thing, washing dishes. The only contact I had with the guests occurred when they slid their trays across the metal counter to me. I was glad I was in the back since talking to strangers isn't my strong suit. I barely had time to glance at their faces. All the little kids reminded me of Travis.

I was hauling a load of trash out to the Dumpster when I recognized the lanky figure with greasy black hair heading around the corner of the building. *Iggy?* After tossing the plastic garbage bag, I followed him. Just as I made it to the front of the building, I saw Iggy open the door and head inside the shelter. Maybe he was volunteering. Then I thought about the skinny jeans and threadbare shirts he wore daily to school. I'd always thought he was aiming for a grungy, rebellious look. I felt a stab of guilt. I hesitated a moment at the side of the brick building, and then I headed back to the rear entrance and into the kitchen.

I joined Mom at the dessert table. "How's it going?" I asked her as I scanned the room.

Mom handed a plate of pumpkin pie to an elderly man before turning to me. "Everything's fine," she said. She actually smiled. "You doing okay?"

I spotted Iggy standing in line with a tray. When the serving lady turned away to get another tray, Iggy pocketed an extra roll. "Yeah," I said to Mom. "Okay, well, I guess I should head back to the dishes." I maneuvered through the crowd to avoid Iggy seeing me, but when I got back to the sinks, I kept an eye on him. I watched him take his tray to a corner seat away from everyone else. He hunched over his food. No one else noticed him wrap the turkey in napkins and stuff them in the pocket of his hoodie. He didn't open the milk carton either. Instead he tucked that in his hoodie, too. After he went to the dessert table, he slid the slice of pie onto a piece of plastic wrap and hid it. Unlike most of the people, Iggy didn't bother to bring his tray up to the counter or clean his place. When he was finished, he stood up and disappeared out a side door.

"I'll take the trash out," I announced to the other washer, a guy from church, even though the bag was only half-full. I peeked out the door and waited until Iggy passed by before I went out to the Dumpster.

I left the bag leaning against the building and used the cars in the parking lot to conceal me. Iggy sauntered through the car-lined rows toward an abandoned building adjacent to the shelter. He hopped up onto a ledge and pulled up his hood. A few stray black hairs stuck out from under it. I took in Iggy's black hoodie, the brick wall covered with graffiti, his worn jeans, and the broken glass littering the ground.

Why wasn't he at home with his family? Come to think of it, I had no idea where Iggy lived. I thought about Iggy's little sister, Rose. She'd been in the ensemble of the play. Maybe there had been a blowup at his house, and he'd decided to clear out for a few days.

The scrawny cat I'd seen earlier leapt up from behind the ledge of the wall. Its back left foot dangled, useless. Even from the distance, I could see the sores on its body and its matted fur. It had a feral look about it, wild-eyed and suspicious, but it took a tentative step toward Iggy. He didn't react to the cat. If anything, he leaned away, which in turn made the cat take another step toward him.

I rubbed my hands together to warm them.

Did Garrett know? No way. If Garrett knew, Iggy would be sitting at their dining-room table.

I headed back to our car, unlocked the door, and grabbed Pearl's Canon A-1. It was overcast, a gray day. A flash could reveal me, and I didn't want Iggy to know I'd seen him, so I'd have to hope there was enough natural light. I arranged myself between the cars and adjusted the dials to ensure the best photo. Iggy's body filled the lower right corner. As I lined him up, he shivered and tucked his hands into the sleeves of his hoodie. I lowered the camera. It was cold. I should go get some of that coffee for him to hold in his hands. Or maybe I could find a decent coat or a pair of gloves.

Would I want Iggy to do that for me, if I were sitting in the cold? No.

I pressed my lips together and lifted the camera again just as Iggy retrieved the napkin out of his pocket. He tore a piece of turkey off and tossed it off the wall. The cat lunged for it, disappearing behind the bricks. A minute later, the cat was back, closer this time to Iggy. Iggy waved a hand at it to swoosh it away, but the cat reached a paw up like it thought there might be something tasty in Iggy's grasp. The cat walked a tight circle, and then sat watching Iggy expectantly. I saw

Iggy's shoulders slump, and he tore off another piece of turkey. This time he tossed it onto the ledge, but farther away from him.

The cat even ate suspiciously. It took a quick bite, then turned to glare at Iggy and stand guard against potential predators. Iggy got the roll out of his pocket. Then he tucked his skinny legs up in front of him and rested his head on his knees. He broke a piece of the bread off and nibbled at it while he watched the cat eat. Their backs curved at exactly the same angle. When I took the picture of Iggy and the cat huddled in the corner of the brick building, it was at the exact moment their eyes met, sort of glaring at each other.

❖

When we got home from the shelter, there were two messages on the answering machine. I figured it would be from Aunt Sharon wishing us a Happy Thanksgiving, but instead Levi's gruff voice came over the machine. "Call me when you get home from sainthood training. I got leftovers."

The second message was from Dad. "Hi, it's me. We're going to Helen's folks to celebrate with them tomorrow. Just make sure you wear something nice. See you after church."

Mom deleted both the messages and started to unload the dishwasher. "Do you have anything to wear?" she asked me.

"I've got my khakis. Is that okay?"

"I'm sure it's fine." She handed me one of the bowls we stored up on the top shelf of the cabinet.

"Are we going to church tomorrow?" I asked as I tucked it on top of the matching bowl.

Mom paused. "Do you want to go?" she asked.

We used to go to church every Sunday, but everything had changed since Travis died. "Do you?" I asked.

She sighed and crossed her arms in front of her. "Honestly, I don't know. John will be there."

John?

Mom ran a hand through her hair and asked, "Are you going to call Levi?"

I shrugged. "I guess so."

Mom took my hand. "It wasn't a terrible Thanksgiving, was it?"
I let her hold my hand. I looked down at the veins visible under her flesh. She looked so old. I thought about Iggy and wondered what would have happened if I'd approached him. "No, it was nice helping people. You were right."

She smiled, but her eyes looked all shiny with tears. She patted my hand. "Good," she said. Then she walked out of the kitchen, leaving the dishwasher wide-open and full. I knew she was headed down the hall to Travis's empty room. I started to put the dishes away, but one of the forks still had crud on it. I dunked it in my water-filled glass in the sink to loosen it up. I wondered if Pearl's Thanksgiving had been any better than ours. I'd left a bag with replacement cans on her front step, and when we returned from the shelter, the package and her car were gone. I hope she had time to make her casserole.

Levi nuked a plateful of turkey, mashed potatoes and gravy, sweet-potato casserole, and stuffing in my microwave.

"Just looking at food makes me want to hurl," he said. "I loaded up four plates. And then I decided to have more when they were packing up leftovers. Dude, you're lucky you got anything."

"Did you bring pie?" I asked.

He dug around in a brown paper bag and pulled out a clear plastic tub. "Compliments of Aunt Bertha."

Levi's Aunt Bertha baked the best pies on the planet, and her coconut cream was particularly delicious. "I love that woman," I said and grinned. It was the kind of thing Garrett would say.

"Me, too." Levi sighed. He pulled out another tub. "I brought some key lime for your mom. Where is she?"

"Travis's room."

We listened to the hum of the microwave for a minute. The timer beeped.

"She doing okay?"

I shook my head yes, then no, as I took the plate out of the microwave. It was complicated. Sometimes she was perfectly fine, like today at the shelter. But then she'd disappear into Travis's room for hours at a time. "She has good days and bad days."

Levi nodded. He lowered his voice. "Does she know? That *you* know?"

"No!" I didn't mean for it to come out so hostile, but I couldn't imagine Mom's reaction if she knew Levi and I had discovered her secret. "No. I don't know, Levi. I think it would put her over the edge or something."

He angled toward the hallway, and for a second I thought he was going to join her in Travis's room.

"Levi, leave it alone," I hissed.

"It's hard," he said, lowering his voice. "If I'd known Travis was my half-brother, maybe I would have done things differently, you know? Maybe."

I shook my head. "You can't do that. You can't what-if it." But then I heard the bedroom door open, so I took the steaming hot plate over to the dining table and sat down.

"Are you interested in some key-lime pie?" Levi asked her.

Her eyes were puffy from crying. She didn't answer.

Levi hesitated and glanced at me. I nodded approval, and he went into the kitchen to get the container. Mom sat down at the table, and Levi brought her pie. He even remembered to bring a fork and napkin. He sat down at the table. Watching Levi being nice freaked me out a little.

Mom stared off into space for a minute, but then she seemed to notice the pie and Levi. She cleared her throat. "Did you have a good Thanksgiving?" she asked, her voice hoarse.

Levi shrugged. "Ate way too much. Lots of good games on TV. I got a nap in."

Mom tried to smile. "Sounds like fun," she said, and then she took a bite of the pie. "It's good."

"Aunt Bertha," Levi said.

"She's always made such good pies. What is it your dad used to say? They should be illegal."

Levi tensed up in the chair at the mention of his dad, but he said, "All the good things are."

Mom scowled at him, and she took another bite while I dug into the stuffing.

"There are more leftovers in the fridge," I told Mom. "If you want something other than pie."

Mom stared at the wall while she chewed.

"So how did the moochers make out?" Levi asked. "You get 'em all fed?"

I thought about Iggy. "I was on garbage detail."

"Oh man, that sucks. What a way to spend Thanksgiving."

"We couldn't be here," Mom said hollowly, and she motioned toward Travis's empty chair. She covered her mouth with her hand. Her face contorted and turned red. "I'm sorry." She grabbed her half-empty plate and started for the kitchen. "At least this way someone benefitted from it," she choked out as she rounded the corner.

It was unusual to see Levi at a loss for words. That sort of freaked me out, too. I finished eating in silence. Mom didn't join us at the table. She stayed in the kitchen for a while—probably until she stopped crying—and when she came back out, she stopped at the table. Mom rested a hand on Levi's shoulder. He didn't move. She couldn't see his bulging eyes focused on me, trying not to blink. Then she bent over and kissed him on top of the head, like she used to do with Travis.

I thought she might head back to Travis's room, but instead she settled onto the sofa and turned on the television.

Levi let out a ragged breath and leaned across the table toward me. "Is she always like this?" he whispered.

"You don't have to stick around. I wouldn't blame you." I took my plate to the kitchen and put it in the sink. Levi and I ambled toward my room. I thought he was right behind me, but when I plopped into my computer chair, I realized he hadn't followed me. He might have stopped off in the bathroom, but after a few minutes, I poked my head into the hall. The bathroom door was open with the light off, but Travis's bedroom light was on. I found Levi sitting on the corner of Travis's bed holding Og, the nasty stuffed dog my little brother used to drag with him everywhere he went.

"I didn't even go to the funeral," he said. "My dad asked me if I wanted to, but…"

I sat down next to him on the bed. "It's okay," I said. "He didn't look like himself."

Levi studied me.

"Travis," I explained. "I opened the casket. He didn't look like himself. I don't know, for some reason that made me feel better."

He tossed the stuffed animal back onto Travis's pillow. "You're lucky. You believe in all that shit," he said. "The whole dying thing. I don't know. I think we're just gone."

"That's what I mean. He wasn't there in the casket. The Travis part *was* gone."

"How's that make you feel better?"

"Well, he has to have gone somewhere else then, right? If this"—I motioned to my body—"is a shell, then the other part, it went somewhere."

Levi's bottom lip stuck out like he might cry, so I busied myself staring at the books on Travis's shelf. We used to make ramps out of them, and Travis raced his Matchbox cars off the ledges. The memory of his rumbling and screeching noises, the crashes of cars against the wall, made my heart hurt. Levi blamed himself. He was the last person to talk to Travis before he hit his head and drowned at the pool, but I was the one who was supposed to be watching him.

"You want to see my hermit crab?" I asked.

Levi made a grunt sound. "You got a hermit crab?"

"Yeah. It's Travis's, really. Remember that kid, Bobby, that Travis got in trouble with?" Levi nodded at me, a grin slowly spreading across his face. "Turns out he lost a bet with Travis. Hector, the hermit crab. He's in my room."

Levi wiped his nose with the sleeve of his shirt. "No shit. I can't believe your mom let you have a hermit crab."

"It's Travis's." I rubbed my hands together and stood up. "Come on. I'll show you."

Levi hauled himself off the bed and followed me into my room.

CHAPTER EIGHT

I tugged at my collared shirt and shifted against the wooden pew as people mingled in the aisle. I always dressed decently for church, but Mom insisted I look particularly nice to celebrate Thanksgiving with Helen the Homewrecker's family. We didn't call her that anymore, now that Mom decided she wasn't entirely evil. I guess Helen's parents would be my step-grandparents. I'd never known my real grandparents. The ones who were alive when I was born lived in Illinois, so I'd only met them a few times, and I was too young to remember. Mom has pictures to prove it, though.

The Methodist church bulletin rested next to me. Mom circulated through the room, basking in the glow of concerned people—our hiatus from church had been noticed—while I fidgeted. I wondered what she was telling them. *Sorry we haven't been here. I freaked because my ex-husband showed up for the grief counseling session to mourn the loss of a child that wasn't his.*

I couldn't muster the energy to feel mad. From across the room, her baggy beige slacks and pointy shoulders under her thin, flowered shirt were more noticeable.

A hand rested on my shoulder.

"Hey."

It was Garrett. He wore jeans and a T-shirt that read, *You Need Jesus, Bro.*

"Fancy," he said in response to my looking decent.

"I got this thing after church."

"No, you look good." He was the only person I knew who gave compliments like that. "You going to youth?" he asked.

I flipped the bulletin open. "Are they having it?"

"We had it the last two weeks with John. It sucked with Gabby, but it's all good now."

Miss Gabby did the Cherub Choir and stood in for our youth pastor, John, when his wife died. John, who might be my mom's new boyfriend.

"Yeah, I'll go," I said.

"Cool. It wasn't the same without you." Garrett flashed his smile and my stomach muscles crunched. I tried to focus on the bulletin, but after that I had a difficult time concentrating. I kept noticing Garrett up front, sitting with his mom, dad, and sister, Emily. Likewise, he continually turned around to wave at me. I thought about his hand trailing down Iggy's arm and sat up taller in the pew. Garrett's family knew he was gay, and there they all were, sitting front and center at church. No big deal.

After the call to worship, Pastor Cole held his arms open wide and announced, "To start us off today, we have a special treat. One of our new members, from the Adams family…well, not *that* family"—chuckles rose from the congregation—"is going to sing for us. If you didn't catch his performance in *Godspell,* you certainly missed out."

Applause rose up from the pews as Garrett stood, grinned nervously, and walked to the front of the church. He wiped the palms of his hands against his jeans and got situated behind the microphone stand next to the organ. "Hey," he said, cupping his hands around the microphone.

More laughter. They loved him.

"Is this on?" he asked.

I wondered why Garrett hadn't worn something nicer than jeans and a T-shirt, but instead of giving the impression that he didn't care, it made him seem genuine. When I heard the first notes of the hymn, I braced myself. "It Is Well with My Soul" was one of my favorites. We usually sat close to John, and his booming, deep voice always sounded so convincing that I found comfort in it. This time John's voice was silent. He listened along with the rest of us.

As soon as the music started, Garrett seemed to forget the rest of us were even there. I had the eerie sensation that I was eavesdropping on his private song to God. Garrett sang softly at first, like a whisper, but we all knew the words seeking peace and comfort. When he said,

"It is well," a smile spread across his face, and he radiated joy as his volume grew. Yes, it truly was well with his soul. Anyone could see. For a second I wondered if Garrett was performing, but my instincts told me no. He made it look so easy, being open to a loving God, but I knew better. And the temptation to ride his wave of conviction was so great, so powerful, that it took every ounce of my willpower to refrain from joining him.

When Garrett finished, enthusiastic applause burst from the audience. He wiped his face with the hem of his shirt, exposing his flat stomach. Somehow Garrett looked genuinely surprised by the response, and he awkwardly returned to his seat. Other people in the pews overtly dabbed at their eyes. Even Mom reached over and gently patted my hand, like this was hard, but just what we needed. She had no idea.

Pastor Cole addressed Garrett. "Thank you, Garrett."

Garrett's head slid lower in his seat.

Pastor Cole clasped his hands together, and then turned to all of us. "Originally I asked him to sing something from the show, but he requested to sing his favorite hymn instead." He arranged some papers on his music stand. Pastor Cole rarely spoke from behind the pulpit. He preferred to preach closer to the congregation. "I hope we'll hear more from you in future services. It does my soul good. Can we get an amen?"

"Amen!"

"And now a passage from the gospel," Pastor Cole said.

I hadn't noticed John sitting in the pew behind us until he stood to head up front to read. Next to the light jacket he'd left in his spot sat the woman I recognized from the Italian restaurant at homecoming. She looked all polished, and I glanced at my mom. She was studying the woman, too. Mom didn't even try to avert her gaze. Finally she leaned over to me and asked, "Who is that woman?"

I considered telling her I'd seen them together before, but I didn't trust her to be okay. Was it lying if I didn't tell her? "I don't know," I said as I slid across the pew to leave. "Time for youth group." A part of me felt bad leaving her there, but John would be leading our group, so I figured she would be okay. I waited for Emily and Garrett at the door, but people kept stopping Garrett to shake his hand.

"Hey," he said breathlessly as we closed the door behind us.

I tried to think of something to say, but it seemed to me everyone in the congregation had probably already said it better than I ever could. I settled on, "Nice job."

Garrett scrunched his face.

"He didn't want to do it," Emily said.

He didn't seem to mind it once the song got started, but I kept quiet.

When we approached the chain-link fence, I paused and opened my mouth to remind Travis to be good. It was where I used to drop Travis off. I stopped myself before the words were out, but it was like I'd gotten hit in the gut. For just a second, I'd forgotten he was dead.

"You okay?" Emily asked.

I composed myself fast. "Yeah." I picked up my pace. We rounded the corner to the cement building and went through the door to the youth room. Chubby Vince was carrying Bibles to the table, but when he saw us, he dumped them and ran to hug me.

"Asher's back! Dude," he said into my shoulder, "I missed you."

I stood awkwardly, waiting for him to let me go. "Vince," I said, "I saw you two days ago at school."

"Yeah, I know. It's been way too long ago." He patted my shoulder.

Vince never went to the service. He only showed up for youth group. John entered the room, his long sleeves rolled up, carrying a pew Bible. "Hey, guys," he said. "Is it just us today?"

Since it was Thanksgiving break, many families had headed out of town to visit relatives. Today it was just Vince, Garrett, Emily, another girl, and me. John slid the Bible over to me. "Pastor Cole asked me to give this to you, Asher."

I froze. The morning before Travis died, we'd gone to church. He'd ripped a page from the Bible during the service. Mom almost lost it, she was so embarrassed. It wasn't until later, when we were going through his backpack, that we discovered he'd stolen it. Mom told me to keep it, but then I'd read the words on the page he'd ripped out and pieced together God's message to me. Not only had Travis's page predicted him sinking in the water, God had seen me with Garrett. He knew what I'd done. When I'd gone to ask Pastor Cole more about the passage, Mom insisted I leave the Bible with him. Now it had found its way back to me. I steadied my breath. I'd stuff it in my drawer. Something else to hide.

"So, how was everyone's Thanksgiving?" John asked, sitting down at the table. Vince folded his hands on the table in front of him.

"Evan and his girlfriend came into town from Miami. Turns out they're going to have a kid," Vince said. "I'm going to be an uncle."

That got my attention. Evan Llowell a *dad?* Levi was going to have a fit. As the star athlete at our high school, Evan Llowell was the epitome of cool to Levi. I wondered how he would react to his idol changing diapers. Then I remembered Evan's movie-star wife. She sure hadn't looked pregnant back at the football game, but what did I know about pregnant people?

"Wow, that's exciting," John said. "How're your folks feeling about being grandparents?"

"My mom was all excited and congratulated them, but my dad…" Vince shrugged. "He kind of let Evan have it." He rolled a pencil back and forth on the table. "After they left the house, Mom was talking about how young they are and worried about whether or not they were ready. Josh thinks it's funny."

The weight of it hit me, that Josh had no idea how close he'd come to being a dad himself.

John rubbed his hands together. "It's tough, isn't it? Parents want things for their children, and they worry. They want things to be easier, and having a child at any age is difficult, but it's a beautiful thing, too."

"I guess," Vince said.

John didn't have children. How would he know?

"Well, since it's just us, how about we talk about relationships? Starting with our relationship with God," John offered.

I glanced at the Bible sitting in front of me. My relationship with God seemed a bit one-sided. I wanted to ask John about his relationship with the woman in church, but I couldn't figure out how to do that. They'd held hands at the restaurant, but I pushed my judgment out of my head. He was probably comforting her. John helped tons of people and always put himself last. There was no way he'd launch into a relationship so soon after he'd lost Meredith.

"Anyone want to start us off with prayer?" he asked.

Vince lifted his hand up off the table.

"Vince?"

I joined my hands together and bowed my head.

"Okay, God," Vince said. I loved listening to Vince pray. He was always so *Vince*. "Hey. How's it going? So, thanks for bringing us all together. It's cool having Asher back." A prickling guilt rose up in me. I squeezed my clasped hands together a little more tightly. "And would you please spend a little extra time with Evan and Candace and my family and the little guy? And bless the people here, while you're at it. Help us to get closer to you today, okay? Thanks. Uh, amen."

By the expressions on everyone's faces, I wasn't the only one who enjoyed Vince's prayer.

"So, if our goal is to be close to God," John said, opening his Bible, "why do Christians struggle to keep him close?"

Emily tucked a piece of hair behind her ear. "We put what we want in our lives ahead of what he wants for us."

Garrett reached over and squeezed his sister's hand. I wondered if there were things about her I didn't know. I couldn't picture any circumstance in which Emily wouldn't have what she wanted. Her tall, athletic frame and long brown hair made her instantly sought after by the cool senior guys. She only had to glance at Vince, and he turned stupid. And the only time I'd ever seen her impatient was with me, when she thought I was getting people to turn on Garrett. The second she discovered that wasn't the case, Emily turned right back to nice.

"We don't have to be perfect for God to love us," John said. "That's the beauty of God's grace."

"Right?" Garrett said. "And who are we to be harder on ourselves than *God* is?"

I realized I was drumming my fingers on the Bible and stopped. Emily swallowed and looked down at her nails. I could tell she was uncomfortable, so I racked my brain trying to think of a way to change the subject. John beat me to it.

"It's not unusual for God to take the form of a father figure," John said. "It's a comparison we can understand. What is the ideal father like?"

"Loving," Garrett said.

"Wise and patient," Emily added.

"Ideal dad?" Vince said. "I think a dad should be forgiving."

The way he said it made me wonder if he'd downplayed his dad's reaction to Evan's girlfriend being pregnant.

"How about you, Asher?" John asked.

The ideal father? I searched for an answer, and I thought about Dad buying me a digital camera and putting sports posters up in my room. I said the first thing that popped into my mind. "The ideal dad knows his children," I said. "I mean, really knows them." But then I glanced down at the Bible. *My sins are not hidden from you.* I felt a little sick.

John opened the Bible in front of him. "Yes, Asher. In fact, in John, it talks about the love our Father gives us. How we're called his children."

"If God is like *my* dad," Vince said, "we're all screwed."

I wondered if someone was going to address that. It seemed like Vince had stuff on his mind. We sat silently, waiting for someone to say something.

Emily took a breath like she was going to speak, but then stopped.

"Emily?" John asked.

She shifted in her chair. "Well, I was just thinking that dads aren't perfect. They can't be," Emily said, staring pointedly at Garrett. "You have to be careful about putting faith in people. They'll hurt you."

"Yes, I know," Garrett said, but his voice didn't show a trace of disappointment.

"How do you feel about that?" John asked.

Garrett considered it for a moment. "I feel pretty okay with that. I mean, we're human, right? We're going to make mistakes. We're going to hurt each other, even when we don't mean to. We're going to say and do the wrong thing and regret stuff." He glanced at me then. "Even stuff we shouldn't regret."

I sat absolutely, perfectly still. He was talking about the day Travis died. He was thinking about kissing me—I knew he was—after I told him I wasn't gay. I told him I was sorry. Still, I didn't let him go. And then Travis died.

"But God, he knows everything," Garrett said. "And anything's possible with him."

I wanted Garrett to stop talking.

"Our relationship with Jesus in the only one we can truly count on," John said and gently closed his Bible.

"That's kind of beautiful," Vince said.

Emily had been sitting there so still and stoic, I didn't notice she was crying. Her face didn't squish up or anything like mine did when

I was unfortunate enough to lose it. She wiped her face. "My brother *is* beautiful, and God *is* great," she said. "But people still need to be careful about putting themselves in dangerous situations."

Garrett shrugged. "Jesus pushed the boundaries. He put himself in dangerous situations."

"And they crucified him," I whispered. I hadn't meant to say it out loud. Everyone stared at me, but it was Garrett's expression that hit hard. Why did it feel like he could see right through me? Maybe because he'd already seen things about me I could hide from other people. I wanted to slide under the table.

"Asher's right," Emily said.

It was silent. I heard the wall clock tick. Garrett was wrong; it wasn't that simple. God had made it pretty clear, if you asked me. That moment I'd kissed Garrett, Travis was dying. My little brother, who I was supposed to be watching, had died *right then*. Maybe I could have convinced myself it was just a coincidence, but God had sent me a message, loud and clear, straight from the Bible. *You know my folly. My sins are not hidden from you. I sink in miry depths.*

John opened his mouth to redirect the conversation, but Garrett beat him to it. "She worries about me," Garrett told us, motioning toward Emily. "She thinks I take too many chances. But I think God is most present when we take chances."

"So, what kind of chances are you talking about?" Vince asked. "Because I'm pretty sure if I jump out of a plane without a parachute, God isn't going to weave a net for me, you know?"

Garrett spread his hands out on the table and took a deep breath. "The thing is, whether she, or anyone else, likes it or not, I'm not hiding who I am. I really wanted to ask someone to homecoming, but I didn't. Because of what people might think."

"Garrett," Emily said. "Just don't."

"You shouldn't let others keep you from doing the right thing," John said.

"Exactly," Garrett said. "So, next time I'll ask him. And I'll let him decide if he wants to go or not, instead of assuming people wouldn't understand."

The clock on the wall ticked. *Him.* I was afraid to look at Garrett, scared he meant me.

"You know, if you take a guy to homecoming, people are going to think you're gay," Vince said. "Just sayin'." We stared at Vince. "Oh," he said. "So that would make you—"

"Gay," Garrett said lightly. "Yes."

Vince leaned back in his chair. "Oh. Okay. That's cool," he said, nodding slowly.

That's cool?

John's expression was absolutely unreadable, but he opened his Bible again and said, "Why don't we wrap up with prayer?"

We bowed our heads, and John said, "Our gracious Father, guide us in our journey along your path. Remind us to live in your word, so we may know your glory and share the good news with all in our lives. And all God's people said…"

"Amen."

"We celebrate when we can get together," my step-mom, Helen, explained from the front passenger seat of the Land Rover. She flipped open the visor and studied her reflection in the mirror. Her eyes were lined in gray and mascara. She applied a layer of pink lipstick and smeared her lips together. When she gently pushed a stray blond strand off to the side, the rest of her helmetlike hair didn't move.

She kept on talking about the people I was going to meet, as if I'd remember. Apparently, unlike Dad and Mom, both Helen's parents were still alive. They live in an old Florida house with a wraparound porch and a tin roof. Several cars lined the driveway as we pulled up. Huge, sprawling oaks with Spanish moss hanging from the branches crowded the long driveway. I also recognized mango and orange trees. Up by the house, the yard turned a thick green. Planters around the house looked professionally landscaped.

"Nice place," I said.

"We pay to have it kept up," Dad said. "Helen's folks are getting too old to maintain it."

"It wasn't easy getting them to let us hire people." Helen turned around in her seat to face me. "My dad fell and broke his hip, so he couldn't take care of the yard. I told Mom, *Your job is to take care of him, so let us get someone to take care of the yard at least.*" She got kind of quiet, and Dad reached over and patted her hand.

It reminded me of Levi and Jennifer.

"My dad is a good man," she said. "But he's…" She struggled for the right word.

"Helen's dad is the most cantankerous person you'll ever meet in your entire life," Dad said. "But you take him with a grain of salt. It's going to be fine."

As Helen walked up, a heavyset woman with gray hair and thick glasses wobbled down the wide front steps. I thought she was headed for Helen, but instead she came right up to me. She extended her arms to hug me, and my absolute panic must have shown on my face because she stopped just shy of me and clasped her hands in front of her instead.

"You must be Asher. I'm sorry, but I just have to squeeze you," she said and bear-style hugged me. She made this *mmm-mmm* noise.

She smelled like cookies. I patted her on the back a bit and shot my dad a horrified look. He had the audacity to smile.

Thankfully, Helen pried the woman off me. "Asher, this is my mom, Penny."

"Penelope, but everyone calls me Penny," she said as she slowly led us up the steps. "My grandpa had a thing for mythology. His name was Paris. Of course, he was named after Paris, France, because his daddy had read this book set in Paris, but my dad told everyone it all had to do with the battle of Troy." She opened the french door that led into the house.

"Oh my land! Is this him?" called another voice as I stepped inside. "Steve, you did not *tell* us he was so handsome."

I was afraid I was going to get hugged again, but instead the skinny woman extended a hand. Her hair was as stiff as Helen's and she wore big pearl earrings. "It is so nice to meet you," she said. "I'm Leda, the older and much better-looking sister." She nudged Helen.

"It's the truth," Helen said, and they hugged.

Dad placed a hand on my shoulder and led me out of the foyer while the women fussed over each other.

The house was old, but immaculate. It had a colonial vibe and tons of huge windows and really tall ceilings. A small group of middle-aged men sat in front of a huge flat-screen television watching a football game. Bowls of chips and salsa, cheese and crackers, and plates of raw vegetables and dips were all over the table. The whole house smelled like fresh-baked ham.

"Hey, Steve!" one of them called. "That your boy?"

"Yep, this is Asher."

The group called various hellos, but then something major happened on the TV and they whooped and hollered.

A separate sink, island, and fridge were located off in the corner of the living room. The back counter housed various alcoholic beverages. Dad led me over, opened the fridge, and asked me what I wanted. Every drink you could imagine was in there, but I didn't see any blue Gatorade.

"Is that sweet tea?" I asked, gesturing to the pitcher.

"Is there any other kind?" Helen's mom called from the kitchen. I hadn't realized I'd spoken loudly enough for anyone but Dad to hear.

Dad poured me some into a tall glass and grabbed a beer for himself. Penny rounded the corner, drying her hands, and saw my dad hand me the tea.

Penny said, "Asher, if you want something, you just go and get it. That's how we do here. There's enough food for an army, but if you're looking for something else, we got a pantry full of God knows what. You help yourself."

"They're real informal here," Dad said.

A voice from a room off to the side called, "That Steve?"

"Earl," Dad said as he moved into the doorway of the room, "what are you doing in here all by yourself?"

I followed him. Inside there was a couch, a small television set sitting on a table, and an old recliner. A heavy man with an egg-shaped head sat in the recliner, two plastic tubes inserted in his nostrils. Dad sat on the couch across from the man.

"Idiots want to watch the wrong game," he said, tilting his head toward the men in the other room. "This your boy?"

"Yep. Asher, this is Earl, Helen's dad."

"Hi," I said, and I joined Dad on the couch.

"Asher. What kind of name is that?" He focused on dad. "You pick that name out?"

"His mom did, actually. It's from the Bible."

Earl chuckled at me, but I couldn't figure out what was so funny. "He's kind of skinny," he said. "You play sports?"

"No."

Dad rested a hand on my shoulder. "Asher's into photography."

"Photography?" Earl asked. I nodded. "You don't play sports?" I shook my head.

"You're tall. You don't play basketball?"

What was wrong with this guy?

"Why not?" he asked. "Tall boy like you should play sports. We need boys like you playing sports. All those black boys on the teams. Need some white boys out there, too."

What? Dad's grasp on my shoulder tightened. "Well, Earl, he doesn't want to play. What can I say?"

"Why don't you make him play? Huh? Boys need to play sports. Teaches them discipline. Shows them how to work on a team. Trouble with kids these days is people care what they think about things. No one gave a damn about what I thought." Earl sat forward and rested his hands on his knees. His belly sagged, and I wondered if it was possible for him to get his knees to touch one another with his belly in the way. "Hey, Steve. Did people care about what you thought when you were little?"

Dad laughed. "Nope, and look how awful I turned out."

"See there? People want to make kids feel good. Be happy. Who the hell thought that up, huh? That's what's wrong with this country. People think they got a right to be happy," he said. "You happy?" he asked me.

I swallowed. This guy scared the crap out of me.

"See, he can't even talk. They don't teach kids right today. No one cared if I was happy. If I didn't respond with a *yes, sir* or *no, sir* when a grown-up talked to me, my daddy woulda whupped me. You get whupped?"

"Uh, no, sir," I said.

"See that? He's smart," he said to my dad. "You're smart," he said to me. "I told you that, and right away you know to say *sir*. People think kids are just different today, but you see that? *No, sir.* Catch on fast. Just need people to hold them to it. Whupping is good. They'll report you now, if you whup your kid. Did you know that? Parents afraid of their own kids. Damned if the world ain't all screwed up when kids tell the parents what to do."

My skin prickled.

"You talk back to your momma?" he asked.

"Uh," I said. I wasn't sure how to answer him. I couldn't say no, because that would be a lie. But my mom was sort of nuts sometimes.

"Your parents split up," Earl said. "So there's no man around the house keeping you in line. See, a man shows his son how to treat a woman. But when your daddy leaves your momma, what's that teach the boy about respecting women? Huh?"

Dad stiffened.

He turned on my dad. "You got your hands full here, Steve. Don't know how you're gonna teach that boy to be a man when you only see him part-time."

"Earl! You leave that boy alone, now!" Penny shouted from the other room.

Earl rolled his eyes and pointed toward the kitchen.

"See there? She's part of the problem. Thinks everyone should be nice all the time. No one ever did nothing by being nice. You think I'm nice?" he asked me.

"No, sir," I said.

He hooted with laughter and slapped a hand on his knee. Earl rocked back and forth on the sofa. It was like I was the funniest person on the planet. "You hear that, Penny?" He called to his wife. "The boy said I'm not nice. He's right, I'm not nice at all. No." He wiped his eyes with the back of his hand.

Penny came in from the kitchen followed by Helen. "You don't have a nice bone in your body," Penny said and swatted him with a dish towel. "Don't you listen to a word he says. He's a big softy."

"No, I'm not."

"He's a big ole softy," Penny continued like he hadn't said anything, and she wound an arm around Earl's neck. "He likes getting a rise out of people is all." She kissed him on top of his bald head. "Don't you let him get a rise out of you."

"I got Steve here upset. Look at him," Earl said.

Sure enough, Dad's face was almost purple. He looked like he was barely containing his rage.

"He wants to hit me. He would if he could, Penny. Won't whup his boy, but he wants to whup me for talking about it."

Helen took my dad's hand and squeezed it. "How about we go see how the football game is going?"

"People don't know how to take you," Penny said to Earl. "You shouldn't do that."

"Do what? I'm not doing anything," he said.

All the tension drained out of me as I started to follow Dad and Helen into the other room. "For Helen," I heard Penny say quietly. "She wants the boy to like her."

"She wants this boy to like her?" I heard him say to his wife. She tried to shush him, but I already knew Earl wasn't the type to be shushed. "How's he gonna like her? When his daddy chose her over his mom? Ain't nothing Helen can do to make that boy like her."

"Well, that was fun," Dad said when we got in the Land Rover.

Helen was silent in the seat next to him as we headed down the driveway and turned onto the street. My stomach pushed against the waistband of my khaki pants. Helen's house reminded me of the time I'd gone with Levi to his uncle's: tons of delicious, homemade food, lots of loud people shouting at the television screen, and completely awkward. The hardest part had been being around my dad and Helen. They were so uncomfortable. Funny that Helen was uncomfortable around her own dad, but then I thought about my own relationship with my father. Maybe it wasn't so weird.

"I'm sorry," Helen said, and it took me a second to realize she was directing the apology toward me.

For what?

Earl reminded me of Pearl. *Earl* and *Pearl*—one letter off. I smiled and rubbed at a spot on my pants where I'd spilled a bit of gravy. The thing that made Earl so scary was that he said what he thought. I wondered if it was an old-person thing, not caring if you offended people. There were so many things I'd had to figure out for myself because I couldn't ask anyone. What if I *could* ask? "Why are you sorry?" I asked.

It took so long for Helen to respond, that I thought maybe I hadn't spoken out loud. "My dad can be a little..." She hesitated.

"Difficult." My dad finished for her.

"Yes, but it's more than that." Helen sighed. "It's like he enjoys making people feel uncomfortable. He's always been inclined that way, but it's gotten worse as he's gotten older. Oh my gosh, in the hospital. The things he said to the nurses."

My dad started laughing.

"It's not funny!" she said.

"What did he do?" I asked.

My dad chimed in. "One of the night nurses was Asian." Helen groaned. "Really nice girl," Dad continued. "So we're sitting there, and she comes in for her shift, and Earl asks her if she's there to give him a massage."

"I honestly could have killed him," Helen said. "I was mortified."

"She just smiled and said no, that wasn't part of her job description," Dad said. "Helen thought it was awful."

"It *was* awful," she said. "But I imagine with this older generation, people in the medical field have to deal with a lot of situations like that." We drove in silence for a few minutes. "Still, it's hard, when he gets on a roll. He tries to get under your skin. Like the sports thing. In his generation, if you're a boy, you play sports. End of story."

"I like him," I said.

Dad glanced at me in his rearview mirror. They didn't ask me why, and I decided to leave it there since I didn't know exactly why either. It wasn't that I believed it was a good idea to insult or hurt people, but when people are nice all the time, you can't really trust them. Plus, when I'd gone back in to see him after dinner, he'd let me take his picture.

CHAPTER NINE

S o your new theory is to be brutally honest? Like the old guy?" Levi asked me on the way to school the next day.

"Yeah. Earl."

"He sounds like a prick."

"You should talk."

Levi curled his lip at me.

"See?" I said. "Just flies off the tongue."

"You might want to learn some self-defense techniques to go along with this shitty theory of yours," Levi said.

The temperature outside was around sixty, but it would probably be eighty again by this afternoon, so Levi and I both wore short-sleeved shirts.

"You got football after school?" I asked.

"Yeah, this is it though. Friday's our last game," Levi said. "And I'm gonna kick ass."

"I have no doubt you will," I said.

"You taking the bus home?"

"Yeah."

Levi took a corner fast. I gripped the handle of the door. "You trying to flip this thing?" I asked.

"I know exactly what I'm doing. You're one to talk. How many hours have you put in driving?" he asked.

"I don't have my learner's permit yet."

"Are you shitting me? You're going to be sixteen in three months. Dude, you should have had your permit for ages now."

I scratched my head. "Yeah, well, not everyone has a new car waiting around for when they turn sixteen."

"Screw you. It has nothing to do with that. My dad would give me hell if I didn't put in the hours."

I paused. Normally I'd just sit quietly, but instead I blurted out, "So when exactly would have been the best time to mention it to my mom? After Dad left or after Travis died?"

"Jesus, Asher. Settle down. It's just you might want to look into it, now that you've got parents competing for your attention," he said. "Might land a car for your sixteenth birthday if you play your cards right." Levi winked at me.

"The benefits of being an only child," I said dryly.

"Some benefit, right?" Levi said, and I knew we were both thinking of Travis. We pulled up into the parking lot. I braced myself as Levi swerved widely into his assigned parking space. We'd barely gotten out of the Jeep when I saw Mr. Boatwright, our school principal, marching up to us.

"Levi!" he bellowed. "If your mother saw you driving like that, your butt would be on the bus permanently."

"Told you," I said to Levi through the interior of the Jeep.

"Shut up," Levi said.

He slammed the door of the Jeep and slung his book bag over his shoulder. "Oh, come on, Mr. Boatwright. I had it under control."

Mr. Boatwright planted his feet in front of Levi and crossed his arms over his chest. They stood the same height, but even though Mr. Boatwright was half as wide as Levi, he had this way of puffing himself up to seem bigger. "Is that right?" Mr. Boatwright asked, blocking Levi's path. Rumor had it Mr. Boatwright had played football in high school and had made something of a name for himself on the field by tackling everything that moved. I believed it.

Levi pretended to deflate and said a woeful, "It won't happen again, sir."

"Good." Mr. Boatwright moved to the side to let us pass. "How's that leg of yours?"

"Got the all clear to play," Levi said as he sauntered past the principal toward the building.

"Bring us a win on Friday," he hollered to Levi.

"I'll do my best, sir."

I thought Mr. Boatwright was continuing past us to inspect the parking lot, but instead I heard his heavy footsteps following us. Garrett and Iggy had moved from the sidewalk to lean against the red brick building. When Garrett reached over and held Iggy's hand, I heard the sharp intake of breath behind us.

"Perfect," Mr. Boatwright muttered. Then he puffed into his principal mode. "Adams!" Garrett dropped Iggy's hand. Iggy backed away from him. "What do you think you're doing?"

"Just talking to Iggy."

"It doesn't look like you're just talking." He appraised Iggy. "You okay?"

"It's cool," Iggy said, which isn't the same thing as being okay.

Garrett shook his head.

"You got something to say, Adams?" Mr. Boatwright asked.

Garrett pointed across the parking lot where Manny leaned against his car with his arms wrapped around his girlfriend. Her body pressed against his. Mr. Boatwright huffed and meandered back out to the parking lot.

"Manny!" he bellowed. "Get a room!"

Garrett and Iggy headed through the doors of the school, but Levi and I stayed glued to the sidewalk. Manny and his girlfriend parted, but when Mr. Boatwright got up close to them, he shook Manny's hand. Probably wishing him luck on the football game.

"Mr. Boatwright," I muttered. "He's such an ass."

Levi hit my arm.

"Ow. What was that for?"

When I looked at him, he was grinning. "You said *ass*."

On the way home from the bus stop, I spotted Pearl watching me from the window. I was headed up the driveway when she opened her front door and called to me.

"Asher," she said. "Come over here."

I redirected to her front yard. She hobbled over to me. It wasn't until she got close up that I noticed she was holding something in her hand. "Here. If you're going to do head shots, make sure you give them these instructions. Make the people follow them. Otherwise your life is going to be hell."

Pearl gave me a weathered piece of paper. It had purple writing on it, and it looked like it had been copied a bunch of times. The name at the top was *Samantha Miller, Photographer.* Who was Samantha Miller?

"And you left this at my house."

It was the photograph of Mom and Levi's dad, in broad daylight. I'd spent so much time hiding it, that I had to fight my instinct to snatch it from her hands and bury it somewhere. Just then our minivan pulled up in our driveway. Mom was home. Perfect. "Uh, no. That's not mine," I stammered. "I'm pretty sure it's yours. Isn't that one of the pictures from your portfolio?" I knew it was. I'd taken it out of her portfolio so I could look at it more closely, and then I'd shown it to Levi as evidence of our parents' affair. But it wasn't my photograph. And I needed to get Pearl back inside before my mom got out of the van. I felt all fight-or-flight. *Maybe I should grab the photo from her hand and run.*

Pearl stared at the picture again. "Why would I have a photograph of your family?" she asked.

I readjusted my book bag on my shoulder. My foot started tapping unnaturally fast. *Keep calm.* I didn't have time to remind her about how she'd used it as an example of people being natural on camera, but that the composition was totally off. How could she forget that? "Search me," I said. *Keep it casual. No big deal.* I started to walk away from her, but she ambled after me.

"Well, I don't want it. You take it," she said.

It was everything I could do not to shove her extended hand away from me. "Uh, that's okay."

Mom turned the ignition off. Pearl stopped following me and stared down at the photograph hard. Her eyebrows knitted together with worry. I couldn't help but notice the thick lines in her face and the way her flesh sort of hung on her.

What I really wanted to do was bolt for my house. Instead I traipsed back over to her. "You showed it to me in your album. Remember? You'd looked at my poster with the photographs on it, and you told me they were crap."

She nodded. "Well, they *were* crap."

"Yeah, you were pretty clear about it," I said. It figured she'd remember that. "But then you showed me some of your stuff. This photograph was in there."

"Well, what the hell was it doing on my floor?" she asked.

I held my hands up to show I was clueless. So much for being brutally honest. I saw my mom walking up out of my peripheral vision. Then I snapped my fingers, like I'd had an aha moment. "Maybe the other night when you were getting me my photos, it slipped out," I said. "Yeah, I'll bet that's what happened." A lie. I knew better. Maybe lies were okay if it meant protecting people. I purposely turned toward Mom. "Hey, how was work?" I asked her.

"Fine," she said suspiciously. "What's going on here?"

"Oh, she was just asking me about something," I said as I started to move away from Pearl. "But we got it all figured out." I took a gamble that Mom would follow my lead and walk away.

She didn't. She headed right up to Pearl. "What's this?" she asked.

No.

This couldn't be happening.

I thought about the hours Mom spent holed up in Travis's room. I thought about how guilt ate at me, and how it must eat at her. A part of me wanted to go into the house and let her deal with this on her own, but I felt tied to her reaction, like it mattered. Pearl held the photo out to her with a shaky hand. Mom took it.

She smiled. "Oh, Asher! Look, it's you and Levi!" She hadn't noticed the background.

"Yeah," I said. I waited.

"Look how little you guys are. You must have been around the same age as…" She was going to say Travis, but caught herself. "Did you take this?" she asked Pearl.

"I don't remember taking it, but wise guy here says I did," Pearl said.

I walked back over to them and pointed at the photograph. "Look at the angle the picture is taken from. It would have been taken from your yard, see?" I gestured toward the back of Pearl's house. A long moment of silence followed. Pearl squinted toward the backyard and back at the photograph, but I was really watching Mom. She had this nostalgic smile on her face, looking at Levi and me.

I'd spent all this time trying to hide the truth from her, and now

I *wanted* her to see the background. I wanted to see what played on her face when she saw herself leaning in to Levi's dad, all chummy. I wanted her to gasp and hide it so no one could see it. I wanted her to tuck it in a picture frame and stuff the evidence in the back of her drawer.

But she didn't. She tried to hand it back to Pearl.

"Oh, no. You keep it," Pearl said. "None of those people mean a thing to me."

Mom laughed like it was a good joke. Pearl didn't joke. Old bat.

"Okay," Mom said. "Thanks, Pearl." Holding the photograph in her hand, Mom followed me up the driveway. I retrieved my key from my pocket, unlocked the front door, and held it open for Mom. "How was school?" she asked as she turned on the light.

"Okay."

I slung my book bag onto the floor by the front door and kicked off my shoes, but I kept the photograph in my line of vision. She didn't put it down beside her purse and keys on the table. I followed her into the kitchen and searched for something to discuss with her. Keys. I remembered my conversation with Levi.

"I was wondering if you could take me to get my driver's permit," I said, "since I turn sixteen in February."

Mom's free hand was in midmotion to the kitchen cabinet. "We were going to do it this past summer," Mom said as she lowered her hand and faced me.

"It's okay."

She leaned against the kitchen counter, still holding the photograph. "How about tomorrow after school?" she asked as she tapped the edge of the picture against the counter.

"That's Tuesday," I said. "I'm with Dad."

"I work late Wednesday and Thursday."

"I could ask Dad."

She stared at the photograph. "No, I want to take you," she said. "I told you I'd take you." Then she put the picture on top of the stack of mail on the far corner of the countertop. "How about Friday?" she asked.

"Okay. Yeah. Friday."

"What about the paperwork? Have you done everything you need to do? There's a test they make you take," she said.

"I can do it online. I need my social security card. Birth certificate, I think."

"I've got those." Mom opened the fridge and searched the shelves. "What do you want for dinner?"

I shrugged. My attention was on the stack of mail with the photograph on top. I'd gone to so much trouble to take it, hide it, and then return it, and now it was just sitting on top of the mail. No big deal.

"We still have Levi's leftovers. How do you feel about a turkey sandwich?" she asked.

"Sure." I walked over to where Mom had tossed the photo and picked it up. There they were, in the background of the photo. How could she have missed it? The two of them leaning into each other. It was oddly quiet in the kitchen. I looked over at Mom. She was framed in front of the open fridge door digging stuff out for dinner.

We ate dinner in front of the television. After dinner, I went to my room to finish the paper on occupations for English class. When I passed by the living room on the way to the kitchen, Mom was curled up on the sofa. I took the Gatorade out of the fridge and took a swig, then I checked the stack of mail again.

The photograph was gone.

❖

I finally pegged it. I'd been trying to figure out who the counselor reminded me of, and it was my third grade teacher. They both had this benign voice, like nothing fazed them. My teacher used the same tone, always, whether it was *Johnny, please read for us* or *Johnny, please put the gun down.* Not that anyone brought a gun to school. But I was pretty sure that's how she would have said it.

"How do you think your mom would describe you?"

I raised my eyebrows. Seriously?

"Okay, how about your friends?"

Friends. Levi popped into my mind. "Probably that I'm sort of quiet. Levi thinks my photographs are weird."

"And this is a friend?"

I nodded. She wrote on that legal pad again.

"Anyone else?"

"Most people think I'm nice."

"Are you?"

"Yeah. I try to be."

She paused and tapped the eraser of her pencil against her temple. *Tap-tap-tap.* Pause. "Who do you think knows you best?"

I thought about that. Levi knew me the longest, so he knew my history. He knew about Travis. But Kayla had seen me cry. No one saw me cry. Garrett popped into my mind. The way he looked right through me. "I don't know."

"Do you think your parents know who you are?"

"Which one?"

"Let's start with your dad."

"No." No hesitation there. She scribbled on the pad. Maybe I should have hesitated.

"What is it about you that he doesn't understand?"

"They decorated my room with sports posters."

"They?"

"My dad and Helen."

"You don't play sports."

I nodded. A statement, not a question. Even she knew that.

"And they won't let you decorate your room?"

Dad and Helen had encouraged me to make it my own. They'd buy me whatever I wanted. "I can change it."

"So you're going to take the posters down?"

I shrugged. I didn't plan on spending much time there.

"You'd rather leave the posters up?"

They hadn't decorated a room for Travis. Before Travis died, the room that should have been for my little brother was an office. They'd never planned on having Travis there. Ever. "I'm not there much."

"How often do you go to your dad's?"

"Tuesdays and Sundays."

"Do you like it at your dad's house?"

I thought about the french doors, the remodeling, and the paved road. It looked like one of those places you see in magazines, where you feel a lot of pressure to take your shoes off at the door. "It's nice there."

"You don't want to hurt their feelings by taking the posters down?"

"They went to a lot of trouble."

"It sounds like you'd rather not make any waves."

Waves. Ripples. "They have a pool."

"That's awesome. I worked as a lifeguard during one summer when I was in college. Do you like swimming?"

I studied her face. She didn't know how Travis died. Otherwise she would never have said that. So I said, "My brother drowned."

Her mouth opened to say something, but then it closed again. Her face flushed, and she pressed her lips together. "I knew your brother died, but—"

"I know. It's okay."

She put her pencil down and leaned forward. "I'm sorry. I didn't know."

That's when I decided I liked her.

Chapter Ten

In all fairness, figuring out new holiday traditions wasn't easy. Last year had been our first Christmas without Dad, but Mom had been feeling pretty ambitious about keeping things normal, so she'd pulled the decorations out of the garage the day after Thanksgiving. That afternoon and evening, Travis, Mom, and I assembled and lit the tree. She had made hot chocolate even though the sun was shining and people outside wore shorts. We found this station that played classic Christmas songs, and after we decorated the tree, we watched those ancient Claymation *Rudolph, the Red-Nosed Reindeer* and *Frosty the Snowman* movies. It hadn't been bad at all, really. Dad rarely participated in the decorating anyway.

Of course, Mom had been a wreck when we'd gone to the Christmas Eve service. We went to the early one, but we'd had to idle in the minivan near the parking lot entrance to make sure Dad wasn't going to show up. By the time we'd gotten inside, we'd missed the opening hymn, and there weren't any places to sit, so we stood in the back. We cut out ten minutes early in the middle of "Silent Night" in case Dad and Helen came early to the candlelight service.

Christmas morning had been rough, too. Mom had only been working for a few months, and we were behind in bills and didn't have any money. Aunt Sharon sent Mom a check, so even though I didn't expect anything, I ended up with rolls of film and some clothes. Mom made sure we knew it was all from Aunt Sharon, though. Apparently Dad had called the house to arrange a time to bring presents over, but he and Mom got in a huge fight over the phone. Eventually he sent something because about a week after Christmas, Mom gave Travis and me fifty dollars each and told us it was from him.

This would be our first Christmas without Travis.

The day after Thanksgiving, we didn't even talk about Christmas decorations since I'd gone to Helen's. There was no telling how it was going to go this year, but the call from Aunt Sharon in Chicago changed everything.

"Six days," Mom said after she hung up the phone. "I don't know if they'll give me that much time off from work. I don't know. What do you think, Asher?"

Christmas in Chicago.

We'd avoided Thanksgiving. Now we were going to dodge Christmas, too. Maybe our new tradition was to avoid tradition. "Are we going to put up a tree?" I asked.

Mom stared at the phone in her lap. "Do you want to?"

I thought about Travis insisting no one move his ornaments even though he crowded them all in one spot on the tree. And how he screamed "Jingle Bells" repeatedly since he knew it annoyed me. Something sort of caught in my throat.

"I will if you want to," she said.

"No."

"Six days," Mom repeated. "Sharon said we just need to give her the dates. She'll take care of the tickets. What do you think?"

I said, "Honestly, I think it sounds good." Maybe I'd finally get to see snow.

❖

"Maybe she has old-timer's disease," Levi said as I studied the overcast sky.

"You mean Alzheimer's?" I said. "Here." I handed him the reflector from the trunk.

"Why the hell wouldn't Pearl remember the picture? She took the damn thing. Wouldn't you remember something like that?" He turned the reflector over in his hands. "What is this?"

"It's used for lighting," I explained and handed him an old bedsheet, too. "Pearl gave it to me to use for today."

"Aren't you worried that she'll claim you stole it," Levi asked, "like with the camera?"

I hadn't really thought about it. The idea of Pearl getting old and forgetful depressed me. "I sort of wondered, when she showed me the picture in the first place, if she was trying to clue me in. Like she thought I should know about my mom," I said. "Now I'm not so sure. I told her to keep it, but then my mom came up and saw it."

"Oh shit." A blast of wind nearly blew the reflector out of Levi's hand. He gripped it tighter.

"Careful with that. Pearl will kill me."

"Wait, your mom saw the photo?" Levi asked.

"Levi, she didn't even notice the background."

"But she saw the photo," Levi said.

"Yeah, and she was fine."

Levi whistled. "Bet that pisses you off."

I got Pearl's lens and camera out of the back and closed the trunk. He was right. It made me furious. "Why should I be mad? I mean, the whole reason I didn't want Mom to see the photo was to protect her. I should be happy she's okay, right?"

"But you're not," Levi said.

I hesitated. He was right. "No, I'm not," I admitted.

"You'd rather she sliced her wrists or something?"

"Don't be an ass."

Levi grinned, and we both said, "Asher said *ass*."

Another gust of wind blew as we started up the driveway to Jennifer's house.

"Kind of crappy day for pictures," he said.

Sure, the wind blew harder than I'd like, but I couldn't complain. When we'd first headed over to Jennifer's house, the sky threatened to clear up. I'd been worried about taking photographs in direct sunlight. The last thing I wanted was squinty photos of Jennifer in harsh light, fighting the shadows bright light made. I trailed after Levi to Jennifer's front door. Her mom answered.

"Jennifer, the boys are here!" she called as she opened the door. "Come on in. She's still getting ready."

I didn't like the way Levi dumped the reflector and sheet onto the leather sofa. I scowled at him.

"We was thinking, over here in front of the bookcase," Jennifer's mom explained. "Sort of sophisticated."

The room with the bookcase lacked natural light. The one window was shaded, so I turned on the table lamp and light switch to see how it would look. My eyes kept shifting to the back of the house where they'd taken the photos at homecoming. I'd told Jennifer we would take the pictures out there, not inside the house.

"I picked up the film," she said, "but I saw that it was for outside shots. It's been so windy today, so I bought the 400 speed instead since the website said it pretty much covered everything."

They hadn't picked up the film I'd requested. I had an extra roll, but that wasn't the point. Why had they bothered to ask me what I needed if they weren't going to listen?

"Hello!" Jennifer skipped down the stairs, squeezed Levi, and then she spun around in a circle for me.

"I know you told her to stick to solid colors," Jennifer's mom explained, "but we just bought this shirt. Doesn't it look great on her?"

"It's okay, isn't it?" Jennifer scrunched up her nose at me. I guessed the gesture might make her disarming or irresistible to some people, but I found it annoying.

Pearl had warned me to be specific, so I'd written it down for Jennifer: no patterns, no bright colors, and apply makeup to look natural. Instead, she wore a low-cut bright-pink blouse with a distinct stripe, and a pencil skirt with tall heels. Her lipstick matched her shirt.

This was why I didn't like people. "Uh…"

"It really captures my personality," she said brightly. "It's okay, right? Pink is my favorite color."

I took a deep breath and started to say sure. But then I remembered how I didn't want to do this in the first place. Pearl had warned me, and she would absolutely berate me for taking crappy photos. I wouldn't blame her. I'd promised myself to be honest. "What else do you have to wear?" I asked.

Jennifer blinked at me.

"Because that shirt won't work on film," I said. "And this lighting won't work either."

Everyone stood there looking at me. Finally Jennifer's mom took a tentative step toward me. She said, "We can bring in the lamp from—"

"We're taking the photos outside," I said and started to gather up my stuff. "Tell you what, Jennifer. You go change, and I'll meet you in the backyard in five minutes." I reached the door. "I did a lot of research to figure out how to do this. I want the photos to turn out right."

Jennifer tugged on her satiny pink shirt.

"Trust me," I said. "Levi?"

He'd been standing there so still that he actually jolted when I said his name. "Yeah?"

"Bring the reflector."

CHAPTER ELEVEN

The school library was home to our computer lab and had the only two printers students were allowed to use. Usually the school maintained them really well, but since the occupation papers were due first hour in Ms. Hughes's class, one was jammed, and the other was overloaded in the queue.

"Do not press print multiple times," Mrs. Kurtz said from the printer. "Jason Freedman, you have three copies sitting here. Three!"

"I forgot the header," he said. "And I didn't know the Works Cited page had to be double-spaced."

"Your lack of proofreading is not my problem," she said. "I'm going to talk to Mr. Boatwright about this. We need to charge a fee for this type of thing. Don't any of you have printers at home?"

Honestly, you would have thought we had the whole class in there, but it was just Jason, Shelly, and me.

Jason grabbed his papers from Mrs. Kurtz and rushed out of the library. Shelly stood by the printer, bouncing up and down.

"That won't make the printer work faster," Mrs. Kurtz said.

The paper slid slowly out of the machine. Shelly gripped the edge of the paper before it was even released.

"You'll smudge the ink," Mrs. Kurtz warned. "Just let it sit in the tray until it's done."

Shelly eyed the clock. We both had reason to worry. The first bell had already rung, and Ms. Hughes was a stickler for being on time. That meant for class and for the paper.

I opened my document from the flash drive and selected print.

Then I dragged the icon to the trash, pulled my flash drive out, and waited by the printer for Shelly to finish.

"Paper jam?" Shelly groaned.

"That's what happens when you grab the papers. Rose?" Mrs. Kurtz called. "Could you help over here? There's a class coming in first hour, and I need to made sure the laptops are charged."

Iggy's little sister walked over to us. I hardly ever saw her at school. It wasn't just because she was a ninth grader either. Everything about her was small. Rose was under five feet tall, so she wasn't visible in crowds. She had one of those pixie haircuts and a tiny nose. I could totally picture her pocket-sized and winged, hanging out in a garden, doing some sort of Tinker Bell thing. Although Rose had gone out for the play, she wasn't strictly a drama kid. She mostly fell into the studious and artsy crowd at school.

"It's okay," she told Shelly. "It does this all the time." Rose opened the top of the machine, pulled a single page out, took out the ink cartridge, and slid it back into place. The printer hummed for a moment.

"Should I print again?" Shelly asked.

Rose shook her head and gently held up her hand to indicate Shelly should wait. Sure enough, a few seconds later, the last page drifted into the tray. Shelly looked to Rose for permission to take it, but instead Rose took the pages from Shelly's hand, straightened them, and stapled the upper left corner.

"Here you go," Rose said.

"Thanks." Shelly grabbed the paper and raced out of the library.

My paper was already printing. Rose's eyes scanned the page. I got nervous that she was going to find an error or think I was stupid, although I knew I'd done a fairly decent job on it. Then she stared out the window while we waited. "There's a nest in this tree," she said. "It's empty now, of course, but I like it anyway. Do you take photographs of things like that?"

She must have read my title, fine-arts photographer. While I waited for the last page to fall into the tray, I looked in the branches, and sure enough there was a bird's nest tucked in a crevice. It was mostly made of sticks, but the bird must have come across some shredded paper because several long white strips with numbers still visible on them stuck out. Like a paranoid accountant was trying to dispose of documents. I pictured the bird rifling through a Dumpster and inadvertently finding a credit card statement or something. "Yeah. Things like that. Sometimes."

When Rose picked the stack up to staple it for me, something flickered across her face. She appraised me, like she was debating over something. "You're friends with Garrett, right?" she said.

My body tensed, but I shrugged.

She lowered her voice. "My brother hangs out with him sometimes," she said. "He doesn't, you know, do drugs, does he?"

"Garrett?" I asked. "No."

"You're sure?"

"Absolutely," I said.

Rose's whole body relaxed and a grin spread wide across her face. I wanted to ask why she wanted to know, but I felt like it wasn't my business.

She handed my paper to me. "Photography is cool. I'm more of a writer," Rose said. "You used the wrong font on your header."

"Great."

"You don't have time to fix it," she said. "If you go now, you'll make it to class on time."

❖

I stepped foot in the classroom the moment the bell rang.

Sure enough, Ms. Hughes said, "Please take out your papers and a blank piece of paper."

I already had my paper in my hand, so I put it on my desk and rummaged through my book bag for a loose-leaf sheet. Josh raised his hand.

"Ms. Hughes? My computer—"

"Please wait and follow directions, Josh."

Josh slouched in his chair and muttered something under his breath.

"On the blank piece of paper, I want you to write me a note," Ms. Hughes said. "Please tell me to what extent this paper represents your best effort. Did you throw this together last night? Is it the best paper you've ever written? Are there any errors you found in your paper just now that you want to tell me about? And Josh, this is your opportunity to tell me what happened with your computer."

I thought about the header with the wrong font. I chewed on my lip, and then I started writing.

Ms. Hughes.

Should I make it formal? Was this a test of our letter-writing ability? I decided to play it safe and do it right.

> *Dear Ms. Hughes,*
> *I'm actually really proud of my paper. I've known for a while that I want to be a photographer, but it wasn't until this project that I realized I wanted to focus on Fine Arts. I pretty much understood everything, but I did notice I used the wrong font in the header. Sorry about that.*

"When you are finished, please pass both the letter and the paper to the front. They are due now. If they are not turned in now, they are late, and late papers are automatically reduced by a letter grade."

Josh's hand shot up again.

"Yes, Josh?"

"There's a reason I don't have my paper. You can call my dad."

"I'm sure you've explained the whole situation brilliantly in your letter to me," Ms. Hughes said.

"Yeah, but you aren't going to take points off, right?"

"I'm not discussing that right now. Right now, we're moving on to our final project before winter break," she said, and she dimmed the lights to show us a slideshow.

As she talked, she distributed a handout. Apparently we were reading novels independently. We had our choice of five different books. Ms. Hughes described each one, read a short excerpt, and we were supposed to document what we liked or didn't like about the book as an initial impression. Afterward, we ranked the books according to preference. Then she broke us up into groups. We all stood up and maneuvered the tables for groups while Ms. Hughes flipped through our choices.

"Group two. Asher, Garrett, and Josh."

Garrett grinned at me.

"Hey, I chose the same book as Manny. Why isn't he in my group?" Josh demanded.

Ms. Hughes ignored him and continued to call out names.

I sat down at the table in the far corner of the classroom where Garrett had already put his stuff. Josh sauntered over and threw his folder on top of the table.

"This sucks," he muttered, and he immediately put his head down on the table until he heard Ms. Hughes call Manny's name.

"Can we switch groups?" he called without lifting his head.

She continued to ignore him.

"Bitch," he mumbled. "I hate this class."

Garrett raised an eyebrow at me. "Have you read *Lord of the Flies* before?" he asked me.

"No."

From under his arms, Josh said, "Manny said there's a movie of it. This sucks."

A white, lined, official-looking form landed next to Josh. I glanced up as Ms. Hughes leaned in close to Josh. "You may go see Mr. Boatwright now," Ms. Hughes said quietly, and then continued to instruct the class.

"Why?" he asked loudly. "What did I do?"

"Uh, insubordination and profanity," Garrett said.

Josh glared at him.

Garrett pointed to the referral. "Well, that's what it says."

"Why don't you shut your face, faggot."

Ms. Hughes spun on him. Her measured voice was firm and cold. "Leave this classroom. Now."

Josh slid his notebook across the desk, stood, and ambled the long way around the classroom to the door.

Ms. Hughes stood stock-still, her feet grounded to the floor, watching him, and when the door clicked closed, she resumed. Like nothing had happened at all.

CHAPTER TWELVE

Hey, sport," Dad said when I opened the door to the maroon Land Rover and stepped inside.

"Hey." *Sport,* as if I had a single athletic bone in my body. I wondered why it bothered me so much lately.

"Good day?"

"Yeah." I buckled my seat belt.

"You got a lot of homework?" he asked.

"I've got to review for science," I said. "And read a chapter. I'm working on my DATA course, but I can do that whenever. It's online."

"Data?"

"To get my learner's permit."

He put the car in drive and we eased into the line of cars heading out of the high school.

"That's right," he said. "Sixteen in February. I was waiting in line at the DMV the day I turned fifteen to get my permit."

I considered what his life had been like at fifteen: married parents and a single child. "Things have been kind of crazy."

We drove in silence for a few minutes.

"How do you feel about picking out a Christmas tree?"

When I was little, before Travis, our family tradition was to buy a tree from the guy at the lot. The Christmas-tree guy set up the lot about a week before Thanksgiving, but we never bought our tree until at least a solid week into December. We'd haul the tree home on the roof of our car. I remembered that Dad adjusted the stand, moving the tree a little to the left or right as Mom instructed. Once it was in the corner, he'd lie underneath and rotate it until Mom figured out which side was best.

No matter how much Dad watered the tree, pine needles layered the floor by Christmas morning. But when Travis was born, we bought one of those fake trees. Mom bought a candle that smelled like pine, but it wasn't the same. Even now, I occasionally came across pine needles stuck between the carpet and the wall.

The fake tree was up in our attic right now. It wouldn't be making an appearance this year, since it was too hard. I guess things weren't as hard for Dad and Helen.

"So what do you say, sport?"

"Sure."

I finished my homework, so we headed to the Christmas-tree lot after we picked Helen up from work. It was located next to Llowell's car dealership. The same guy ran the place every year. As we pulled up in the field, I spotted the old guy wearing a thick hoodie, a money belt, and a Santa hat. He was making change for this businessman type who had a little girl clinging to his leg while Manny from high school lifted a big tree into the back of a blue F-150. A bunch of kids got seasonal jobs working at the lot.

Dad, Helen, and I stood there, looking at the line of trees facing us and waiting for the guy to finish. A moment later, Wild Bill strolled out from the maze of trees, wearing a weathered flannel shirt, grungy jeans, and a gapped grin. Bill had graduated from high school the same year as my dad, but Levi would say life rode him hard and put him away wet. Bill hadn't been quite right since he'd run over and killed a toddler back when he was a teenager. He couldn't keep steady work, but folks around town who knew his background hired him for odd jobs.

"Evenin', Mr. Price," Bill said.

"Mr. Price is my father," Dad said. "Am I ever going to get you to call me Steve?"

"I reckon I could try."

"How are you, Bill?"

"I ain't dead, so I suppose that's good," he said. "Helpin' Mr. Hamilton with these here Christmas trees. We got the pines up in front. Spruces and firs in the middle section."

"Not the spruce," Helen said. "Remember my parents' tree last Christmas? Not a needle left on it by Christmas morning. It was a spruce."

"You want a pine?" Bill asked.

My dad took Helen's hand. "Helen prefers the softer needles. Maybe we could look at the firs?"

"Sure." Bill lowered his voice. "We got the older ones up front here, see, so people will buy them first. But I'll take y'all back to the trailer. A shipment came in this mornin'. Don't tell folks, but I'll take y'all back there."

"That's kind of you, Bill," Dad said.

"Thank you," Helen said.

I followed Dad, Helen, and Bill through the maze of trees. Groups of people walked around. Christmas lights hung clumsily above us, draped from one pole to the next. Staticky piped Christmas music played from a speaker clamped onto a telephone pole. The sun was just starting to set, and someone turned on a bright floodlight to illuminate the selections up front. In the back by the trailer, the trees were still wrapped in yellow twine, leaning against one another.

"See here, this one's a fir," Bill said. He pulled it out of the stack of trees, retrieved a pocketknife out of his worn pants, and cut the rope. The branches released but mostly stayed upright.

"Looks a little narrow, doesn't it?" Helen said.

Bill thumped it onto the ground a few times and pressed down the branches.

"They fall once you got it in the stand," Bill said. "Branches'll fill out. This here's a nice 'un."

Helen shook her head. "It's got that bare spot," she said, poking a skinny finger at an empty patch. "I don't know. Can we look at another one?"

Bill tugged it back into the stack of trees.

We moved down the row a bit, but Helen hesitated. "What about this one?" she asked.

It stood a good four feet taller than I am, and I'm six foot.

"Well, that is nice," Dad said. "Do you think that would fit? It looks a little tall."

"Oh, I don't know. I think it would. Can we see that one?"

I looked back and forth between Dad and Helen. She must have spatial issues, because even Travis would have known Dad's ceilings were too low to accommodate that monstrosity. Why was Dad letting Bill go to all that trouble when we both knew better? Maybe I was missing something.

"Where do you guys usually put the tree?" I asked.

"In the family room. Next to the french doors."

No way.

Bill started to wrestle with the tree, so I stepped up to help him drag it out. We hauled it away from the others, and he cut the string.

"Oh. That's lovely. Isn't it perfect?" Helen said.

"How high is your ceiling in there?" I asked.

"Standard."

"Does it say how tall the tree is?" I asked.

"Says here," Bill said as he struggled to get to the tag. "Eleven feet."

"Oh, it will fit," Helen said. "Don't you think?"

I raised my eyebrows and made a noncommittal noise.

Dad patted Helen's back. "Maybe we should keep looking."

I helped Bill yank the tree back into place. As they continued down the row, I kicked at the dirt and shuffled over to the trees on the other end. I touched their spiny needles. This was the kind we'd gotten when I was little. I remembered hanging ornaments on the branches, my fingers little and clumsy. I breathed in the scent of them.

"What are you looking at, Asher?" I heard Dad call.

"Oh, nothing," I said.

But he was already moving toward me. Helen was down at the other end, having Bill pull out another tree. Dad joined me by the spruces. As we looked at them, I wondered if Dad was remembering, like I was. He ruffled my hair.

"Hey, Helen," he called. "Come take a look down here."

Wild Bill put the tree they'd been looking at away, and then he followed her down to where we stood.

"Can we take a look at this one?" Dad asked.

"Sure," Bill said.

He yanked it out, cut the twine, and shook the branches loose. Then he peered underneath it.

"No needles yet," he said. "Guess that's good."

"Isn't that a spruce?" Helen said.

Dad put his arm around Helen and squeezed her. "Yes."

Helen pursed her lips. "It's not very full, is it?"

"I kind of like it. What do you think, sport?" he asked me.

It wasn't even symmetrical.

"This one won't break the bank," Wild Bill said.

We couldn't afford nice, fancy trees when I was growing up. "I like it," I said to Dad.

Helen and Dad exchanged a look. She shook her head slowly from side to side, but then she smiled. "Let's pack it up," she said.

I know it's stupid, but that night, I felt better than I'd felt in a long time. Helen made hot chocolate, and it didn't even irritate me that it was some fancy chocolate and not from a package. Out front, I helped Dad saw off the bottom of the tree. We brought it into the family room together and arranged it in the stand. Afterward, we hauled plastic bins in from the garage and unpacked some of Helen's expensive glass ornaments.

"Crystal, actually," she corrected me. "Let's stack the boxes by the wall until we find the lights. Careful now."

Even that didn't bother me. It was a relief that nothing was familiar. I didn't have to encounter any memories here. I was disappointed when Dad announced it was time to take me home.

"It's too bad we couldn't finish up tonight," Helen said.

"The branches really do need to settle first," Dad said.

"Oh, well. We'll finish up on Sunday," she said.

"Sunday?" I asked.

"Well, we aren't going to decorate without you," she said. "Maybe I'll get your father to put the lights on, but I'm not putting a single ornament on the tree until you can help me." She stopped herself short. "If that's okay, I mean. If you want to," she said. "You don't have to."

"No," I said. "That would be nice."

Dad and I rode, just the two of us, back to my house. We traveled in silence for the first few minutes, but then he reached over and turned on the radio. It was on one of those stations that play music from the 60s and 70s. Dad flipped through stations and settled on some rap song. He bobbed his head a little. "What are you listening to these days?" he asked.

"Lots of things, I guess."

He nodded. I thought about Earl.

"Not this."

"Oh," he said. "Sorry." He turned the radio off. "Good. I didn't really like it either."

"The first station was okay," I said.

He started to turn it back on, but I held my hand up. "Really, Dad. It's okay."

He took a deep breath. "Right." He was quiet for a minute. "It's just, Helen was wondering what kind of music you like. What bands. I don't even know. We wanted to get music for you, so when you wake up Christmas morning, you have a few things you actually like."

Christmas morning? Wait. "Uh…"

Dad pulled up into my driveway. "What?" he asked.

"Yeah. About Christmas. I think Aunt Sharon wants Mom and me to visit her in Chicago."

"Aunt Sharon?"

I nodded.

"No," he said. "Absolutely not. Your mother had you for Thanksgiving. I get you for Christmas. That's the deal."

Deal?

He put the Land Rover in park. And turned off the ignition. "We'll settle this right now."

No. "Dad."

"She's had you for every holiday since we divorced," he said. I thought about how he worded it, *We divorced.* Mom always said, *He left.* "Christmas is mine."

"But Aunt Sharon—"

"Your mother can go to Chicago if she wants to. That's fine. But I get you for Christmas." He hit the steering wheel. "This is so typical." Dad rushed out of the car and strode up to the front door.

I usually just walked in, I mean it's my house, but with Dad there next to me it got all awkward. Instead, I rang the doorbell. I could picture Mom inside, sitting in her sloppy T-shirt and sweatpants, watching television while she waited for me to come home. I heard movement, probably Mom looking through the peephole. She unlocked the door.

"Hi, Steve," she said. "Is everything okay?"

"I don't know. You tell me. What's this I hear about you taking Asher to Chicago for Christmas?"

Mom glanced at me, then back to Dad. "Aunt Sharon called *yesterday* to invite us to Chicago," she said. "So yes, there is *talk* about us going to Chicago for Christmas."

"Just to be clear, Asher is with us for Christmas," Dad said. "And I don't appreciate you undermining our plans with promises of trips."

Mom laughed. "First of all, I didn't initiate Chicago. My *sister* did. To be nice. Not as some plot to undermine your plans. I *am* sorry," she said, dripping with sarcasm, "I just haven't gotten used to you giving a damn about what we do."

"Of course. Because I'm the bad guy," he said, gesturing his hands upward in frustration. "Whatever, Margaret."

"I'll let you know what we decide to do," she said. "Come inside, Asher."

I hesitated, but then I stepped inside our house. "I'm sorry," I said before she slammed the door, but I'm not sure if I was apologizing to Dad or Mom.

CHAPTER THIRTEEN

Turns out every person on the planet goes to the DMV on Friday afternoons. Mom and I knew we were in trouble the second we pulled up in the parking lot. We had to squeeze into a space behind the building in the last row. Inside, the people crowded against the wall and filled every chair. One woman working the counter was trying to tell this old guy how to line up for the vision screen. The other heavyset woman with big brown hair straightened a stack of official-looking papers, moseyed over to a digital screen that posted the number *73*, and called, "Seventy-four!"

A man wearing loose-fitting shorts with a button-up shirt stood up and hoisted up his waistband. He put a form on the counter and said, "My driver's license expired. I got this paperwork here."

She adjusted her glasses and said, "I need to see your driver's license."

He pulled his wallet out of the back pocket of his baggy shorts and slid his driver's license onto the counter.

"Do we need a number?" I asked Mom.

She wove through the crowd of people and pulled a number off a device attached to the wall. Her face looked grim as she came back to me.

"Ninety-eight," Mom whispered to me.

She checked the time on her phone and angled the screen toward me. It was a little after four. The DMV closed at five.

"Should we come back another day?" I asked.

"I took off work early to get here."

She said that loud like maybe people would leave or give up their spot in line to accommodate us. I figured a lot of people took off early to get here. The old man finished his vision test, and the lady told him to go sit down and she'd call him back in a few minutes.

"Is anyone getting their license today?" she called to the waiting room.

Mom nudged me.

"I'm getting my learner's, not my license," I hissed at her.

She humphed at me, and then she stepped forward. "He's getting his learner's permit," Mom called out.

The lady took her glasses off to see us better. "Do you need to take the test?"

Mom elbowed me.

"I took it online," I said.

"And passed it. We have all the paperwork here." Mom waved the papers at the lady and started to head for the counter, but the woman held her hand up to stop her.

"Number seventy-five!" she called.

Mom decided it would be a good idea for me to drive us to Harmon Photo to develop my film. I wasn't so sure. Harmon Photo was forty-five minutes away and involved highway driving. She argued that if I wasn't so fussy we could always take the film downtown to the grocery store instead. I had the distinct impression she was trying to show me how awful it was to drive out to Harmon.

"We'd save money on gas and film," she argued. "It's color film, so it doesn't require anything special."

"Have you looked at their machine?" I said. "And the people running that thing have no concept of photography. They push buttons and feed it in. That's it."

Plus we knew way too many people in town who worked at the Thrifty. I was pretty sure Iggy worked in the photo shop. When I'd bought my first roll of film, he was the one who showed me the aisle of 35 mm. Iggy had laughed at me when I chose the last roll of black-and-white film. Plus there were images on this roll from Thanksgiving that I couldn't let Iggy see.

So my first time driving would be to take my film to Harmon Photo.

It had been a while since we'd been to Harmon's. Usually I champed at the bit to get there since I had film waiting to get picked up, but Mom had picked up the last rolls, and I bought the roll of color film at the grocery store. I got my notebook where I kept track of all my expenses, put it in the backseat, and slid into the driver's seat.

Mom handed me the car keys. I sorted through the ring until I found the right one and turned on the ignition. The radio sounded louder than usual, so I turned it off. I buckled the seat belt.

"Check your mirrors," Mom said.

I angled the rearview mirror up slightly and checked both sides. Then I took a deep breath, pressed the brake, and shifted into reverse. I held my foot on the brake while I looked for cars coming on our usually empty street and slowly eased out of our driveway.

Harmon Photo was tucked into a strip mall. When I turned into the parking lot, it occurred to me that the last time I had been there, Travis had been with us. Was it normal to feel nostalgic over all the annoying things he did? I thought about how Travis kicked the back of the seats and how stressed out Mom got driving. I couldn't imagine driving with him in the car, and guilt washed over me. I would have gotten used to it.

The spaces in front of the photo shop were empty, so I had my choice of places to pull in. When I put it in park and turned off the ignition, I realized how tightly I'd been holding the steering wheel. My shoulders felt stiff. I turned to Mom and smiled.

"Well?" I said.

"You drive like an old woman," she said.

Seriously? My shoulders slumped with disappointment. She patted my arm when she saw my expression. "Oh, Asher. You did great. Very cautious."

"Is that bad?"

"No. It's perfect."

I handed her the keys and stepped out of the car into the midday sun. The sky was hazy, but it was still warm for December. Mom and I headed to the entrance on the right. When I opened the door, a bell jingled. I noticed the shelves that were usually lined with camera supplies were almost empty. Signs advertising 50 percent off stood on top of the display case. The cool photographs on the wall were missing.

"No, they're metal," Alice was saying on the phone. "We have two glass cabinet displays. Well, you're welcome to come by and take a look. We're here noon to five Monday through Saturday." Alice glanced at me and smiled. She held up a finger, just a minute, and turned her back to me. "Probably that last Saturday before Christmas. Right. Well, thanks for calling," she said and hung up the phone.

"What's going on?" I asked.

"We're closing shop," she said. "Take a look around and see if anything interests you. Fifty percent off just about everything."

Closing? I didn't look at anything. I stared at Alice. How could Harmon Photo *close*? "Why?"

"There isn't a lot of business," she said. "It's not a huge surprise. There aren't a lot of people using film these days."

"Is there something we can do? Raise money?"

She used that face grownups do with kids, when they think you're cute for being hopeful. Ah, he thinks he can save the store. How cute. She wrinkled her nose at me. "It's all pretty much a done deal."

"Okay, so what about my film?" I asked. "Can you develop my film?"

Alice reached under the counter, pulled out a paper, and rotated it so it was facing me. "These are reputable online stores many of our customers use. And there are still some locals who develop on site."

Mom walked up beside me and glanced at the list of business and links. "Our grocery store has one of those processing machines. What's your opinion on those?" she asked Alice.

"It really varies. A lot of it depends on the machines. With the type of thing Asher does, black and white, he's going to need to send it in somewhere to have it properly developed."

"He does color now," Mom said.

Alice raised her eyebrows. "Really?"

"I'm using a Canon A-1," I said. "My Minolta sort of sunk."

"Hold on, was that your camera? A lady brought in a Minolta a while ago. It had fallen in a pool."

I nodded. "Yeah, that was mine."

"Well, Canon is excellent," Alice said.

"It's not mine. My neighbor is letting me use it."

"If you're using color film now, you have a lot more options. You can try the grocery store if you want, but I get nervous about those types of things. You're pretty particular, aren't you?"

"Yes, he is," Mom said, not bothering to hide her irritation.

"I can't believe you guys are closing," I said. I folded the paper she'd given me and slid it into my pocket.

She shrugged. "That's the way it goes. Why don't you have a look around?"

Of course, I saw a ton of stuff I'd have liked to have: tripods, camera cases, lighting equipment. But I found myself wandering over to the other side of the shop where they had the studio.

"Are you guys closing the studio too?" I called to Alice in the other room.

"Yes," Alice hollered. "We used to get a lot of family portraits, but these days everyone with a camera thinks they're a photographer. If you ask me, you get what you pay for."

This ridiculous statue of an old butler still stood in the front window. Travis used to put his fingers inside the guy's nostrils. It used to irritate Mom. She swatted at his hand and told him not to touch things.

I touched the butler's nose.

I didn't understand. My research suggested the field of photography was growing. The occupational outlook was good, on the rise. So why was Harmon going out of business? I took the paper out of my pocket and unfolded it as I wandered back into the supply area. I wondered what they were doing with their equipment. Alice was looking through the packets of developed film. She looked up at me. "I've got to call all these people," she said, indicating the drawer full of developed photographs. "They've got to pick them up before Christmas."

"That's when you close for good?" I asked.

She nodded.

I held up the paper. "So your customers are just going to these other places?"

"One guy is converting a bathroom into a darkroom," she said.

"That's so cool," I said. "I read about that. You just need access to water. If we closed it in, we could…"

"No," Mom said. "Don't even think about it."

"Mom…"

"All those chemicals? No," she said. "We only have one bathroom, Asher."

"The garage?" I asked.

"Asher," she warned.

Alice wrinkled her nose at us. "Sorry," she said. "I probably shouldn't have mentioned it."

Mom sighed. "It's okay. So what are your plans, Alice?"

"I start school in January," she said. "I've been accepted into a Radiology program."

"Radiology?" I asked.

"X-rays, MRIs, ultrasounds. Basically I'll be looking inside people's bodies to diagnose problems," Alice said.

"So you're still a photographer," I said.

Alice paused. A smile spread across her face. "I hadn't thought about it that way," she said. "Yes. I'll still be a photographer."

I gripped the edge of the countertop and stared up at the blank walls. "Where are the photos you guys had on the walls?" I asked. The old restored black-and-white photographs of old Florida scenes had been so cool. Cars parked on the Gulf shore, airport trucks, car dealerships, and ancient gas stations.

"Those were with us on loan. They're in the back room, packed up to return. I need to drive them out near where you guys live," Alice said.

"What's the address?" Mom asked.

She read it aloud to us, and I suddenly realized it wasn't just out near where we lived. The photographs belonged to Pearl.

❖

When I pulled up in the driveway, Pearl stood in the center of her yard spraying the grass with the hose. She wore a faded blue robe and turned in a slow circle, like one of those rotating sprinklers. Bizarre.

"Look at her," I said to Mom as I turned off the ignition. The hose wrapped around her legs. If she tried to walk, she'd face-plant into the ground.

"Poor Pearl," Mom said. "It must be awful getting old."

We got out of the car. Pearl squinted in our direction. She stopped rotating.

"You let him drive? With my photographs in the car?" Pearl hollered at us.

Alice had called Pearl to get permission to send her packages with us. I wouldn't have been surprised if she had said no, but Pearl had agreed to it.

"Got my learner's permit," I said as Mom and I walked toward her.

"Do you want Asher to bring your packages inside?" Mom asked.

"In a minute. My grass is turning brown."

"Well, it's winter. It usually does that."

"Not my yard," she said.

Mom put her hands on her hips and took in the saturated grass. "It's supposed to get real cold tonight. Be careful with the water or it will freeze and kill everything."

Pearl scowled at my mom. "I think I know what I'm doing." Her slippers were saturated with water and dirt. The hose wrapped around her legs at least three times.

"Why don't you let Asher do that for you?" Mom asked. "Would you like to come inside for some coffee or tea?"

"I can do it myself."

"I know. Your yard is always gorgeous," Mom said, and then she lowered her voice a bit like she was sharing a secret with Pearl. But I could hear her. It was pretty lame. "But honestly, it would do Asher good." I figured she was just trying to convince Pearl to get out of her soaking shoes. The old lady had the hose pointed down right next to her, dumping the water onto her slippers.

"You're making a puddle," I said and reached out for the hose, but Pearl yanked her hand away. "And you're tangled up."

Pearl glanced down at her feet in the puddle.

"Damn it."

She handed the hose to me, and I circled her to unwind it, all the while pointing the nozzle out toward the yard and trying to avoid soaking my mom. Pearl stepped out of the hose trap. Her slippers squished in the puddle.

"Don't just stand there," Pearl said. "Go turn off the spigot."

I hurried around to the side of the house and turned off the water. By the time I returned, Mom and Pearl stood at the open trunk of the car. I joined them and carefully lifted the first framed photo out of the car. Pearl led me to the front door of her house. Inside it didn't stink too badly, but Pearl's slippers sloshed on the floor making muddy puddles.

"Slide it behind the sofa," she said.

"Maybe Asher can hang it up for you," Mom suggested.

"I wouldn't trust that boy with a hammer," she said.

When I brought in the next package, my ears perked up at Mom and Pearl's discussion.

"But if he's looking for a place to develop film," I heard Pearl say, "why doesn't he just do it himself? Can't trust other people to do it right, anyway."

"Mom won't let me have a darkroom," I said as I set down the package.

They both turned to look at me, like they'd forgotten I existed.

"He doesn't know anything about the chemicals," Mom said dismissively.

Boy, I hated that. She had no clue what I knew. "Yes, I do."

"He thinks if he reads an article or watches a video that he's an expert," she told Pearl.

"I know how," I said. "I just don't have a place to do it." Suddenly I remembered the yellow envelope Pearl had given me with my photos in it. "Where do you get your photos developed?" I asked. "Did you use Harmon?"

She huffed. "No. I do it myself."

"You?"

"It's an art. You'll screw it up if you take it to one of those machines. And if *you* try to do it on your own, you'll ruin everything," Pearl said. "Typical teenager. Got all the answers. How many time have you developed film?"

I hadn't done it yet. But it didn't look all that hard. "None, but I've done a lot of—"

"Stop talking about what you think you know. Ask me how many times I've done it."

Pearl irked me. I wanted to go home.

"Thousands of times. Thousands," Pearl said, and she waved

a bony, spotted hand in the air. "Fine. I'll develop his film. In my darkroom."

❖

Pearl's darkroom was located in the center of her house. It was twice as large as the darkrooms I'd seen online, and well stocked. Photographs hung on corkboards and strings tied across the room, and I tried to determine how long it had been since Pearl had used it, based on the images.

"Did you convert this from a bathroom?" I asked.

"I had it built this way," she said.

The photographs resembled the time period when she would have taken the photograph of Levi and me in the backyard, but we weren't in any of them.

She had labeled every item and posted instructions, but a thin layer of dust covered most of the surfaces.

Pearl ran a finger across the countertop. "I don't spend much time in here anymore. Aside from developing that last batch of your photos." She rubbed her fingers together. "You're going to have to clean this place first."

I spent the afternoon checking labels for expiration dates and cleaning. Pearl ordered me around, but I took note of everything she said. I had to admit, she lined up with what I'd been researching online.

"Why do you go by Pearl?" I asked her.

"Because that's my name."

"Then who is Samantha Miller?"

"I am."

"Is Pearl your middle name?" I asked, but then she just ignored me. Old people can get away with things like that.

When it came time to actually develop the pictures, she wouldn't let me touch a thing, which made me paranoid. The photos on the roll included Iggy and the cat, and Earl with his oxygen tank. The second roll was solid Jennifer. I had a distinct picture of what I wanted them to look like in my head, and I didn't want Pearl to screw it up. I mean, she'd done a great job with the other roll, but what if her memory slipped?

But what choice did I have, really?

I ended up leaving my stuff with her and heading home for dinner. But there wasn't any dinner. Mom said she wasn't hungry so I scrounged around for something to eat. While Mom sat in Travis's room, I nestled up to my computer and searched for photographers from 1960 to 1990 named Samantha Miller.

And that's when I discovered my crabby old neighbor had taken photos of riots on college campuses during the Vietnam War. She'd been nominated for a Pulitzer for photojournalism.

Chapter Fourteen

On Sunday morning, I woke up late to a quiet house. I rubbed my eyes and squinted at the clock. We'd missed church again. The youth group was supposed to help Miss Gabby with the Christmas program for the little guys this morning, so I wasn't as disappointed as I might have been. Every time I looked at those kids, I kept expecting to see Travis. Still, I missed seeing my friends in youth group.

I stretched out in bed for a while, looking at the ceiling. Mom must have changed her mind. John hadn't stopped by this week for grief counseling either. I rolled out of bed, pulled on pajama pants, noticed they were too short, and headed down the hallway. Mom's bedroom door was open a crack. I knocked gently.

"Mom?"

A muffled voice called, "What?"

"No church?"

"I can't," she said, barely audible.

I opened the door.

"Her name is Sara." Mom's room was pitch-black. I moved across the room and sat on the edge of the bed. Her frame didn't move, and her voice was monotone. "The woman John sat with at church. He said they're taking things slowly."

"So they're dating?"

"I guess. I don't care. I don't. It's just…I'm tired, Asher."

My eyes adjusted to the dark and I noticed she was staring blankly at the ceiling.

"How long have you been up?" I asked her, but she didn't answer. I saw the pills on her dresser. "When did you last take one of these?"

"I'm okay," she said. "I'm just tired."

"When did you take one?"

"Are you going to your dad's today?"

"Mom."

Her eyes finally shifted to me. "Last night was hard. I took one last night. Just one," she said. "Maybe two." Then she took a deep breath and sat up. "Seriously, I'm okay. Are you going to your dad's? Because I need to do Christmas shopping."

Mom propped herself up on one elbow and said, "Tell me what you want for Christmas."

Last year I asked for camera accessories and film. I'd resented that we didn't have money and complained. Not as much as Travis, but I'd done plenty. This year I'd moved into candid, and a whole different set of accessories came with it, but I said, "I can't think of anything now that I'm using Pearl's darkroom. What do you want, Mom?"

"I can't get what I want," she said matter-of-factly. She threw the covers off. "So, how about some breakfast?"

❖

After Dad picked me up from home, he apologized for arguing with my mom about Christmas plans. "I shouldn't have put you in that situation," he said. "Your mom and I will work it out. I try not to, but when I think about how much time she's had with you, and how much I've missed…" He shrugged. "My point is, we'll work it out," he said. "Okay, sport?"

At his house, we decorated the tree with Helen's crystal ornaments. When we finished, she brought out a small box wrapped in red paper with a gold bow and handed it to me. It wasn't one of those bows with the sticky adhesive underneath. It was a hand-tied bow, so you actually pulled the ends and it came undone. And there wasn't any tape holding the paper in place. The ribbon actually held it together.

Inside the box was a glass ornament. It was a black vintage camera with my name engraved on the front. I pressed my lips together.

"I wanted you to have something of yours on the tree. I hope it's okay," she said.

"Thank you," I said, and I was surprised by how grateful I felt.

Helen exhaled slowly. I noticed how she clutched her hands in front of her. Dad wrapped his arm around her and kissed her on top of the head. I hung it on the tree in the middle of all the crystal ornaments. I liked that it didn't match the set.

❖

Josh folded a piece of paper into a small triangle while Garrett and I completed the literary-term page Ms. Hughes had given each group.

"Protagonist?" Garrett asked.

"That would be Ralph," I said.

Garrett wrote the name in the blank. His penmanship looked exactly like the bulletin board examples they used to teach kids to write in grade school.

"Jack," Josh mumbled.

"Pretty sure he's the antagonist," Garrett said. "Seeing as how he represents the whole downfall of civilization on the island."

"He likes hunting. I like hunting."

"He hunts *Ralph*."

"So?" Josh stretched his arms up high over his head. "Ralph seemed kind of like a know-it-all."

I was all set to be impressed that Josh had read any of it, but then he said, "I only watched the first half of the movie."

"Uh, I don't think they're exactly the same," Garrett said. "Okay, next one. Who's the antagonist? Majority rules. I say Jack. Asher?"

"Smasher," Josh muttered.

I pretended Josh wasn't there. "Yeah, Jack is the antagonist. Watch the rest of the movie, Josh. You'll see."

Ms. Hughes strolled over.

"How's it going?" she asked.

"Fine," Garrett said. "We're halfway finished with the first page."

"How are you liking the book, Josh?"

"Oh, it's good as far as books go," he said. "Survival stuff. And it's just the guys, since that pilot dude takes off."

Ms. Hughes picked my copy of the novel off of the desk. "You liked that part, did you? Funny, I don't remember the pilot taking off."

Garrett made eye contact with Josh and did this subtle head shake.

"I've been watching the movie, too," Josh covered.

"So you're reading the book and comparing it to the movie?" she asked.

"Yeah, I have a hard time picturing what happens when I read, so I've been doing both," he said. "Sometimes I get stuff confused."

"Maybe you should just stick to the book," she said. "They aren't exactly the same."

Ms. Hughes moved toward Jennifer's group.

"Good cover," Garrett said.

"I don't care what that bitch thinks," Josh said. He put his head back down on his desk. "She gave me a referral."

Garrett focused on the paper again. "Right," he said. "Okay, so the bell's going to ring. Should we try to get together outside of school to finish this up? Plus we've got the project. We need to talk about which one we're going to do."

"Yeah, I'm busy," Josh said, but football was over, so I couldn't imagine why he'd be busy.

"How about we meet up over at my house around six?" Garrett suggested.

"Are you shitting me?"

"It's a group project," Garrett insisted. "You're in our group."

I pictured the anime drawings Garrett had all over his bedroom walls—the one of the two of us. My heart started pounding at the thought of Josh standing in Garrett's bedroom, taking it all in. Josh would have all the evidence he wanted. But if the way he behaved in class was any indication, Josh would ditch us anyway. Which led to my working on the project with Garrett alone.

"Maybe we should go to the library," I suggested.

"Yeah, but Emily will be home, and she might be able to help. What do you say, Josh?" Garrett asked.

"Your sister's hot," he said. The bell rang. "Yeah, I'm in," Josh said. "I'll see you tonight."

❖

Our science teacher used the upcoming holiday as an excuse to give us a taste of chemistry. We had to use a gas chromatography machine to isolate unknown components. Or, as my lab partner, Kayla, would say, we looked at pretty colors. I got our goggles and gloves and reviewed the safety tips.

"I hate this time of year," she said as she pulled on the gloves. She didn't wait for me to ask why. "Do you know more people suffer from depression around the holidays than at any other time of the year? Most wonderful time of the year, my ass." Kayla fiddled with the stud in her eyebrow. "Oh, and my parents. They're throwing the annual Christmas Eve party. Guess what my mom wants for Christmas."

"Uh, what?" I asked as I secured my goggles.

"For the party, would I please look *normal.*" She made this guttural growl. "Maybe I should ask Jennifer if I could borrow her cheerleading outfit again. I can even do a happy cheer. *Merry, merry, merry year. Jesus is born, go have a beer.*"

I laughed.

"Seriously. You don't know my mom. Everything has to look perfect. She slaves away to get everything just right so it *looks* perfect," Kayla said. "And my dad gets shit-faced."

"We're not doing Christmas this year," I said.

She waited for me to explain more, but I didn't say anything. Kayla punched my shoulder while I was pouring the acetone.

"Hey! What if this were hydrochloric acid?"

"Sorry, but you can't drop that crap into a conversation and not explain."

I added the other chemicals. "Swirl this," I said. "Okay, so with my mom. It's just we're not doing a tree or decorations or anything."

"Why not?" Kayla's eyebrows knit together with concern.

"Travis, I guess," I said, then nodded toward the solution. "I think you're supposed to cover it now."

"Oh"—Kayla covered the mixture and sighed—"you are so lucky."

Lucky? I must have made a noise, because she nudged me.

"At least it's honest. Your mom isn't pretending."

I made another noise, because of course my mom was pretending. She pretended she didn't have an affair. She pretended Dad was Travis's dad.

"Use the dropper," I said. "Put it here. I'll measure and mark it."

"You think it's better to fake it?" Kayla asked.

"I don't know," I said. "I still get to have Christmas. My dad and

Helen got a tree and stuff. Plus, my aunt wants to fly us to Chicago, but my dad says I'm supposed to spend Christmas with him. It's all sort of complicated." I reviewed the instructions. "Okay, let's see about the next thing here."

"I hate science," Kayla moaned. "And Christmas."

My parents arguing made me wish we could just skip the holidays. Everything was such a big deal. And it wasn't like I was a little kid, so why did people get all upset about everything?

"Every year is exactly the same with us," Kayla said. "Put up the tree, bake the damn cookies, put them in tins, hand them out. She writes this Christmas letter telling everyone how great we're all doing. She asks me to make a list of the things I want for Christmas, like I'm six years old. It makes me want to throw up."

I pictured the tree we'd picked out from the Christmas-tree lot and how happy I was to get one just like the kind we'd had when I was little. "You'd miss it," I said. "If she stopped doing those things, you'd miss it."

"No, I wouldn't."

Dad left, Travis died, and everything changed. "You would."

"I just want her to be *real*."

I thought about that. Mom avoiding Christmas didn't make her real. And it didn't make her brave either. I looked at the spread of the color on the paper and the color itself.

"Okay, last one, Einstein. What's the answer, partner?" Kayla asked.

I said, "Iron and copper."

"A poor substitute for silver and gold, don't you think?" Kayla said, and the bell rang.

Chapter Fifteen

The outside of Garrett's house was lined in colored Christmas lights. We arrived at his place at exactly six o'clock. When I didn't see Josh's red Silverado truck in the driveway, I couldn't decide if I felt relief or concern.

"You want to call when you need me to pick you up?" Mom asked.

"I can walk."

I swung my book-bag strap onto my shoulder, got out of our vehicle, and walked up to Garrett's front door. I rang the doorbell. It was growing dark outside. Mom waited in the driveway, headlights on, until the front door opened. Garrett stood in the silhouette of the doorway.

"Hey," he said. He wore dark blue jeans and a black T-shirt. No shoes. Guitar music played somewhere in the house. "Come on in." Garrett opened the door wide for me.

It wasn't the first time I'd been in his house. It was the third. The first time was way back when the house belonged to Evan Llowell, Josh's older brother. Garrett's family had put a Christmas tree up in the corner. It didn't look real, but it didn't look fake either. Garrett saw me looking at it and said, "My mom actually made it. Cool, huh?"

It really was. I'd never seen anything like it. It was covered with homemade decorations. Nothing on it looked store-bought except for the lights.

"You hungry? Thirsty?" he asked. "I've got blue Gatorade."

He remembered. I hated that my face got warm. "No, thanks." I scanned the rest of the house. I hadn't noticed any cars in the driveway, but maybe they actually had room for cars in their garage. Garrett led me through his family room down the hall to where I knew his bedroom was. I stalled at the entrance to the hallway. I wasn't sure how I felt about being alone with him.

"How about we work at the dining table?" I suggested. "More room to spread our stuff out, you know?"

"Okay, we'll move there when Josh gets here. Come on."

It occurred to me that Josh might not show up at all, but I didn't say anything. I followed Garrett down the hall. His bedroom door was partially open. The music came from inside, an acoustic guitar. It wasn't until Garrett swung the door open that I realized we weren't alone. Iggy sat in a black swivel office chair underneath Garrett's window. His bare feet were propped up onto Garrett's bed. His guitar crossed in front of him, and he picked the strings and repositioned his fingers along the neck without glancing down to check. He played with his eyes closed and hummed another tune. He didn't acknowledge our coming into the room, and Garrett didn't interrupt Iggy's concentration. Instead I could see the pride swell up in Garrett as he watched Iggy play.

I searched the wall for the picture Garrett had drawn of the two of us, but he'd hidden it away or thrown it out. I wasn't sure if I felt relieved or disappointed. The *Lord of the Flies* novel sat on top of Garrett's end table. Sticky notes stuck out of it. A drawing pad was flipped open next to the book, a pencil casually resting on top. The top page showed a partially drawn guy, his hair long and scraggly, his clothing ripped and weathered. He held a large shell in one hand and a torch in the other. I pointed to the drawing.

I mouthed the word *Ralph*. Garrett mouthed back *yes*, clearly pleased I'd recognized the character.

One of the project options was drawing pictures of the main characters in the novel, including elements representing the values of that individual. Without discussing it with us, Garrett had already started working on the group project. I'd been leaning toward the bit on symbolism, thinking maybe I could photograph images and then Garrett could write about what each object symbolized. At least I didn't need to worry about Josh's ideas. I'd bet money he hadn't thought about it at all.

Iggy played his last note, and I asked, "What was that?"

"Oh, hey," he said, although I found it hard to believe that he'd been so into the music he hadn't realized we'd entered the room. "Just something I'm playing with."

"You made that up?" I asked.

Iggy did this little head tilt that I guessed I was supposed to take as something between a nod and a shrug and played a series of chords. Garrett plopped down on the bed next to Iggy's feet.

"I know, right?" Garrett said to me. "He's always coming up with stuff. It blows me away."

Iggy acted all into his music again, like he hadn't heard Garrett's praise, but the way he stepped up his game, playing faster, I knew he was playing to impress. Whatever.

"So, should we get started?" I asked, moving closer to the doorway.

"I thought we'd wait for Josh."

Iggy snorted. For once, I agreed.

"I don't think we should count on Josh showing, Garrett," I said. "I mean, he hasn't really—"

The doorbell rang.

"Ha! Screw both of you," Garrett said lightly, and he hopped off the bed. "I got it!" he called as he ran down the hallway.

Iggy continued to play guitar.

"Are you coming?" I asked.

"No way. I already passed tenth grade."

I hesitated in the doorway a second before moving down the hall after Garrett. Josh stepped inside the doorway, and seeing him standing there took me back two summers ago. I pictured Josh's hand possessively placed on Kayla's hip. Kayla, fresh-faced and goth-free, blinking adoringly up at Josh's face. My hand rested on the hallway wall.

Now Josh took in the new decor. "Well, this is different," he said as he took inventory, walking around the room.

"That's right, your brother lived here. I keep forgetting that."

He strolled into the dining room. "Evan had a pool table right here," he told Garrett. "One of the guys bought it off him when he moved to Miami. Pain in the ass to move." Josh pointed to the wall farthest from the front door. "Okay, he had this crazy big-screen television over there. A couch there, and then a table over here with chairs," Josh said. "And a liquor cabinet like you wouldn't believe. This place has seen some action."

"Yeah, not so much these days," Garrett said.

Josh meandered down the hall to the first closed door. He pointed to it. Garrett knocked on the door.

"Mom?"

"Yes?"

"I've got friends over. Is it okay if I show them your work room?" Muffled through the door. "Uh, sure. For a second."

He opened the door. Garrett's mom sat in the center of the room on the floor in sweatpants and a button up shirt that swallowed her. Patches of purple and green stained the front of the shirt. She had paint on her hands, but she was staring at a blank canvas.

"Josh, this is my mom."

"Hi," she said, though she didn't look up at him.

"Asher, you know my mom."

"Yeah."

She looked up at me. "Hello, Asher. It's nice to see you again." People tended to be nicer to me since Travis died. It was a weird side effect. I never knew what to make of it. "How are you?" she asked.

"Fine."

"Your mom?"

"She's good. Going to Chicago for Christmas."

"Oh, that's lovely! Are you going, too?"

"I don't know yet. I'm supposed to go to my dad's, but…yeah. I don't know."

"Well, you're welcome to come here," she said.

Couldn't she hear? I had too many options already. "Uh, thanks."

"You boys have fun," she said.

Garrett closed the door, and we continued down the hallway toward his bedroom.

"That," Josh whispered as he motioned toward the work room, "was my brother's bedroom. The first time I ever got laid was in that room. Jesus, this brings back memories."

Kayla. His first time was with Kayla in that room. And she'd gotten pregnant, and he didn't know.

"Huh," Garrett said.

"You know Kayla, right?" he said. "She was normal back then, pretty hot if you—"

"Don't." I cut him off.

Josh and Garrett both stopped in the hallway to look at me.

"Seriously. About Kayla," I said. "Don't."

Josh grinned. "You like her?"

"She's a friend of mine."

"*Riiiight*," he said. "Well, she's real sweet. A nice piece of—"

I shoved his shoulder. "I'm serious."

Josh howled laughing. He clapped his hands together. Another door swung open, and Emily poked her head out.

"What's going on?" she demanded.

"Uh, study group," Garrett explained, but he looked like he wasn't too sure. I don't think he'd counted on a potential fight.

Josh shouldered past Garrett. "Hey, Emily. How's it going?"

"Fine. So why are you in the hall?"

"I'm getting a tour. Can I see your room?"

"No, you can't. I'm studying, too. Finals next week. College applications and scholarship essays due. Enjoy junior year while you can, Josh. Senior year is not cake."

"Sounds stressful," Josh said. "Maybe you should take a break?"

"I'll take a break when the last bell rings a week from tomorrow."

"Let me take you out that night," Josh said. "You know, to celebrate."

Emily leaned against her door frame. "You want to take me out?"

Josh ran a hand through his hair. "Maybe. Unless you think you're too good for me or something."

She made a choked noise. "As tempting as that sounds, I'm not interested." Emily raised her eyebrows at Garrett. "So, good luck on that project."

She shut her door. I eyed Garrett's bedroom at the end of the hall and wondered what Josh would think of Iggy sitting in there.

"Maybe we should just get to work," Garrett said.

❖

Josh proved to be less useful than even I could have predicted. He spent the entire evening trying to make up excuses to pester Emily. Garrett and I managed to get a decent review in for the test, regardless.

"Okay, so what about the project?" Garrett asked.

"Yeah, what are you guys planning on doing?" Josh asked as he grabbed a handful of popcorn. "Because I'm not sure how I'm going to do on this test, and I need a decent grade on this project to pass."

"What about the picture you drew?" I asked. "The one of Ralph. Maybe we could combine the character and symbolism ones. You can finish the drawing, and then Josh and I can write—"

"Whoa, whoa. I'm not writing."

"You're such an asshole," Iggy said as he rounded the corner. He pulled on the hoodie I'd seen him wearing at Thanksgiving.

"Iggy!" Josh stood and greeted Iggy with outstretched arms like they were best buds. "Have you been here the whole time?"

I eyed the hoodie. It was too cold outside for only a hoodie.

"I'm just hanging out."

Josh leaned toward him and lowered his voice. "With Emily? Is that why she wouldn't let me in her room? You've got to be kidding me."

I couldn't help but look at Garrett. He was waiting for Iggy to correct Josh—*no, I'm with Garrett*—but Iggy just pulled this smug expression.

"Jealous, Josh?" he said.

"Yes. Definitely. How the hell did you pull that off?"

Iggy shrugged.

Josh laughed, then he said, "Hey, I need to talk to you. You leaving?"

"Yeah."

Josh pulled out his phone. "I'm off, too." He stood up and stuffed his blank notebook into his book bag. "So, you guys figure out that project, okay?"

He and Iggy started for the front door, but just as they reached the handle, Iggy turned to Garrett and asked, "Is it cool if I leave my guitar here again?"

Garrett made a *hmm* noise, like he was amused, only it wasn't funny. He said, "Maybe you should ask Emily."

Iggy rolled his eyes, pulled up his hood, and headed for the door with Josh. "See you guys tomorrow," Iggy muttered, and then he and Josh were out the door.

Garrett sighed. "Where were we?"

"The project," I said.

"Right," he said, but I could tell his brain wasn't with me.

"We could combine the symbolism and character projects into one," I suggested. "You want me to write it up tonight? You can take a look at it in the morning."

Garrett rubbed his hands over his face. "Yeah, I can't do this anymore tonight."

I should have just tucked my novel and notes into my bag and left, but something about Garrett slumped in his chair held me in place. I closed my novel and slid it away from me. "Are you okay?" I asked.

He stretched his arms over his head, and I couldn't help but notice the way his shirt clung to his chest. Then he shook his whole body, like a dog shedding excess water. He raised an eyebrow at me. "Yeah," he said. "It's fine."

"I wasn't trying to pry."

He rested a gentle gaze on me. What was it about Garrett that made me feel like he could see right through me? "I know, Asher," he said. "With Iggy, sometimes it's hard. He gets distant, like he won't let me get too close."

When Iggy was in grade school, he told everyone he had magic powers and threatened people with curses. In middle school, he started the grunge thing, listening to music no one had ever heard of and getting surly with teachers. But still he managed to navigate the crowds at school pretty well in high school.

I slid the novel closer to me and tapped the edges to keep my hands busy. It occurred to me that Iggy had plenty to hide. And why had Josh wanted to talk to him? Why was Iggy so tight with all of those different groups at school, when he worked so hard to be a loner? I hesitated. "Is he still clean?" I asked.

"Yes." Garrett's whole body stiffened. "That's a deal breaker. If he uses, then we're done. He knows that."

I glanced at the door. "He doesn't, you know, sell. Does he?" I asked.

Garrett angled his head to the side and examined me.

"Why do you hate him so much?"

"I don't *hate* Iggy," I said. "I don't hate anyone."

"But if you were going to hate someone, Iggy might be a good start?"

I took a deep breath. "Look, I get that he's creative and talented and all of that. Okay? That's great."

Garrett waited.

I didn't say anything.

"But…? There's a but to follow that, right?" Garrett finally said.

I dropped the novel. "It's your business. Not mine."

He reached over and rested a warm, steady hand on my shoulder. I could feel the heat of him through my shirt. My heart started thumping. "Is there history between the two of you?" he said. "Because…"

I shrugged his hand off my shoulder. "Because what?"

"You act differently when he's around," he said.

"No, I don't."

"You do."

"Look, we don't have history. Unless you count his drug paraphernalia out in the woods at my dad's place *history*."

"Drug paraphernalia?"

A couple years ago my dad found all this stuff on the property, and then Iggy was bragging about the good times he and his friends had out at my dad's property. "Look, everyone knows he's done drugs. And rumors about him being bisexual have been going around for years. But I just saw you with someone…" I lifted a shoulder. "I don't know. Someone different."

"Like?" he asked.

I searched my brain for the right person. Faces from school flipped through my brain, but honestly, there wasn't anyone. "Someone who doesn't do drugs."

"He's clean."

"Someone you have things in common with."

"We're both creative."

"Yeah, but…" I sighed. "Someone who bathes."

Garrett leaned back in his chair and his mouth twisted. "That's mean, Asher."

"No, seriously. Does he bathe? Why the stringy hair?" I pushed the image of Iggy at the homeless shelter out of my head.

Garrett raised his voice. "But Kayla's okay?"

"What does that have to do with anything?"

"Why is it okay for Kayla to wear black, smoke, all that, but not Iggy? What's the difference?"

There was a reason Kayla chose to dress in black. There was a reason Kayla developed a thick skin. But Iggy, he had always been like that. "So you're saying you…that you find"—I fumbled with words— "Iggy, the way he is…attractive?"

"Do you think Kayla's pretty?" he countered.

Kayla, with her maroon hair and pierced lip, eyebrow, and tongue, *was* pretty. It was like all she'd suffered through made her beautiful. She just wore her pain on the outside.

"Yes," I said. "Kayla's pretty."

"Well, that answers that."

"What?"

"I thought there was something between you and Kayla. Now I know," he said. I shook my head, but he continued. "So I guess if you're asking if I'm attracted to Iggy, the answer is yes."

My body went cold and clammy. I rubbed my hands together to warm them. Why did I care?

"He isn't the type I usually go for," he continued, "but the more I've gotten to know him, the more attractive I've found him."

A spark lit in me. I avoided eye contact, tried to stop myself from asking, but I couldn't. "So." *Keep it casual. No big deal.* "What type do you usually go for?"

Garrett stayed quiet for so long, I had to look at him. He had this pained expression on his face, like I'd hurt him. His eyebrows were drawn up together, and he was breathing heavy. "Why are you doing this to me?" he asked.

Doing what? I'd crossed some line, but I didn't know which one.

"You like Kayla, right?"

"We're friends," I said. "Of course I like her."

"You know what I mean."

I didn't *like* her. At least I didn't think I did. It was hard to know the difference. I opened my mouth to deny it, but Garrett cut me off.

"What type do you usually go for, Asher?"

My mouth closed. I didn't know how to answer that question. I didn't like anyone. All that romantic stuff, it didn't appeal to me. It never had, really. People lusted after each other all the time in high school, but I just wasn't wired that way. I didn't get carried away. The day at the pool started to surface in my memory, but I shoved it way down inside, next to the Bible passage and my memories of Travis.

"I don't think I have a type," I whispered, and then I stood up. "I should go." I wanted to block this out. I wanted to be home in my room with my walls full of photographs.

Garrett slid out of his chair and approached me. He was close enough for me to smell coconut oil. I averted my eyes from him and steadied myself against the table. My breath came fast, and he moved closer. For a second, I thought he was going to wrap his arms around me, but he only rested a hand on my shoulder. I sensed how near he was. He leaned over me, his face near mine. So close.

I didn't want to stay away from him. I wanted to turn and lean against him. I remembered the way he felt next to me, close. I craved his warmth. I wanted to listen past his thudding heart to the depths of his soul.

But instead, Garrett dropped his hand from my shoulder and said, "I can't do this, Asher. You should probably go home."

CHAPTER SIXTEEN

The Santa-hat clad flight attendant stood by the airplane door as Mom and I filed past.

"Happy holidays," she said, a smile plastered on her face. Her lightbulb earrings and necklace blinked.

Green wreaths woven with red-and-gold ribbon hung from the airport ceiling. LED lights dangled as well, like stars. The piped-in music played Christmas medleys. A sign hanging above our heads pointed toward the gates and baggage claim. I waited for Mom to lead, but she stopped in the middle of the path of people exiting the plane. They swarmed around and past her, like salmon avoiding a rock in the middle of a river.

"Uh, baggage claim, right?" I said, and Mom nodded and followed me.

We headed down the long, narrow path, sticking to the right. If I hadn't been there, Mom would have just kept on going, but I saw the sign pointing down the escalator. I made sure to get on before Mom did, just in case she spilled forward and got her hair stuck or something. I spied Aunt Sharon at the bottom of the escalator before Mom did. She wore a long brown coat—the same shade as Garrett's hair—and a black hat and scarf. Aunt Sharon slid her gloves off and waved them wildly at me. I waved back and nudged Mom. "She's right there," I said.

Mom scanned the crowd and then lit up. "Sharon!" she called, and flung an arm up in the air.

Aunt Sharon bumped people aside to get to Mom. They gripped each other hard and stood in a long embrace while travelers walked around them. I waited off to the side, grateful to be on solid ground. Both their faces squished up like they were going to cry, and when they pulled away and looked at each other, Aunt Sharon looked horrified.

"Oh, Ret," Aunt Sharon said. The only person on the planet who called my mom *Ret* was her sister. She put her hands on Mom's waist. "You're so thin." She covered her mouth with her hand.

"I'm okay," Mom said.

"Your clothes," Aunt Sharon said and pulled Mom to her again.

"Don't," Mom said into Aunt Sharon's shoulder. "Please. Don't."

Finally they let go of each other, and Aunt Sharon turned to me. "Asher," she said, and she hugged me. Aunt Sharon stood a solid two inches taller than I was, and at six foot, I wasn't short. Everything about her seemed strong and solid, even her blunt haircut. With Aunt Sharon standing next to me, I suddenly felt exhausted, like maybe I hadn't rested easy in months. "You survived the flight," she said.

"Yep." I hadn't slept much the night before. Images from 9/11 flipped through my brain all night, and I imagined terrorists plotting the demise of all the passengers on our plane, of course. Even at the airport, I studied every person in the boarding area. I'd had some suspicions about this one guy with a knapsack, but then his girlfriend had joined him. It seemed like he had something to live for, so I'd felt better. Once we were on the plane, I read every bit of the literature they gave us. I couldn't believe the number of people who ignored the flight attendants while they gave the instructions. We were in the seats behind the emergency exit, and I wasn't sure the businesswoman they'd put in the row had what it might take to lead us out. I paid close attention to the instructions she received, too, just in case. I'd white-knuckled the takeoff and landing.

But the flight had been fine, even with temperatures below freezing in Chicago.

"I already got a cart," Aunt Sharon said, always practical. "And your baggage claim is over there." She led us through the crowd to the claim section. Sure enough, our flight number was listed above the conveyor belt. Just as we walked up, the machine kicked on and luggage started spewing out to be claimed. Now I understood why Mom insisted on putting purple ribbons on the handles of our suitcases. Nearly every bag sliding onto the belt was identically black. When I spotted ours, I started to maneuver through the crowd to catch it, but

Aunt Sharon tugged my shoulder and said, "Just wait for them to come to us. It's okay."

She was the pro, so I stopped and waited. Still, this was a city, and it seemed to me one of these people could grab our bags and run, but that didn't happen. I hoisted mine off the belt, and Aunt Sharon got Mom's. Mom had tried to give me the rolling bag, but I'd insisted I take the old suitcase without wheels. Like it would be easier for her to lift that heavy bag. Sometimes it seemed like she forgot I was fifteen years old.

Aunt Sharon stacked our bags onto the cart, swung it around, and headed through an assortment of sliding glass doors. Mom and I followed.

"We lucked out with parking," she said as she reached into her purse. She pulled out two pairs of gloves and handed them to us. "I'm right out front."

I didn't feel like putting them on, but I didn't want to seem ungrateful. When we stepped out the last set of doors, a fierce cold hit me. "Holy crap," I muttered, and I tucked down my face. The snow on the ground did not resemble the postcards or movies I'd seen. It looked like someone had dumped gray slushies all over everything. Aunt Sharon pressed a button, and the lights of a car less than twenty feet from us flashed. It started automatically. Another button opened the trunk of her car.

"Go ahead and get inside," she ordered, and Mom and I didn't argue.

Mom hopped into the front seat, and I slid in back. "Mom," I said, my teeth chattering like a cartoon character. "It's so cold."

"I know."

"I mean, really," I said. "People could die."

"I know! They do, every year."

I stared out the window at the gray sky, and a plane flew low to land. I rubbed my gloved hands together, but I still felt the chill. Aunt Sharon climbed into the driver's seat.

"Ah," she said. "It's warming up in here."

I stuck my hand in front of the vent in the backseat, but it didn't feel all that warm to me. "How cold is it?" I asked.

"It is twenty-three degrees," Aunt Sharon announced. "Cold enough to freeze your nose hairs."

Instinctively I squeezed my nose to check on the inside. It seemed fine, but I couldn't help wondering what would happen to me if I had a runny nose.

If Mom thought the driving in Florida was rough, I was sure she was having a heart attack up front with Aunt Sharon. Lanes and lanes of dense traffic covered the icy roads. A big truck rumbled past us on the left, spewing grit onto the road. Some of it hit Aunt Sharon's car.

"What is that?" I asked.

"Salt. Keeps the roads from icing over."

"Doesn't that damage vehicles?" I asked. "All that salt?"

Aunt Sharon shrugged. "I'd get more damage if I slid into another car. I'll take the salt. It's okay. If you take your car in to be cleaned every so often, it's fine. It's no worse than the sun fading car paint in Florida, right?"

Right.

I expected Aunt Sharon's place to be downtown on a grungy street, but it wasn't. Instead it was nestled in this neighborhood she claimed bordered Lincoln Park and Lakeview. As we got closer, I paid attention to the signs. We turned off of Diversey, passed a small dry cleaner's, and hung a right into a narrow street. Driveways lined either side of the road, facing identical garages with short walkways up to front doors. More ash-colored snow piled up on the sides of the driveways. The buildings went straight up, three stories. Aunt Sharon pulled into the first one on the left. She pressed a button in her car, and the garage door opened. It didn't seem to me that her car would fit into the narrow space, but it did.

"You might want to get out on your mom's side," she said.

I slid over in the seat and carefully opened the car door.

Aunt Sharon was already at the back of the car with the trunk open by the time I squeezed through the garage. She hauled our bags out and motioned for me to help her.

"We'll take them through the front door, okay?" she said.

I stepped out into the open. Long, deadly spears of ice hung from the roof. Icicles. I ducked under fast in case one dropped. They looked so cool. I made a mental note to take a picture later. I expected to hear sounds of the city, but instead it was quiet. The buildings must have muted the traffic a block away. Not a single person stood outside. Only two other cars were visible in the stretch of driveways, even though today was a Saturday.

"What is it?" Aunt Sharon asked, her breath foggy.

"It's so quiet."

She smiled. "Yeah. We like it."

We. Aunt Sharon used her key to open the front door, and we pulled the luggage inside the foyer. She showed us where to hang our newly purchased coats in the closet. "There are plenty of gloves and scarves here, too. Help yourself," she said, showing us the shelf above the rod. "Let's leave the luggage here for a bit. I'll give you a tour before you worry about settling in, okay?"

She led us down the entryway, pausing to reach inside the laundry room to press a button to close the garage door. The first level of Aunt Sharon's place included the garage, a small bathroom, and an office. French doors led off the back to a small porch edged with tall fencing and dead vegetation.

"We grow tomatoes, beans, and squash in the summer," she said. "It's not much to look at right now. Let's head upstairs."

A narrow flight of stairs on the right side brought us to a massive open room. Outside the tall windows that lined two full walls I saw the crooked tree branches. A spiky-branched Christmas tree with festive colored lights and silver tinsel blinked in the corner of the room. Unlike my dad's tree, this one was a hodge-podge of completely mismatched ornaments. I recognized some of them. One year my mom arranged for Travis and me to make ornaments as presents. We'd spent a full day slopping goopy dough into wreaths and candy canes, baking them, and painting them with watercolors. Then Mom sealed them with shellac. I must have been around eleven. I remember thinking the whole craft thing was lame, but I'd helped Travis, who was only four, roll the dough into strips. I'd held his hand, pressing the dough into shapes. I encouraged him to put the dots I made onto the wreaths wherever he wanted. On the back of the candy cane hanging on Aunt Sharon's tree, my finger traced where I'd carved the year. Underneath, Travis had made his mark, too—a lowercase *t*. I thought we'd escaped the memories, but Travis was here, too.

A white sofa with straight lines divided the room into two sections. It faced the front windows, and a low iron coffee table with a tall unidentifiable-metal centerpiece took up the middle of the room. Two comfy brown recliners rounded out the seating area. Even though the entire floor was covered in wood, Aunt Sharon had put thick, warm rugs on the floor to divide up the areas. It felt cozy.

"In the summer, you can't see anything but the trees. It feels like we live in a tree fort," she said as she pressed a button on the wall. A fire erupted in the fireplace.

"How did you do that?" I asked.

"It's a gas fireplace."

I nodded like that cleared it up. A vase filled with glass tulips sat on top of the mantel. Aunt Sharon saw me admiring them.

"We got those in Amsterdam," she said.

We.

The room included a wooden dining-room table with an ornate wooden bench on one side and two straight-backed dark wooden chairs on the other side. An open doorway led to the spacious kitchen with black granite countertops, dark cabinets, and stainless-steel appliances. Something Aunt Sharon called a Juliet balcony stood off the back but was a million times smaller than the balcony I'd seen in the *Romeo and Juliet* movie we'd watched in English, freshman year.

"Sharon, this is beautiful," Mom said. She put her purse down on the kitchen counter and wandered back into the giant, open room.

"Carol had her eye on this neighborhood for ages, so when the unit came available, we picked it up," she said.

Carol. That was the *we*. When I'd asked Mom about why Aunt Sharon had never married, she'd told me my aunt was married to her work. The first I'd ever heard of Carol was a few months ago when I'd been talking to Aunt Sharon on the phone. I'd heard Carol's voice in the background. Still, no one had ever mentioned her to me.

"Do you want to see your rooms?"

Mom and I followed her up the next flight of stairs. Straight ahead was a larger bathroom with a full tub, the walls painted a shade of purple a little lighter than Kayla's hair. To the right was a guest room, decorated in bright yellows with green walls. I'd never seen a house with so much color. I couldn't help thinking about the boring beige and white walls in ours. A full blooming poinsettia sat on top of the tall dresser at the far corner of the room.

"Okay, Ret, all the drawers are empty, so feel free to put your stuff away. The closet, not so much. I shoved things to the side. Carol uses it for storage."

"It's lovely, Sharon." Mom shook her head. "We should have made this trip before. You've lived here for years." For a second, I thought Mom was going to cry, but she just took a ragged breath and sank onto the bed. She touched the thick comforter and slumped over onto the pillows. Her face scrunched up. "Down pillows?" Mom accused Sharon. "Seriously?"

"Hey, we didn't pick those up for you. Nothing special," Sharon said. She sat down on the bed next to Mom and grabbed her hand. "It's okay. You deserve nice things."

Then Mom's face scrunched up. "I don't," she choked out. "I don't, Sharon." Mom rolled onto her side, hugging a pillow against her chest. She buried her face in the pillow.

Aunt Sharon stroked my mom's hair. "You do," Aunt Sharon said, her voice sure and soft. "You deserve nice things. You do."

Across the room on the wall hung a poster of the 1933 Chicago World's Fair. It wasn't a photograph, and the composition of objects—colossal buildings and fountains and Ferris wheels—seemed unnatural.

Mom propped herself up. "I think"—she hiccuped—"I think I just need to rest. Just a little while. Is that okay?"

"Of course," Aunt Sharon said. "How about a glass of water."

The way Aunt Sharon spoke, it was like she was making statements even when she was asking questions. Her voice never went up at the end. Mom nodded and wiped her nose with the back of her hand. Aunt Sharon started to stand up, but I motioned for her to stay. "I'll get it," I said.

"We have distilled water in the fridge," Aunt Sharon said. "Asher, could you also—"

"I will." She didn't have to finish. I knew what she wanted.

I walked downstairs to the kitchen, found a red glass in the cabinet—was everything a color here?—and filled it with water from a pitcher in the fridge. Mom's purse sat on the counter. She took the pills the doctor prescribed when she started to panic, so I opened her purse to get them out of the side pocket. When I reached inside, my hand caught on something flat and slick. Tucked next to the pills, I discovered the picture Pearl had taken of Levi and me.

Had she noticed the images in the background? She must have;

otherwise why would she have brought it? Instead of retrieving only her pills, I brought her whole purse. I stopped by the bathroom on the way back to the guest room to get some tissues, too. When I entered the room, Aunt Sharon was sitting next to Mom. I placed the purse and water on the nightstand, and Mom went straight for the pills. Aunt Sharon shifted uncomfortably on the bed, but I moved back into the doorway to wait. Mom tossed back a pill, took a sip of water, and blew her nose.

"What are those?"

"Takes the edge off," she answered.

Worry flickered across Aunt Sharon's face, so I said, "She only takes them when she needs to." I didn't add that she tended to need them frequently.

"I'll show Asher where he's sleeping and I'll check on you in a bit. Do you need anything else?"

"No, I'm fine." She clamped her hands together on her lap. "I love you, you know."

"I love you more."

Mom smiled. "I love *you* more."

"Nuh-uh."

Mom threw a small decorative pillow at Sharon, and they both grinned. Aunt Sharon closed the door behind us, and we headed up yet another set of stairs. These led to a single room Aunt Sharon called a loft, with a sliding glass door overlooking a full open balcony. From it, I could see the entire Chicago skyline. A fold-out sofa was already made into a bed. It also was the only room in the entire place with a television, hanging on a sky-blue wall. Someone had painted butterflies, lakes, frogs, and all sorts of outdoor things on the wall.

"We call it our room of whimsy," she said, looking around the space. "I know it's a bit ridiculous—that's sort of the point. You and Ret will have to paint something, too. Everyone does. And this is where you'll be sleeping."

I wanted to ask her about everything, who had painted what and when, but I stopped myself. We'd have time. My gaze shifted back out the sliding glass door. I'd be able to look at the skyline while going to sleep.

"It's not as spacious as the other rooms."

"It's perfect," I said.

Aunt Sharon smoothed a wrinkle out of the blanket. "I thought you might like it up here. You know, we've never slept out on the balcony, but we've always talked about doing it. It's too cold now, but if you guys come back in the spring or summer, maybe you could try it out."

I plopped down onto the fold-out bed. I could feel the metal rods underneath, but I didn't care. Aunt Sharon opened a drawer.

"Here's the remote. We only have basic cable. We hardly ever watch television, to be perfectly honest," she said. "The only downside is you don't have a door for privacy."

I stared out the window at the city skyline. The sky was turning dark, even though it was only four o'clock in the afternoon. Lights glimmered from the city.

"You going to be okay?" she sort of asked.

I nodded. It was the most okay I had felt in months. She sat down, her elbows resting on her knees, her torso leaning forward. Something about her stance, the way her feet connected solidly with the floor, made me feel safe.

Aunt Sharon pressed. "Your mom's lost a lot of weight."

"She's eating," I said. "She just gets upset. She sits in his room all the time."

His, meaning Travis. Why didn't I just say his name?

"And how are you?"

"I'm okay." I pulled at a loose string on the bottom hem of my shirt. "Dad's back in the picture."

"So I heard. I appreciate him agreeing to you visiting me." I made a noise of some sort, and Aunt Sharon said, "What?"

"Flying back early, by myself, and spending Christmas with him and Helen—it's just weird," I said. "I don't really know them, you know?"

"You don't really know me either." Aunt Sharon patted my shoulder. "Come on. Let's head back downstairs. I'll show you my room on the way."

Back down on the level below the loft, down the hall from my mom's room, was the master bedroom. It was painted a brick red. Everything else in the room was a neutral color, beige, black, or white. Gauzy curtains covered the windows but let in light. The furniture was a mix of dark brown wood and wrought iron. On the bedside table rested a framed picture of Aunt Sharon and a black woman, their mouths open in midlaugh, clothes blown all wild, a blue lake and sky in the background. It was the kind of photograph I liked. I heard a voice call from below us.

"Hello?"

"We're up here!" Aunt Sharon called.

The sound of footsteps light on the stairs approached. The woman from the picture stepped inside the bedroom.

Her dark hair was shoulder length and tucked back in an orange headband. She wore an orange jacket over a black pantsuit and a sheer orange-and-red scarf. Ornate gold earrings dangled from her lobes. I wondered if they were heavy. Her eyes were both fierce and warm, and the way she set her jaw made me think she might be scary if I got on her bad side. She stood six inches shorter than Aunt Sharon, but she wasn't short. She embraced my aunt, rested a hand on her cheek, and then turned to me.

"You must be Asher," she said, and she sort of floated farther into the room. She moved like a dancer or a predator, and the way her eyes squinted at me, and her mouth set firm, I felt every bit the potential victim. "Well. I am Carol. Carol Johnson." She stood with her legs and hands clasped together and leaned slightly forward toward me. "It's a pleasure."

"Nice to meet you, too." I bowed my head a little. The way she spoke reminded me of British actors or the royal family or something. She certainly carried herself like royalty.

"He likes the loft," Aunt Sharon said.

"And why wouldn't he?"

They stood there, waiting for me to say something. I swallowed and struggled for a topic. "Aunt Sharon said you found this place?"

"Yes, I did." She took her earrings off and placed them inside a wooden jewelry box on a tall dresser. "We've been here, let's see…"

"It was after my mother died," Aunt Sharon said.

"Just after I moved to the new law firm."

"Under three years."

"You're a lawyer?" I asked.

"Yes. I am," she said, sliding the scarf off her neck and hanging it on a hook behind the door. Underneath she wore a plain gold chain with a dainty silver cross. She kept that on. "And you are a photographer, I hear."

"I'm working on it." I stuffed my hands into the pockets of my pants.

"Mm-hmm," she said, like she was making her mind up about something. Carol glided over to Aunt Sharon and touched her shoulder. "The Art Institute first, I think."

"Agreed. We'll do Christmas Monday. The Drake for tea?"

Carol faced me. "Do you like tea?"

Tea. Like sweet tea? Or hot tea? "Uh?"

"Sharon. Why would a boy want high tea?" Carol said, and she turned to me. "They put napkins in your lap and play the harp and bring out tiny cucumber sandwiches with the crust cut off. It's very fussy. Do you have any interest in attending high tea at the Drake?"

I shrugged. I didn't want to mess up their plans.

"It's Margaret's favorite," Aunt Sharon said.

"Perhaps we will save that for an afternoon with Margaret. When is his flight?"

"Tuesday."

"It's not much time," Carol said, and she made a disapproving noise. She coasted toward me and took my hand in both of hers. Her piercing dark eyes scrutinized my face. Freckles dotted her hairline. It was a weird place to have freckles. I shifted my vision down to our hands. She had entwined her fingers with mine, and I wished I could take a picture of the way our flesh looked together. The skin on her hands felt a little dry and scaly, but her voice was soft.

"Asher. What do you wish to do while you are here?"

I fought the urge to slide my hands from her grasp—I didn't really feel comfortable touching people—but I didn't want to appear rude. Carol kept her hands with mine and waited for me to respond. It was like she had all the time in the world. "Actually, the main thing I wanted to do was what you said—go to the Art Institute." She waited for me to continue. Usually people filled spaces in conversation with chatter. I always felt relieved when they just moved on, but Carol didn't do that. I wondered if that's how she got clients to crack. It seemed like a smart strategy. I cleared my throat. "Online it said they track the history of photography, going back to like the mid-1800s.

And I did this project at school on jobs, and it mentioned the Illinois Institute of Art, even though there are some schools in Florida and New York, too. And then galleries..." I was rambling. "But I'm good with whatever. I mean, the tea thing is cool. You guys know best."

Carol squeezed my hand encouragingly and rose to her full height. "This is not a boy for the Drake, Sharon. You are fifteen, yes?" I nodded. "At fifteen, I didn't know what I wanted. Some people just know. This is a boy who knows what he wants. What do you say we give it to him?"

"Okay," Aunt Sharon said. "We'll go to the Art Institute tomorrow. Right after church."

Chapter Seventeen

The next morning, I expected to crowd into the car and drive to church, but we didn't. Instead they intended to walk. In Florida, adults didn't walk anywhere.

"It's not too far from here," Aunt Sharon explained, lacing up a pair of worn brown boots.

"You are not wearing that sweater to church," Carol said. She wore black pants, a pink shirt with a thick, scarf-like collar, and dangling pink-stone earrings.

Aunt Sharon's brown sweater did look threadbare and rough. She stood up and tugged on the sleeves. "Don't make fun of my sweater. It's my favorite."

"What about that one I bought you?" Carol opened up the closet and handed me a scarf. "This looks good with your shirt," she told me.

"The one from Lord & Taylor? Uh, no." Aunt Sharon turned to me. "Carol thinks everything's better if it has a label on it. I make her crazy."

"You look like you found *that* in the streets," Carol said, sliding her hands in her fitted coat.

Sharon faced Carol. "With the money you paid for that sweater, I could have fed someone for a week."

"There is nothing wrong with having nice things," Carol said, which I thought was funny since Sharon had said that to Mom about the down pillows yesterday. "When someone buys you something nice, you are supposed to say thank you."

Aunt Sharon said, "Thank you."

"And wear it."

"I'll wear it, but not today. You're so bossy."

They continued to bicker as we bundled up in coats and scarves and walked four blocks from Aunt Sharon and Carol's place. Halfway there, specks of white started drifting down from the sky. Snow.

"Flurries," Aunt Sharon said.

"This is the first time Asher's seen snow," my mom said as she trudged through the slushy sidewalk.

"Stop," Carol said, gripping my arm. She tugged me to the side in case anyone needed to get past us. "Now tilt your head back. Open your mouth," Carol said.

"Won't we be late?" Mom asked.

Aunt Sharon and Carol ignored her. I blinked at the misty ice and stood on the sidewalk. Then, with my eyes closed and mouth open, an icy flake landed in my mouth. As the cold melted on my tongue, I heard a click. Aunt Sharon had taken a picture of me with her phone. I waited to see if panic welled up in me, but it didn't. They asked if I wanted to see it, but I shook my head—that would be too much. Mom nodded proudly at me—I guess for not making a scene about it. The truth was, walking in the flurries made me feel like a little kid. No one fussed about hurrying to make it on time. We didn't have to inspect the parking lot to avoid Dad and Helen, not that we'd done that in ages anyway. Maybe anxiety was habit-forming. It had been a long time since I'd gone to church without worrying.

Their church was located in a red brick building with a round stained-glass window on the exterior. A tower extended from one corner. Wrought-iron fencing covered the front of Broadway United Methodist Church.

"Can I have my camera?" I asked Mom.

She dug it out of her purse, and I took a close-up of the brick itself, and then took another photo from the side of the building, looking straight up toward the flurry-filled sky. Mom insisted we put the camera away before we headed inside.

The vestibule was quiet; the service had started. But because Aunt Sharon and Carol didn't seem stressed out about it, I wasn't either. On the walls hung banners with *God knows my struggles, and I am welcome!* written in bright cursive letters. Another banner bore the word

Diversity and another *Love*. Skinny, tall Christmas trees in various sizes stood throughout the building. Tags identifying needy families and kids hung from the branches.

A long coat rack like you'd find in a department store stood against the far wall, so Mom, Aunt Sharon, Carol, and I stored our thick jackets. Carol stuffed her gloves and hat into her coat pocket, so I did the same. A sign warned us to keep our valuables with us. We didn't have that sign in our church. We also didn't have a sign stating:

> We are black, brown, red, yellow, white, and all the colors of God's created rainbow. We are lesbian, gay, bisexual, asexual, and straight. We are transgender, intersex, female, male, gender fluid. We are queer. We are questioning. We are every age. We are every ability. We are every economic & theological location. We are YOU.

It's not that our church didn't welcome people, but we weren't that specific. At least I thought so. I didn't really know.

A tall, thin man with a gentle smile handed us the church bulletin as we entered the sanctuary. I scanned the open room. The pews formed a half-circle around a small open area. The light through the stained-glass window colored the inside of the sanctuary. Images of doves, crosses, and praying hands covered the pews. A group of teenagers hung out toward the back, dressed in dark skinny jeans and cool scarves. One guy wore a kilt. Even from a distance, I could tell one boy was wearing bright lipstick. I glanced down at my khakis and pulled on the hem of my button-up shirt.

My eye was drawn to the round stained-glass window I'd seen from the outside. I thought about that, the way things appear on the inside and outside, and how out on the busy street you'd never know how quiet it was inside this room. Two women stood in the front of the room, one white, one black, and we'd caught them midprayer. Rather than pretend they hadn't seen us at all, the silver-haired woman waved at us and smiled.

"Good morning, Sharon and Carol. Are these your visitors?"

"Yes," Aunt Sharon said. "We were tasting snowflakes outside."

"Pretty different from Florida, I'd imagine. Wonderful. So good to have you here," the woman said, and then continued. "Is there anyone else who is here for the first time?"

The woman motioned toward the back of the room. I turned in the pew to glance at the man standing against the brick wall. He looked thirtyish, dressed casually in jeans and a button-up shirt. His arms were tightly braced across his chest.

"Welcome!" she said warmly.

He snorted. "This is the first time I've been in a church in twenty years."

"We're delighted to have you. You are welcome here."

"Yeah, well, I've been told otherwise," he said, bitterness and defiance challenged her claim. What was his problem? And then a chill raced through me—gay. He was gay.

"Whoever told you that *lied*," the woman responded. She said it with such authority and conviction and truth, I couldn't look at her directly. I didn't dare turn around to see the guy's reaction in the back. I tried to imagine the people from my church sitting in these pews—Miss Gabby with her perpetual sour face, John with his steady grip, Garrett with his impish grin. I buried myself in the brochure and read the stuff every bulletin has: welcome, visitor information, Bible studies, childcare. On the adjoining page was the Call to Worship, which they called Centering Words: *May God know my honest heart, and may that be enough, for God's love is for all.*

The opening litany talked about oppression and speaking for those who can't speak for themselves. It occurred to me that this might be the kind of church Garrett used to attend in Orlando. Maybe in bigger cities it was like this.

Music started up front, and a man who looked a lot like John walked up to the front of the congregation. I glanced around at the people. A man and woman held hands at the other end of our pew. A couple of young families. A lot of people sitting alone. There was one guy probably in his twenties sitting by himself a few rows up and on the left. He rested his head on the pew in front of him, and his lips moved, but no sound came out. The hair on my arms prickled as I remembered sitting in my church pew back home, Og cradled in my hands, a jumbled prayer playing on my lips. I had to look away.

When they called for children's time, a bunch of kids raced up to the front. I tried to picture Travis among the kids, tried to imagine what this trip would have been like if he were with us. A lump formed in my throat.

Better without him.

Easier without him.

I felt ashamed.

The pastor held up an embroidered bookmark thing, one of those plastic pieces old ladies stitch messages into and give away to people. When the pastor asked the kids to identify what word they saw in the stitching, they were stumped. "Nothing?" the pastor asked. Then he flipped it upside down. "How about now?"

Still nothing. People in the pews smiled and leaned forward to see.

"Hmm, try focusing on the red instead of the white."

I saw it. It was the word *JESUS*. It was sort of like one of those optical illusions. Cool.

"I've had this for a very long time," he said, and it made me wonder who had stitched if for him. "What we're going to talk about today is how people see things. Because when we look at things, sometimes we don't really *see* them. Jesus calls on us to see things differently. And sometimes we don't want to, but it's important that we find him."

Carol made this *mm-hmm* noise whenever anyone said anything she thought was important. It made me grin. Turns out, the service was all about taking time to slow down so we can recognize the needs of others this time of year.

"I get so focused on lists and gifts," the pastor said, "that I forget to see what's important."

Carol made her mm-hmm noise.

"On the way here today, I passed a man huddled in an alley, and he called to me and I pretended I didn't hear. I can rationalize. The man could have harmed me. He could have robbed me. People are desperate this time of year." His voice trailed off. "People are desperate. So the better thing, the safer thing, was to ignore him. Never mind changing *how* I see people. I chose not to look at all. How often do we do that?"

I thought about me and my camera focused on Iggy feeding scraps to a stray cat, keeping a secret he hadn't even asked me to keep.

"Christmas isn't about rushing. It's about slowing down and taking the time to attend to others." He looked down and reverently touched the cover of the Bible. "Jesus saw people. He sees us. And he loves *all* of us. And he wouldn't give anyone a gift certificate to their favorite restaurant unless they were hungry. He sees our brokenness. He heals." The Bible passages were familiar to me, and the message seemed louder and clearer. If we could see the pain people carried inside, we would love every person we met.

I thought about that and the people I knew. The ones I cared about the most were the ones whose pain I knew, but sometimes I punished them for it. But then there were people I didn't really think about, like Pearl. What kind of pain did she carry? And what about Iggy? I knew his pain, and what had I done to ease that? Nothing. I stole a glance at my mom. She usually wore her pain loud and clear, but she seemed strangely relaxed and at peace as she sat in the pew next to me.

While we sang the last hymn, the pastor exited down the aisle. At the end of it, another man about the same age stood up to greet him.

"Who's that guy with the pastor?" I asked Aunt Sharon.

"What?"

"The guy talking to the pastor."

"You mean Michael?" Aunt Sharon said. "The two women who started the service are our pastors. Michael's a guest speaker. He works for the health department, helps people in the city with HIV. That's his partner, Paul."

I studied Michael. He looked healthy. But the guy he was talking to now, Paul, looked too thin, too pale. It hurt my heart to look at them.

Afterward, everyone we met talked about how they couldn't fathom why anyone would willingly visit Chicago this time of year. I wondered if any of them had ever seen a Florida cockroach. One guy asked about the camera around my neck. Turned out he owned an art studio in another neighborhood. He invited us to stop by while we were in town.

"No singing today?" one lady asked Carol.

"Carol sings," Aunt Sharon told Mom and me, like we didn't pick that up from the exchange.

"Not today," Carol said, "and not very often. And not very well."

"Don't be fooled by her. She's talented."

"Your aunt thinks *all* black women can sing," Carol said, and the two of them hooted and leaned into each other, sharing an inside joke.

❖

After church, we ate at this restaurant where Aunt Sharon and Carol were regulars. They only served breakfast, and the menu was thick like a book. Each meal included a description of where all the ingredients came from: the location of the farm, the names of the people who owned it, and a story about them. The cheapest thing on the menu—scrambled eggs—was still twenty-five dollars. And that didn't include orange juice or coffee. Aunt Sharon and Carol refused to let my mom pick up the tab. That type of generosity usually put Mom on edge, but she didn't argue.

On the way to the L track, we passed an art gallery. I hesitated at the window for a moment, looking at the artwork propped up in the window. Some twisted sculptures sat atop boxlike displays. There were a series of them, five in all, but one resembled a crooked tree.

"Check it out," I said to Mom, pointing.

"What is that?" she asked.

"Doesn't it look like the twisted pine tree?" I asked. "Like in my photo?"

"Oh. Sure," she said absently.

I don't think she saw the similarity, but that was okay. I took a picture of it through the window, read the name of the studio—Exposure—and followed Aunt Sharon and Carol down the sidewalk into this blocky, run-down structure. Thick tracks ran above our heads, and I ducked a bit. All I could think about was people throwing nasty stuff onto the folks below. No one else seemed concerned, so I followed Aunt Sharon, Carol, and my mom into the building and up to a set of turnstiles. Aunt Sharon slid a card into a slot as each of us walked through.

"Up the steps," Aunt Sharon instructed, and I followed Carol onto a windy platform.

I squinted against the freezing wind and repositioned my scarf to cover my face.

"Come over here," Carol said, and I joined the three women in a huddle. "It helps to turn your back to the wind."

I glanced around at the old man sitting on the bench, the couple holding hands, and the stray people. When Aunt Sharon pointed out the train coming, I couldn't help thinking about it flying off the tracks and annihilating us all, but everyone around me seemed unimpressed by the rushing train. I figured the screeching stop must be normal, too. A series of low chimes sounded, and a voice announced the name of the stop and that doors opened on the right. I started for the door as it opened, but Carol gently touched my arm.

"Give people a chance to get out first," she said, and two couples and a businessman and an elderly woman and a mom with a kid filed out before she pushed me forward. "Okay, now." We stepped inside just as the voice announced the doors were closing. I couldn't imagine traveling like this all the time. I'd be a nervous wreck.

No one on the train talked as we bounced along the track, the hum building as we increased speed. Some people read books or newspapers. Others focused on electronic devices. One girl with stringy pink hair sat with her knees tucked up under her chin and stared blankly out the window. She wore mismatched clothes and black eyeliner. Her gloves had the fingers cut off, and chipped black nail polish covered her nails. Normally when someone catches me looking, I look away, but when she turned to me, I didn't. I held up my camera and tilted my head as a question. The corner of her lip curled up, and she slightly lifted her left shoulder like *whatever*. She settled back to staring out the window, and her awareness of me evaporated. I took her picture. She didn't even glance at me when she got off at the next stop.

❖

The thick glass door leading into the lower-level photography gallery required strength to open. I gripped its heavy metal handle and pulled. It was difficult to tell if you pushed or pulled to get in, but either way, a person strained to enter. The carefully lit wall facing the doors welcomed viewers to The Universe Next Door. Aunt Sharon and Carol stood there to read the details of some photographer from Cuba, but I stared at his black-and-white photograph of the lightbulb.

In the photo, a makeshift cardboard camera was taking a photo of a lightbulb, and its darkened image showed in the reflection inside the box. Photoshop? Was this real? How did he do that? I moved closer to read the description of the work.

"Asher," Mom said. She motioned for me to join her. Mom pointed at a sentence toward the end of the passage describing the artist. "*His work in in black and white then shifted to color*," she read, then turned to me and curved her mouth into something like a smile. "Sounds like someone else I know."

I swallowed. I had this eerie sensation of being on display, like the place was a giant frame and I was the subject. Mom studied me too closely. I hadn't thought about roaming through this with people watching me. Maybe this wasn't such a good idea. I shot Aunt Sharon a panicked look.

"Margaret, I wanted to show you the camera-obscura section," she said nonchalantly. She'd picked up on my discomfort. "It's around the corner."

I waited for them to shift into the other room before moving away from the entrance. Then I edged along to the right. Every photo along the wall was in black and white. This section focused on the use of light. Light shimmering through holes into a room. Light and dark. But then I started thinking about the setup, how the photographer arranged items, and I couldn't shake this sense of the images being planned. The impact was there—the light poking through—but if the artist drilled holes to get the effect, if the light beyond those holes was a spotlight, I'd be disappointed. It mattered to me if the source was the sun. If it wasn't, it was empty.

Why did it matter?

Why did I care?

I moved into the center of the gallery. The first photo I saw was of a house lit with Christmas lights. The photographer had lined it up so the house was being viewed through a window. I read the title: *New Year's Eve*. New Year's always seemed like such a letdown, with all the presents opened. It was strictly a grown-up party, and the picture would have made sense to me if the house across the street in the photograph showed lights in the window. That would mean a child looking out his dark window to across the street where adults partied and cheered the passing of one year into the next. It made me wonder about what had happened inside the house across the street. What had happened to keep their windows dark? It wasn't abandoned. It had the trappings of festivity—the outside Christmas lights were lit. But the truth, what was inside, was dark.

Like our house, ever since Dad and Travis left.

I looked up on the wall to identify a reference, a clue, as to what this gallery section was about, and I read the word: Childhood. I took a steadying breath. Okay.

An image of stubby, well-used crayons, as if taken right from the tin in Travis's closet, was framed on the wall. The colors of the crayons were identifiable since they were printed on the sides, but the image itself was in black and white. Did the artist arrange the crayons or were they just like that?

It bothered me.

It mattered to me.

Why?

I moved along the wall. The view from the top of a metal slide— did the photographer polish the metal to make it look like that? Was the sand naturally in disarray? Did he happen upon this spot and just take the photo? Did he wait for the lighting to get just right? Was this a park he played in as a child?

I rubbed my face.

Images started forming in my mind, Travis's room, his kid-sized baseball glove hanging in his closet, his stack of dirty clothes Mom refused to clean, and his nasty stuffed dog, Og.

I wanted to be home now.

I wanted to photograph it all.

Oh God. I couldn't do this. I blinked back stupid tears. Jesus. I glanced around, but the only people in the gallery were a few people standing silently, observing the art. No one even glanced at me. It was so quiet, like a library. No, like a church. A sanctuary. When anyone did speak, it was a whisper, a respectful, sanctified whisper.

Then I saw the photograph of the bathroom.

There was a tub on the upper left, a bath mat spread out in front, and the wet imprint of feet on the floor. I covered my mouth as tears sprang to my eyes. Damn it. Watery, evaporating footprints. Like the ones Travis's feet made on the concrete at the pool. Oh God. I spun away from the photo and rounded the corner. I aimed for the heavy door, and it didn't feel as solid on the way out as it did on the way in. I searched the signs on the wall and bolted for the men's bathroom, rounding the corner and securing myself inside a stall. I paced in the small space and let myself cry a bit. Then I saw the writing on the wall. At first I was irritated. Really? Graffiti on bathroom stalls in the Art Institute? But then I read what was scribbled on the door.

Art is life, printed in blue ink.

Art is a heart set free, responded someone in pencil, a loopy cursive.

Art is the part of your mind that most inspires and frightens you, inscribed in black Sharpie in bold capital letters.

It was a conversation.

I took my pencil out of my pocket and scanned the door. I found a space up toward the top where I could barely reach on tiptoe. I wrote in small lowercase letters, *art is truth*. You'd have to search to see it. Because truth isn't something you create. It's something you discover.

Chapter Eighteen

I pressed the button at the bottom of my phone and slid my finger to unlock it. The icon at the top left indicated I had one text. I shifted in the plastic chair at the terminal gate. It was a message from my mom.

How are you?

I typed back, *About to board.*

Aunt Sharon, Carol, and my mom had given me a phone for Christmas. And not just any cell phone; it was a smartphone. Mom caved when they were at the Apple Store talking about my flight home. The idea of my getting on the flight by myself and potentially getting stranded somewhere sold her.

I love you. So much, she sent back.

I decided to text Aunt Sharon, too. *Thank you for everything. Tell Carol.*

Turns out I'd done a decent job giving Christmas presents, too. I'd sort of hoped Mom and I would buy presents while we were in town, but there hadn't been any time to ourselves when we were out shopping. Plus, it wasn't any secret we were short on cash. I'd stayed up late writing them a letter on loose-leaf paper. Kind of lame, I know, but I was thinking about what the pastor had said about gifts. In the letter I told them how much I appreciated everything they'd done for us the past week: taking us to galleries, ice skating, shopping—they'd bought me a bunch of clothes—and out to eat at all these cool restaurants. I tried to include details, so they would know how much I'd gotten out of it. The real present would come after I developed the photographs from the trip. I couldn't wait to take them over to Pearl's.

The gift I'd gotten for Mom had traveled from Florida with me, and I had second-guessed my choice. When she opened the wrapping paper and saw the color photograph I'd taken of her sleeping in Travis's bed, she covered her mouth with her hand. I moved beside her to explain before she could cry. "See the way the light softens the color? And look, there's Og in the corner, and the book is here," I said.

"You took a picture of me when I was sleeping?" she asked.

"It's the first color photo I ever took."

"Of me?" She gazed at the photo, her eyes wide. Her mouth curved up into a proud smile. "Look at this," she said to Aunt Sharon and Carol.

They took the photograph from her and studied it, their heads tilted.

"You didn't use to take photos of people," Aunt Sharon said. "What made you change your mind?"

"That," I said, indicating the photograph.

Mom gripped my hand. "Thank you, Asher."

But even though I knew they'd be going to the Drake Hotel for tea, I envied Mom's remaining three days in Chicago. I dreaded going to my dad's house and experiencing the potentially awkward moments. I'd quickly adjusted to sleeping in the loft, where I'd painted a rudimentary curved tree on the wall, and the lights of the city in the distance comforted me. I felt less alone, lying in the fold-out bed with a million lights reminding me other people weren't asleep either. Travis's room felt far away, a part of some other overexposed life. Even though the sky was gray in Chicago, it was an honest gray. And the artwork on the walls of the Art Institute reminded me that I might be strange in Florida, but photographers like me dated back to the 1830s.

Aunt Sharon and Carol belonged to this other world. No one stared at them when they walked down the busy Chicago streets holding hands, but they wouldn't make it down an aisle of the Thrifty Foods without catching glances. But did I really know that? Maybe it wasn't such a big deal.

They called my flight for boarding, so I hoisted my bag over my shoulder and stood in line. I glanced at the other passengers headed to Florida. Several families were geared up for Disney World and beach trips. A few businesspeople milled around. I spied couples holding hands and grinning. Over in a corner, between the wall and the window looking out on the tarmac, slouched a guy who looked like he might be in his early twenties. He wore a short green military-looking jacket and had spiky black hair. His eyes were lined in black and his pierced lip pouted as he bobbed his head to some song on his iPod. The bleached skinny jeans magnified his emaciated frame, and I turned away. He reminded me of Iggy. And as luck would have it, he sat right next to me on the plane. At first I didn't think I'd have to talk to him, but after he'd tucked his worn leather satchel under the seat, he said, "Hey."

"Hey."

He dug around in his pocket. "Gum?" he offered a stick. His voice was softer with a lilt. Now that we were sitting closer, I could tell he was wearing powder or something on his face, too.

"No, thanks." His nails were turquoise. I buckled my seat belt and pulled the safety manual out of the pocket in front of me.

He leaned back in the seat. "My ears always pop when they take off. It kills."

Since I was a travel pro now, I knew ear popping didn't kill. "It's never bothered me," I said as I pretended to scan the manual.

"Business or pleasure?" he asked, crossing his legs at the knee.

"What?"

"Travel purpose." He blinked at me. "Are you traveling for business or pleasure?"

"I live in Florida. So neither, I guess," I said. And then I thought it might be rude not to ask, so I said, "How about you?"

He took a minute to think. "Neither for me, too, now that you mentioned it. My mom moved to St. Pete, and I have to visit her for the holidays."

Have to. "You live in Chicago?" I asked.

"I go to school there."

"What are you studying?"

"Web design," he said.

"I'm thinking of going to the Art Institute when I graduate," I said.

"Oh, you're still in high school. What a nightmare. What year are you?"

"Sophomore."

"God, I think I blocked that year out entirely. High school was the bane of my existence." He surveyed me. "But I imagine you do okay. Let me guess. Basketball?" he asked.

"Uh, no." I laughed.

"And that's funny because?"

"Everyone thinks that, because I'm tall. I'm not the most coordinated person, is all."

"Hmm. Me neither. But you like school?"

I shrugged. "I wouldn't say I *like* school, but it's okay. It's sort of small, so everyone knows everyone."

"Sounds like my school. We had just under four hundred kids. And I did not play basketball," he said. "The best day of my life was when I left that cesspool."

I wondered if he looked the same then as he did now. I wanted to ask because it seemed to me you were sort of asking for trouble when you looked so different from everyone else. Then I remembered Kayla, and I felt like a jerk.

A bell sounded, and then the plane started to move across the tarmac. The flight attendants gave the safety instructions, and I followed along closely like before, but I realized they said the exact same thing. Still, I listened. When they finished, the pilot announced *Clear for takeoff* and then we were jarred up off the ground and into the sky. I avoided looking out the window. Most accidents occurred during the first few minutes of takeoff or during the landing.

When the plane steadied, my ears plugged and popped. It hurt. The guy next to me chewed on his gum. I would have asked him for that piece of gum after all, but he'd tilted his seat back, put in his earbuds, and closed his eyes. He had this peaceful expression on his face.

I thought about my mom, and how every emotion she felt just surged to the surface. She couldn't contain it. Her grief covered everything. What if she started dressing like her pain as well, and she walked around like a grownup freak in black? It was bad enough she'd dropped twenty pounds since Travis died. How do you ever get back to normal if you decide to look like you're broken? *She wants me to pretend.* What a luxury, to be the one who gets to grieve.

I pulled the in-flight magazine from the bin and pretended to be engrossed in it, even though I'd pretty much read it on the way to Chicago. The guy next to me drifted off to an easy sleep.

❖

"How's your aunt?" Dad asked once I joined him in the living room.

A boys' choir singing Christmas carols played softly in the background. Helen stood at the kitchen counter, making some sort of dip. Dad reclined on the sofa. I noticed a few pine needles under the tree.

"Aunt Sharon? She's great. They've got this really cool place, and I got to sleep in a loft with a view of the city skyline."

"Is she still in Belmont? I don't remember a loft."

"I don't think so."

Dad chuckled. "It was this one-bedroom place with no air-conditioning. We stayed with her for a week the summer she graduated from college. Do you have any idea how hot it gets in Chicago? I thought we were going to die from heatstroke. We lasted two days, and then we made an excuse to go stay with Margaret's parents instead."

I sat down at the farthest end of the sofa from my dad. "Must have moved," I said. "Their place is like four stories tall. They've got a fireplace."

"I guess they pay social workers better than they used to," Dad quipped.

He sounded so smug, so in the know. Like he had any idea about who Aunt Sharon was, or her business.

"It's the nicest place I've ever stayed in my life," I said pointedly. "And we went to the Art Institute. And I got to check out art galleries."

"I hope it wasn't too hard to cut the trip short," Helen said. "It sounds like you were having a great time."

I didn't say anything. The truth was, I'd wanted to stay. "Carol said they want me to come back this summer," I said.

Dad raised his eyebrows. He pointedly exchanged a look with Helen. "So you met Carol."

Of course I met Carol. But it got me ticked that Dad had known about Carol, and I hadn't. I played it like it was no big deal. "Well, yeah. She works at this place downtown. We stopped by her office, and it's up on the sixteenth floor. Two sides are solid glass, floor to ceiling, and if you stand right up against it, you feel like you're falling off the edge."

"So you know."

"Know?" I asked.

"About Aunt Sharon and Carol?"

"You mean that they're lesbians?"

"I was wondering how they were going to handle that. You know, if they were going to convince Carol to leave town or pretend to be roommates or what."

"Why would they do that?"

"Your mom didn't want to tell you. Or anyone, really."

"It isn't a big deal," I said. "And Mom was fine. She likes Carol."

"Of course she does. But I always thought it was interesting that she hid it."

I drummed my fingers against the arm of the sofa and said, "No one is hiding anything."

"Yes, and that's great. I'm not saying—" He stopped. "Never mind. Let me try again. I'm glad you got to meet Carol."

I crossed my arms in front of me. Dad set his face into a cool mask and turned his attention to Helen. "What can I do to help?"

"You can chop these onions if you want. Asher, do you like eggnog?"

Nasty. "Uh, not really." I wished I could be back in Chicago with Mom, which reminded me that I promised her I'd text her when I landed. I pulled my phone out of my pocket and typed: *I'm here. Sorry forgot to text when landed.*

"What's that?" Dad asked. He'd stopped chopping.

"A phone. Mom and Aunt Sharon got it for me. For Christmas."

"She got you a *phone?*" Dad slammed the knife down on the counter. Helen put a hand on his arm, but he pulled away from her and paced the kitchen.

"No. I talked to her about this," he said. He stopped and turned to Helen. "I told her what we were doing."

Uh-oh.

"I can't believe the nerve of that woman."

"She probably forgot," Helen said. "So what? It isn't like that's his only gift. It's not a big deal."

"She didn't forget. This is intentional." His face looked grim. "I'm calling her."

"Steve."

"No, she knew. Helen, I've had it."

The phone was in his hand, ready to call, and I said, "Dad. Don't." He looked up at me. "I don't think it was on purpose. Seriously." I took a deep breath. "You don't know how messed up she is." I didn't want him to call her and yell. I didn't want him to make her upset. In Chicago, she almost seemed normal.

"I know exactly how messed up she is," he said.

"No. You don't. She barely holds it together. Look, she spends hours in his room holding stuffed animals and sniffing clothes. I find her keys everywhere—in the freezer and the mailbox. She has trouble remembering to pay bills, and the pills just make her fuzzy."

Dad's expression changed, and I thought I'd convinced him she wasn't being a jerk. I expected him to drop it, but instead he put his phone away and narrowed his eyes at me. "What kind of pills?" he asked, his voice measured.

"I don't know," I lied. "The doctor gave them to her."

"Is she going to therapy?" he demanded. "I know she isn't attending the sessions at church."

"Steve," Helen warned.

He held his hand up, like he was stopping her words. "This matters," he said, not taking his gaze off me. "This is about Asher, not her."

I cleared my throat. "She's getting help. John brought the book over. They talk about it at the house." But he hadn't been over since he'd started seeing that lady.

"John isn't a professional counselor, Asher. She needs professional help. It doesn't sound like she's functioning." He rubbed his hands across his face before asking, "Is she missing work?"

She'd missed a few days here and there, when I couldn't get her out of bed, but I didn't tell Dad. "No, it's not like that."

"Asher."

"It's not. It's just that I don't think she remembered you were getting me a phone. We were in the Apple Store, and they were talking about me flying back alone, and Aunt Sharon suggested it," I said. "That's all."

Dad pressed his lips together, which meant trouble. Oh, he believed the phone purchase had been an oversight, but I had an uneasy feeling I'd just made things a lot worse.

CHAPTER NINETEEN

Helen and Dad hosted a big Christmas Eve party, so I needed to be on my best behavior and dress accordingly. I didn't know half the people there since most of them were Helen's family and friends, so I was excited when I recognized Earl.

"I brought something for you," Earl said as he huffed with the effort of walking from the car to the door. "A python," he said. "It's in the car. I'll send your dad out for it in a while."

A python?

"It belonged to my daddy. He fought the Japanese in World War Two, so he knew a thing or two. They still teach you about that in school?"

"Yeah. And I read a book about Hiroshima."

"Oh Christ. Helen, they've got a bunch of liberal commies running the schools." He turned to me. "Well, you'd better thank your stars they did. I wouldn't be standing here if they hadn't bombed the hell out of 'em. You tell them that the next time they feed you this whole America's-so-sorry shit. Did they tell you what those Japs did to our guys? They cut off their nuts, stuffed them in their mouths, and sewed their lips shut. Sent the bodies back to the battle lines. Thought it'd scare the hell out of the soldiers. Scary as hell, isn't it?"

I nodded.

"But it just pissed our guys off more. Got 'em all fired up to do what they needed to do. Sort of backfired, didn't it? Bet they don't tell you about *that* at school."

They didn't. "It gets pretty real when we talk about Hitler and the concentration camps," I said. Why I felt inclined to defend the school system was beyond me. "We talked about those camps in California."

"Liberal shit." Earl hitched his pants up. "They don't teach boys how to be men anymore. And we ain't got any boys coming up in our family. We've got you for a few days, so I figure your dad and I can show you how to use the python."

It occurred to me the python might not be a snake. Maybe it was some sort of martial-arts move where you squeezed the snot out of your enemy. Or a tight-knit secret society. Or maybe something like a Jedi mind trick. That could be cool.

"You been out shooting?" He lowered himself into a chair near the front window.

"Not as much as I'd like," I said. "I did some in Chicago on the street and subway. They've got street musicians and homeless people selling these papers."

Earl looked at me hard, like maybe I was stupid. "Isn't Chicago one of those antigun places?"

"Uh. I don't know."

"If you shot people in the streets of Chicago I'd have read about that in the news. What the hell are you talking about?"

"Shot people? No, with my camera."

Earl about busted a gut laughing. His body rolled to the right and left. He held his side like it hurt him. So he'd been talking about guns. Got it.

"Oh, sweet Jesus," he said as he wiped tears from his eyes. "You about made me piss my pants. Shooting homeless people."

Great.

"Steve!" Earl yelled. "Hey, Steve!"

My dad came out of the kitchen.

"You need something, Earl?"

"Go fetch me my gun case out of the glove compartment."

Dad hesitated. "Why?"

"I'm old."

"No, why the gun case?"

Earl rested his hands on his thighs, his big belly sagging in the center. "I'm giving it to your boy." He gestured toward me.

"Uh," Dad said, "hold on a second." He walked to the kitchen, calling, "Helen?"

"It's a revolver," Earl explained to me. He shouted to my dad, "Bring the ammo in, too!"

But Dad didn't emerge from the kitchen. Instead Helen came out. "Hey, Daddy," she said. "What's this talk about a gun?"

"You and your sister haven't gotten me a grandbaby, so I'm giving the Python to Asher here."

"You can't just give him a gun without talking to us first."

"Why not?"

"Because you just can't."

"Steve and I will teach him what he needs to know. Where is Steve? Did he go out to the car?"

"No, Steve didn't go out to the car. We need to talk about this."

"Well, tell him to get the ammo, too."

Helen turned toward the other room. "Mom!" she called.

I watched Helen and her mom huddle in the corner. Earl gave them a brief glance.

"Bunch of hens," Earl muttered under his breath.

Penny walked over, obviously flustered. She did remind me of a hen. "Earl. What the Sam Hill you think you're doing?"

"Why'd you get your momma?" he asked Helen. "What do you think she's going to do?"

"Talk some sense into you," Helen said. "Mom."

"Earl, you are not giving that boy a gun." She put her hands on her hips and glared at her husband.

Earl turned to me, his eyes bright. I realized he was enjoying the fuss. "You want it?'

"Uh…"

"He's a boy. Of course he wants it," Earl answered for me. "You've gone and made him all uncomfortable. My daddy gave me my first gun when I was eight years old. Shoot, I'd bagged a hog by ten. I'll bet no one's even taken this boy hunting. You ever been hunting?"

"No."

"Your dad ever teach you to shoot a gun?"

"No." Levi's dad used to take us out in the orange grove and target shoot, but that was with a rifle.

Earl gestured toward me but talked to Helen and Penny. "You see this? This boy's a certifiable mess."

Penny rubbed his shoulder. "Earl, *you* are a mess. Leave this boy alone. This is not the time to discuss this." She left the room.

"Asher, can you help me in the kitchen?" Helen asked.

I followed her.

"Why are you taking that boy to the kitchen?" Earl hollered after Helen and Penny. "What the hell's wrong with giving presents anyway? It's Christmas, goddammit."

Helen didn't stop in the kitchen. She led me into the room they'd made mine, closed the door, and examined my face. "Are you okay?" she asked.

"Yeah."

"I'm sorry. I don't know why he's latched on to you like he has. I'm hoping he'll drop the subject of the gun, but if he doesn't, we'll just tell him no. Your dad's pretty upset."

Dad. I moved over to inspect Hector's cage. Although I'd just asked them to crab-sit, Dad and Helen had bought driftwood for his cage. Hector perched on top of it, so I guess he liked it. He'd eaten part of the lettuce I'd given him the night before.

"It's not like I've never held a gun before," I said, putting my hand against the tank.

"Oh. Your dad said—"

"Levi's dad took us out to the grove. It's been a long time, but it isn't a big deal," I said.

"Oh," Helen said, "do you want the gun?"

I didn't know. It wasn't something I was super interested in, but Levi would think it was the coolest thing ever. "Maybe. I just don't want it to be a big deal, you know?" I said. "Everyone's getting upset, and I think your dad was just trying to be nice."

Helen smiled at me. "Okay. I'll tell you what. We'll let him give it to you, but if you decide you don't want it, we can keep it for you."

According to Levi, I was the luckiest human being on the planet. Apparently the Colt Python was the best production revolver ever made. This one looked kind of rough if you asked me, but Levi sent me links to a dozen websites showing me how much they were worth.

"I can't sell it," I told him. "It belonged to Earl's dad."

"When are you going out to the range?" he asked.

"I'm not sure. Maybe the day after tomorrow?"

"I'm going with you."

I was suddenly the most popular person on the planet as well.

"Seriously," he said. "I have to talk to this guy. You tell me when you're going. Okay?"

Hours after I hung up with Levi, I continued receiving links to the Python's history and photos of different guns. He wanted me to take a picture of the gun and send it to him, but I refused. I still wasn't sure how I felt about digital photography.

He texted: *it's not art it's communication asshole*

I ignored him.

❖

It was well after midnight when I slid between the sheets of the bed in the room Dad and Helen put together for me. The blue sheets reminded me of the bedding in Travis's crib. When Travis was a baby, his whole room was the same shade of pale blue. Unlike those worn blankets, these sheets were fresh-from-the-box stiff. Maybe Helen starched her sheets. I tried to settle into a comfortable position, but this mattress didn't give. My bed at home sagged. It knew my form.

It took me ages to fall asleep. Dad actually had to wake me up in the morning. For the first time in my life, I slept in on Christmas. "What time is it?" I asked.

"Nine," Dad said as he pulled the curtain open. "Helen's got breakfast on."

I smelled bacon. I rubbed my eyes.

Every Christmas since Travis had been able to toddle, he had woken me up first Christmas morning. Sometimes I'd hear his feet padding down the hall toward my room. I kept my eyes closed until he was right next to my bed. *As'er*, he used to call me, like ass-er. Hugely embarrassing in public, but forgivable in private. He tugged on my arm. I'd squint at the clock. Sometimes it was still the middle of the night, hours before dawn. I'd let him pull me down the hall out to our brightly lit tree and point at all the presents. *See?* he'd tell me, Og tucked under his arm. *See, As'er?* I knew better than to wake Mom and Dad before five, so I'd get blankets and pillows and camp out with Travis on the sofa. Sometimes he went back to sleep. Sometimes he didn't.

Now he wasn't here at all. I pulled on a pair of jeans and the new graphic tee Aunt Sharon bought me.

"Merry Christmas!" Helen said brightly as I trudged into the family room.

Dozens of colorful packages in assorted sizes stretched out from underneath the tree. I blinked. "Who's coming over?" I asked, because there was no way this was for just us.

Helen scooped bacon out of the pan with a spatula and placed it on a rack. We didn't have a bacon-grease catcher. Mom used paper towels. "It's just us today," she said and poured orange juice into fancy, long-stemmed glasses. "We'll open presents after breakfast. Do you think you can wait that long?"

What was I, five? "I think I'll manage," I said, smiling.

I helped Dad set the table and tried not to worry about my measly gift for them under the tree.

After breakfast, I cleared the table, but I left the cleanup to Dad and Helen. They had a system, and I had the distinct feeling I was just getting in the way. I sat cross-legged on the sofa and sent Mom, Aunt Sharon, and Carol *Merry Christmas!* text messages.

"What's your phone number?" I asked Dad. He called it out to me, and I added him to my contacts. "Helen?" I asked. "Can I have yours, too?" They exchanged a happy look, and Helen gave me hers. The way they reacted, you'd think adding them to my phone was gift enough.

I responded to a message Levi had sent me earlier. He wanted to know what I'd *scored on Jesus day*. I typed back that we hadn't opened presents yet and asked what he'd gotten. Turns out his folks had gotten him a paintball gun. I grinned and wrote back, *Not a python*. He returned with a stream of obscenities.

"You ready?" Dad asked, rubbing his hands together and approaching the tree. "Helen? Are you coming?"

"Sorry!" She carefully carried two mugs of coffee over to the table. "Oh, did you want coffee, Asher?"

"No, thanks."

She perched on the edge of the sofa. Dad insisted on distributing all the presents first. "Asher," he said, handing me a big box. "And this one. Oh. Here's another one."

I chewed on my lip as the stack grew around me. Occasionally he handed a gift to Helen or himself, but there was only one gift for the two of them from me under the tree. By the time he was finished, they each had about six packages. I had three times as many. No joke.

"Dad." I clenched my hands into fists.

"I'm making up for last year."

"You gave us money."

Dad waved his hand at me. "She wouldn't let me give you gifts. It's not the same."

Helen reached over and squeezed my arm. "They aren't all big things," Helen assured me. "Most of it is small stuff. Really. It's okay."

I eyed the package I'd gotten them. Inside were two framed photos: one from the football game and one of the two of them by the pool. In the pool one, Dad is smiling, but Helen isn't, really. I hadn't wanted to take their picture, and I'd dropped my camera into the pool in protest. Not my finest moment. But I meant for the photo to be a peace offering. I wasn't sure if it would have the right effect.

"Oh, open this first," Helen said, handing me a package.

I took a deep breath and surged ahead.

When I was growing up, we never bothered cleaning as we went. Part of the fun was having piles of wrapping paper strewn about, but Helen believed in keeping things tidy. She had a trash bag handy for all the wrapping paper, and she even had a storage bin for reusable bags and particularly lovely ribbons. Turns out they loved the photographs of the two of them, and they took it as I hoped they would.

And even though I'd gotten a ton of gifts, the text I sent to Levi contained only one word: *KEYS*.

CHAPTER TWENTY

I wanted to drive the new-to-me silver Ford Focus immediately, but Dad insisted we open the rest of the presents first. I'd gotten a ton of cool stuff—a new tripod, film, a book about the history of photography, a new pair of Converse...but nothing compared to the car. After lunch, he took me out to the garage and walked me step-by-step through all the exterior features. We opened the hood, and he showed me how to check the oil and coolant levels. He stood outside the car droning on about its safety features and *Consumer Reports* while I adjusted the seat and fidgeted with the dashboard buttons.

"Can I drive it?" I asked him through the driver's window—*my* window.

"Not without an adult. And by that I mean your mom, Helen, or me. You haven't got your license yet," he warned. "I'll tell Helen we're taking her for a spin."

I ran my hand along the steering wheel. My car. And the trunk had plenty of space for all my equipment. Dad pressed the garage-door opener. Afternoon sunlight filled the space.

"Well, what are you waiting for?" Dad asked when he climbed into the passenger seat and belted himself in. "Show me what you've got."

I slid the key into the ignition and listened to the motor start. It was quiet. I lined the mirrors up and tested the turn signals. Then I pulled out of Dad's driveway and eased down the winding, paved road. I drove cautiously, unlike Levi.

"You can go a little faster," Dad said.

"I know. I don't want to."

He chuckled. "Okay."

I eased over the bridge.

"Nice," Dad commented. "Now look both ways before—"

"Seriously?"

"Okay, okay."

I gripped the steering wheel and checked for traffic before pulling out onto the main road. "I've driven with Mom. We went into Fort Myers," I told him.

"Good."

The brakes were a little more sensitive than in the minivan, so when I approached the intersection, I stopped a little abruptly.

"Easy," Dad warned.

I ignored him and admired the way the sun reflected off the gray surface of the car. My face hurt from grinning. This was so much better than Levi's noisy Jeep Wrangler. I decided to turn right, toward Levi's house.

"When did you pick it up?" I asked Dad. "I don't remember seeing it yesterday."

"Remember Craig? He dropped it off last night at the party."

Craig, one of my dad's friends from high school, worked for Llowell Chevy.

"He picked it up at auction for me. I told him we were on the lookout for something for you. I would have waited for your birthday, but the deal was too good to pass up."

I pulled into Levi's driveway and honked the horn. Seconds later, Levi came out the front door. I rolled down the window.

"Come to rub it in, huh?" he said. "Told you you'd get some keys."

"How's it going, Levi?" my dad asked, leaning forward in the passenger's seat and looking through my window.

"Not too shabby. Merry Christmas," Levi said, then he held up a finger like he'd just remembered something. "Hold on, I got something for you, Asher."

Levi hurried back into the house. Dad was asking me about whether or not I'd ever changed a tire before when Levi came back out of the house carrying something.

"Here," he said, handing a medium-sized plastic tub to me. "It's another hermit crab." He stuffed his hands into his pockets. "You know, to keep Hector company."

Through the clear plastic, I saw several shells. I couldn't tell which one housed the crab, but I'd have a chance to check it out back at Dad's place. It was probably the nicest thing Levi had ever done for me. "Thanks."

He nodded awkwardly. "They'll probably fight at first, just so you know. Check the websites. I got some extra shells in there, too."

"Cool."

I had given Levi one of Jennifer's head shots for Christmas. She was listening to Levi in the shot, leaning forward, her hair billowing in a breeze.

Levi smacked the side of my car. "Okay, so where you guys headed next?"

"Probably my house. Is it okay if we swing by there and pick up some stuff from home?" I asked Dad.

"Sure," he said. "You're driving."

It wasn't until I turned onto my street that I realized I didn't know how I felt about him coming inside the house. Even though he'd lived there for over fifteen years with us, it felt disloyal to Mom to have him there. It also seemed sort of stupid. As I parked the car, Dad said, "Why don't I just wait here?"

Yes. "I'll just be a second," I said.

I fumbled with my key ring, now that I had an extra pair on the chain. As I unlocked the front door and opened it, I heard the familiar sound of the television from inside. I was so accustomed to Mom sitting on the sofa watching TV that I was already halfway to my room before it registered that she was still in Chicago. I froze. The television was on. Did Mom leave it like that? Everything seemed in its place. Maybe some sort of electrical surge turned it on.

"Hello?" I called, but no one answered.

That's when I noticed the sliding glass door standing wide open.

Every slasher movie I'd ever seen rushed through my head as I scrambled back to the front door. I threw the car door open, my breath coming fast.

"That was quick," he said.

"Someone broke in," I said.

Dad glanced at me, and then toward the house.

"Get in," he ordered. I slid in, closed the door, and locked it. Like maybe someone was going to rush out of the house and try to assault us. Dad grabbed his cell phone and dialed while I wrestled with my brush with death. What if the person had still been in there? What if they'd been watching me? What if they'd been poised around the corner, holding a knife or a gun? I wasn't even listening to Dad until he tapped me. "Are they still in there?" he asked.

"I don't know."

"We're not sure," he said to the dispatcher.

"I didn't see anything missing," I told him.

"Hold on," he said, and covered the phone. "How do you know someone broke in?"

"The sliding glass door was open. And the TV was on."

He repeated what I said. I stared at the windows in the front of the house, imagining faces appearing in them, staring back at me. It creeped me out. Dad hung up the phone. "We're supposed to wait here. They're sending an officer."

I nodded. I wondered if Levi's mom was working.

"You didn't notice anything missing?" he asked.

"No," I said, my breath still coming fast like I'd been running. "But I didn't go far into the house."

Dad picked up his phone again and called Helen to fill her in while I tried to picture a stranger walking through our house, on our carpet. My computer was the only valuable item in the house. I kept my eyes open wide while we waited, half expecting someone to come around the corner of the house. They had to escape through the orange grove behind our house; there wasn't anywhere else to hide.

A police car squealed into our driveway. It *was* Levi's mom. Dad got out of the car and jogged over to meet her. I hesitated a moment, looking at Levi's mom and my dad standing in the driveway together. Their spouses had an affair with each other. If that crossed their minds, it didn't show on their faces. I joined them on my cracked driveway.

Levi's mom's dirty-blond hair was pulled back into a low ponytail. Like my mom, she didn't wear any makeup. Her radio crackled, and she said something back in code before turning her attention to us.

"Okay, Asher. Tell me what happened when you went inside," she said to me.

As I talked, another police car pulled up on the street. Levi's mom told us to stay put. Then she and the other officer circled to the back of the house.

Dad leaned against my car. "Well, this is exciting," he said.

I raised my eyebrows. I watched his gaze trail across our neglected yard. I wondered if he'd ever noticed it before—how everything had sort of fallen apart since he left—but I felt too edgy to give it much thought. A noise caught my attention from next door. Pearl hobbled out of her house. Her gray hair lay flat against her head on one side, like she'd just woken up.

"Someone die?" she asked.

"It looks like someone might have broken into the house," Dad said. "Did you see anything?"

He probably should have left those questions for the police, but Pearl said, "No. Did they steal anything?"

"We don't know yet."

Pearl's face pinched. "Bastards," she muttered. "I'd like to see them come into my house. I'd shoot their ass."

"You got a gun, Pearl?" Dad asked as he rolled up his sleeves.

"Of course—.357."

"Good to know," he responded.

I gulped. I wondered how many times she'd come close to firing a round at Levi or me.

"Asher got a gun for Christmas," he said. "A Python."

She snorted and pointed a bony finger at me. "He can barely shoot with a camera. Whose bright idea was that?"

"Thanks, Pearl," I muttered.

Dad kicked a piece of gravel. "My father-in-law's."

"Huh. Must not know this boy all that well, giving a gun to a kid like him."

It bothered me that she was right. Maybe if Earl knew me, he wouldn't waste his time on me. *Like him*...what did that even mean?

"Did they like the photos?" Pearl asked.

I'd told Pearl that I intended to give some of the photographs she'd developed as gifts to people for Christmas. She'd helped me pick them out, but she still insisted they were crap. Except for the one with Iggy and the cat. She'd told me that one wasn't as crappy as the others. Gee, thanks.

"Yeah. So far," I said. "I suppose the developing was decent."

She spat. "Decent?"

The police came out through the front door and motioned for us to come inside the house.

"Stop by before you leave. If there's a hoodlum on the loose, I want to know," Pearl said as she waddled away, her legs taking tiny old-person steps. "Assholes."

"Merry Christmas, Pearl," Dad said, and we headed inside my house.

The television was still on. Levi's mom leaned against the counter in the kitchen writing notes while we sat around the dining table with the other officer.

"We identified the point of entry as the sliding glass door," he said. "It was wedged off the track. You're going to want to install one of those braces as a deterrent, but for now a piece of wood, about so long, can do the trick." He held his hands apart to indicate the length.

"Are you going to check for fingerprints?" I asked.

Levi's mom ignored my question and asked, "Would you mind looking around a bit, Asher, to see if anything seems out of place?"

"Sure."

We began in the entry of the front door. I scanned the room. The cushions on the sofa were off-kilter a bit, like someone had been lounging there. Mom made a huge deal out of straightening up the house before we left. But that didn't seem like the type of thing the cops would care about. Plus, whoever it was had been watching SpongeBob. Mom wouldn't have left it on that station. She was all about chick movies and sitcoms and, ironically, home-improvement shows. I took inventory: television, lamp, coffee table, sofa, pillows, and blanket.

"Everything's here," I said.

They accompanied me into the kitchen. All the appliances were there.

"Did you leave dirty dishes in the sink when you left?" Levi's mom asked.

"No."

You can't leave dirty dishes out. A parade of ants or feisty cockroaches will throw a party. Still, a dirty pan, bowl, two plates, and a bunch of silverware loaded the sink. Someone had raided our pantry. It looked like they'd had a couple of the canned raviolis Mom got for me, and mac and cheese. I opened the cabinet and moved things around to get a look. When I picked up one of the boxes, it was empty.

"They ate all my Pop-Tarts," I said.

Levi's mom looked in the trash can. "And raided the liquor cabinet."

Sure enough, several bottles had been thrown in the trash.

"I know who did this," I said.

All eyes turned to me.

"I went to homecoming with this girl, Kayla. Her parents were out of town, and Josh Llowell broke into Kayla's house to throw a party. He broke in through the sliding glass door." I took a deep breath. "I'll bet he threw a party here."

"Did he know you were out of town?" Levi's mom asked as she jotted notes.

"Levi knew," I said.

Her hand froze for a moment.

"They're friends," I said. "It's just, he might have mentioned it. I don't think Levi had anything to do with it."

She continued to write.

"How about we look at the rest of the house?" the other officer suggested.

He'd left the toilet seat up in the bathroom, and his aim sucked. The shower curtain was left open. A towel sat in a heap on the floor. He *showered* here?

"We didn't leave it like this," I said.

"Towel is still damp," the police officer noted.

The story of *Goldilocks and the Three Bears* suddenly took on a whole new dimension for me when we got to my bedroom, because someone had been sleeping in my bed. My sheets were rumpled. My pillow still had the imprint of someone's head in it. I didn't recognize the surge of anger rushing through me. Josh in my bed? I wanted to puke. My computer was still there. My photographs were untouched.

When we got to Travis's room, I knew as soon as I opened the door that no one had been in there. There was a stillness about it, an emptiness. Nothing had been disturbed. Even so, I surveyed the room from the doorway.

"No one came in here," I said with finality, closed his bedroom door, and walked across the hall to Mom's room. It seemed fine, too.

Just my room. Figures.

We headed back to the living room where Levi's mom took a statement from me and continued to fill out paperwork.

"I'll go check in with the neighbors," the other officer announced.

"I'll be finished up here in second," Levi's mom said, and she started to pack up, too. "Are you staying here tonight?"

"I'm with my dad until Mom gets back from Chicago."

She nodded. "Leave lights on. Television, too. We'll add some extra security in the neighborhood, but I think you're right. Just some kids looking for a place to hang out."

Just?

"Where's your dad?" she asked.

It was then that I realized Dad hadn't accompanied us to the front room. "I'll get him," I said. Maybe he was in the bathroom. But the bathroom door was wide open. "Dad?" I called.

The door to Travis's room was ajar, too. That's where I found Dad, sitting on the edge of Travis's bed holding Og. Seeing him there, memories swarmed me. Dad leading me back to bed while Mom gave Travis his nebulizer treatment, Travis's breath short and shallow. Dad's low voice reading *Where the Wild Things Are* for the hundredth time. An early memory, back when Travis slept in the bassinette next to my parents' bed, Dad holding Travis, studying his face. I wasn't jealous; I figured Dad had held me like that when I was little, too. Maybe he hadn't. Maybe when Dad held Travis, he had been trying to summon the strength to love a child that wasn't his.

"Dad?" I said.

He wiped his face with his shirt sleeve and cleared his throat. "Ready to go, sport?"

CHAPTER TWENTY-ONE

Dad drove home so I could talk to Mom, but when I called to tell her about the break-in, she didn't pick up. I hung up when the computer voice asked me to leave a message. I hated leaving messages. Finally I decided to send her a text: *Someone broke in our house. Nothing stolen. Everything's okay.*

I hadn't received a reply by the time I got back to Dad's house, so I sent a message to Aunt Sharon asking her to tell Mom to check her phone.

Helen got all the details of the break-in while we ate this fancy duck dinner. Duck. I hadn't had it before, but it tasted all right. I practically had dinner with Levi, too, because he texted me the entire time we were eating. I reported the conversation to Helen and Dad—no, Levi hadn't heard anything about a party. He *did* mention to Josh that I'd left town. Seemed to me we'd gotten our man. Served him right. After the way he'd treated Kayla and harassed everyone, he deserved a reality check. You can't just break into people's houses.

I asked Levi if he had Kayla's number. He didn't, but he could get it from Jennifer, who—get this—had surprised Levi with tickets to see a touring musical for Christmas. That made me grin.

I must have typed and erased my message to Kayla half a dozen times before I finally settled on, *Hey, it's Asher. Got your number from Jennifer. Hope it's okay. Do you have a minute?*

My phone rang seconds after I'd sent the message. I hurried out of the dining room to talk to her in private.

"What's up?" she asked.

"Hey," I said, sort of flustered. "Sorry, didn't expect to hear from you so fast."

"You sent me a message."

"Yeah. I know."

"Okay."

Jeez, she made my palms sweat. I rubbed my hand against the denim of my jeans and switched the phone into my other hand.

"You got a phone," she said, filling the quiet on my end.

"Yeah. So, I called because someone broke into my house while I was in Chicago. Through the sliding glass door in the back."

"That asshole."

I knew she'd get it.

"Did they catch him?" she asked.

"No, they think he heard us pull up and took off. When I went inside, the door in back was open, like he'd just run. He left the TV on."

"He'll deny it. Do they have proof?"

"I don't know," I said. "But I told them about how he broke into your house."

"Oh, this is sweet. You just made my Christmas, Asher. Do you know he actually called me?" Kayla said.

"Seriously?"

"To wish me a Merry Christmas." She scoffed. "I mean, really? A Merry Christmas? What an ass."

❖

I blinked into the darkness. It took a moment for me to figure out where I was—Chicago loft? Home? The sports poster across the room came into focus. Dad's house. A cool breeze blew in through the open bedroom window. The clock on the bedside table told me it was after midnight. I rolled over to lull myself back to sleep. Then I heard the noise.

My body stiffened, alert.

Maybe it was just Hector and his new friend. I'd watched them battle it out when I first situated the new guy in the tank. The articles online claimed the behavior was perfectly normal. They were establishing the alpha crab. The new crab won out; he was a little bigger than Hector. I fought the temptation to yank the new crab out of the aquarium. The websites said hermit crabs were social creatures. Hector would be happier with some company, but I wasn't so sure.

I heard the noise again. It was faint, but I could make out the sound of something moving. It wasn't coming from the tank. Inside the house? No, the quiet crunch of pine needles under someone's feet came from outside the bedroom window. Slow, purposeful steps—the sound of someone trying to keep quiet.

"Hello?" I called. The noise ceased, but only for a moment. I heard a low chuckle, not the friendly variety, and a chill inched up my spine. "Who's there?" I said, trying to keep my voice steady.

The movement continued, and I noted the blue light seeping in my window. It was a clear, cool night. Whoever was outside my window wasn't a friend. This wasn't my neighborhood back home where Levi's visits to my window were expected. Dad's house was tucked into the woods. Whoever was outside my window wasn't Levi, and they weren't backing off at the sound of my voice.

I slid out of my bed, keeping low, and maneuvered over to the gun case. I unzipped it slowly, quietly, and held the heavy gun in my hand as I eased over to the wall directly across from the window. I crouched down. "Who's there?" I called out, gripping the gun with both of my hands.

The noise stopped. Maybe the laugh had been my overactive imagination. Maybe it was just a raccoon. I waited, my pulse racing, my eyes wide. Then it started up again: *crunch*. A shadow passed by my window. Crap. Definitely a person. A hand appeared at the screen.

"Go away!" I hollered, pointing the barrel at the window. "Seriously. I have a gun."

But the shadowed figure stood there framed in the window. My phone sat on the other side of the room, on the bedside table. I should have just grabbed my phone. *Damn, damn, damn.* Too late now. My hands shook as I pulled the hammer back. It made a solid *click*. I put my finger on the trigger, closed my eyes, and angled the gun toward the window as I squeezed the metal piece toward me. The cylinder shifted, and I braced myself.

But instead of a loud bang, the gun made another clicking noise, and I heard a voice whisper, "Asher?"

I opened my eyes.

"Asher, I need to talk to you," the voice called from outside the window. "It's Iggy."

❖

Iggy shivered in the entrance to my dad's house. His hands were shoved deep into his hoodie pockets, his arms locked straight, and his shoulders pulled up tight. Standing like that made him look even scrawnier. He wouldn't meet my eyes, which was fine by me. My hands were still shaking. I'd almost killed him.

"Hey," he said.

"What are you doing here?"

Iggy made the same creepy laugh as he had outside my window. I wanted to throttle him. Then he stalled in the doorway, dazed like he wasn't sure why he was here either.

"You want to come in?"

He finally muttered, "Sure." Like he was doing me a favor.

Should I take him to the front room where Dad and Helen might hear us? I didn't want him in the bedroom. Iggy creeped me out. Years of covert operations with Levi instinctually made me want to hide Iggy, but I sort of hoped Dad and Helen would wake up and demand to know what he was doing here in the middle of the night. I wondered the same. I settled on the kitchen. That way if anyone woke up, it wouldn't seem as weird.

"Can I get you something?" I asked him.

"No. I'm fine."

He was lying. Everything about Iggy looked the opposite of fine. I opened the pantry and pulled the half-full bag of crackers Helen used with the dip for the Christmas Eve party.

"I said I'm fine," Iggy repeated.

I opened the bag and leaned against the counter. "Who says I got them for you?" I shoved a cracker into my mouth and handed the bag to him. His one eye visible through his hair gazed steadily at me. He got a cracker. Instead of shoving it in his mouth, he broke off a piece and nibbled on it.

"Sorry about waking you up," he said. "I won't stay long."

I waited.

"I had to give you this." He pulled a folded envelope out of his pocket and handed it to me. My name was written on the outside. "I read it," Iggy said. "It was on your bed."

My bed? I recognized the handwriting. It was Mom's.

"I got this idea in my head that it was from Garrett." He spoke slowly, measured. "The way he is about you, it's just—"

"You were inside my house?" I asked. I'd told the police it was Josh. Panic rose up in me. I'd almost killed Iggy and I'd turned Josh in.

"Yeah. I've had some trouble at home." He shifted. "Okay, it's not cool. I know that. But I knew you weren't there and—"

"If you needed food, a place to stay, why didn't—" I was all fired up to be accusatory—*you ate our food, you slept in my bed*—but I'd never been homeless.

"That's not why I'm here. Look, you need to read the letter." Iggy took a deep breath and said, "I really want to hate you. Do you know that?"

I wanted to hate him, too. I nodded.

"Call your mom, Asher," Iggy said, and he grabbed a handful of crackers and left.

❖

Aunt Sharon picked up on the fourth ring.

"Hello?" she asked.

"Where is Mom?"

"Asher? It's the middle of the night."

"Mom. Go check on her. Now. Aunt Sharon, please."

She brought the phone with her. I heard the rapping on the door. I heard Aunt Sharon call, "Margaret?" I heard the squeak of the door opening. "Hey, Ret?"

Please, please, please. Muffled voices, then Aunt Sharon back on the line. "She's okay. My God, you scared me," she said. "She's fine."

And then Mom was on the phone. "Asher? Are you okay?"

She sounded sleepy, but concerned. She was okay. I should have felt relieved, but I didn't. I shook with anger. "I got your note."

At first I thought we'd been disconnected or maybe she'd hung up the phone. But then she said, "I'm so sorry. You weren't supposed to—"

"I thought you were dead. I thought you left me."

It was silent on the other end, a longer pause than the first, but this time I knew she was still there. Finally, she said, "I thought you'd be better off without me."

Better off? "How does that work?" I demanded, my voice rising. "It's bad enough Dad left and Travis died. So you think I'd be better off if I add you to the list?"

"Asher…"

"So what was the plan?"

Another delayed response. "Pills."

"Perfect," I said, my voice breaking. "That's easy enough."

"I love you. I love you so much," she cried. "You have no idea. I'm not who you think I am, Asher. If you knew—"

"I know."

"No, you don't."

I shook my head at the absurdity. "Yes, I do."

"Asher, you have no idea—"

"I know about Travis," I said. "I know about the affair. I know—"

Something happened on the other end of the line, shuffling, voices muffled again. I heard Mom wailing in the background. I glanced up to see Dad enter the kitchen.

"Is everything okay?" Dad asked. He wore matching pajamas, like something out of a catalog. I waved him away with my hand, but he joined me at the table. I refused to look at him.

"Hello?" It was Aunt Sharon.

"Put her back on."

"I don't think I can," she said. "What did you say to her?"

My mouth formed a grim line. I'd handled it all wrong. All the anger drained out of me, and I felt exhausted. "I know about the affair she had with Levi's dad," I said. "Put her back on. Please."

"Hold on."

Dad was reading the letter I'd left sitting on the table, the one where Mom told me she'd added my name to the bank account, where to find the folders in the filing cabinet, and who to contact to put the house on the market. Any proceeds from the sale of the house could cover collections, and the rest should buy me a car or cover part of college. I wondered what Dad thought of the part where she said I'd be better off living with him and Helen, assuring me that he was a good man who loved me. She'd written that she'd made mistakes, more than I knew, and that I was the only thing she had ever done right.

"Here she is," Aunt Sharon said, and she handed the phone off to Mom. In the background, I heard Aunt Sharon say, "Just listen to him."

Mom wasn't talking, but I could hear her breathing.

"Mom? I should have told you when I found out. I should have just come to you and said something, but I didn't know how you'd react. I was…" My voice caught, so I tried again. "I thought you might hurt yourself. But the thing is, I know you hid it from me because you love me." It wasn't until I said it out loud that I realized how true it was. Or maybe it was true because I'd said it.

"I do," she said, then choked out, "I love you so much."

"I'm not better off without you."

"Yes, you would be. You don't understand."

"You aren't the only one who has lost things," I said. "You aren't the only one who makes mistakes."

"Okay." She sounded tired, unconvinced.

"Do you have any idea what would happen to me if you were gone?" I said. "You think I'd just get over that? Mom, promise me you won't do anything stupid."

I refused to get off of the phone until she finally said a weary, "I promise." But I didn't believe her.

After I hung up, Dad and I sat at the table for a long time not saying anything. I was grateful for that. Eventually he got up, poured himself a drink straight from the bottle, and returned to sit with me.

I chewed on my lip. "I don't want the gun," I told him.

"Okay. You want me to give it back to Earl or—"

"I don't care. I just don't want it."

Dad swirled the liquid in his glass and took a swallow. He set it down on the table and rubbed his hands together. "Who told you?" he asked.

"I figured it out myself," I muttered. "Levi knows. His dad told him."

Dad sighed.

"When did *you* know?" I asked him.

"When Margaret got pregnant, she told me."

"But you stayed."

"We thought he might be mine. We decided to work through it. For the kids. That's what people do." He took a sip of his drink.

"Only you changed your mind."

"Asher, I knew the moment I saw him, Travis wasn't mine," Dad said. "I tried. I really did, but every time I looked at him...and everyone else knew, too. Small towns." He shook his head. "Your mother is not an easy woman to live with."

Anger surged. I still lived with her. I didn't have the choice of leaving. But I couldn't say that to him. No way would I give him the satisfaction. I stood up, walked back into the guest room, and quietly closed the door. No one followed me.

Chapter Twenty-two

I didn't plan to run away. The air in the house felt too thick and heavy, and I needed to feel the crisp December air in my lungs. I slid on my jeans and a sweatshirt, laced up my new Converse, and rinsed out my mouth. I even stopped by Dad and Helen's room to tell them I was going outside for a bit. So they knew. Does it count as running away if they knew? I'm not sure. But before I opened the front door, I tucked my wallet, phone, and car keys into my pocket. And my camera.

Outside it was surprisingly bright. The moon illuminated Dad's Land Rover, my car, and the curved pine tree in the field in blue. I headed toward the tree. The crunchy grass made me think of Iggy, and I wondered if he was lurking out here somewhere. Homeless. I tried to imagine what it would be like from that perspective. I climbed up onto the curve of the tree. The bark felt rough and cool under my skin, but at least it felt real. From this vantage point, I could look at my dad's house from a distance. A faint light shone from Dad and Helen's window. He was probably filling her in on the new developments of my mom's nuttiness.

I hadn't told him about Iggy. I needed more time to think about him. Josh hadn't broken into my house; Iggy had. He'd eaten our food and slept in my bed and read the letter. Mom must have left it in my room. If Iggy hadn't read it, Mom might have died. Or maybe I would have found it anyway when I stopped by the house. But Iggy took it. He didn't have a car. Did he *walk* from my house to Dad's to give me the letter? I did the math. Yep, he'd left my house and come directly here.

Even though he hated me.

It didn't even occur to me to call the police and report that it wasn't Josh. Maybe tomorrow. They'd figure it out. I wondered if Iggy was in the system. As a senior, I was pretty sure he was eighteen. Did that mean he'd be tried as an adult if he got caught? He hadn't taken anything. Didn't we have to press charges or something? I had no interest in getting Iggy arrested.

I shivered and wondered where he was staying now. Maybe he hung out over at the shelter. I thought about the abandoned brick building over by the food pantry where I'd watched him feed the cat. That was the photograph, the one Pearl liked. All that talk in church about helping people, and my first instinct was to fire a gun at someone. What if the gun had been loaded? What if I'd killed him? I'd be responsible for two deaths: Travis and Iggy.

I missed home.

Dad and Helen's house wasn't home. I wasn't sure if it ever would be. I pictured my house: the cracked driveway, my room with my black-and-white photographs. I still hadn't hung up a single color one. The trouble was I had the perfect number of pictures spaced out, and it would be a hassle to try to figure out how to integrate the color ones into the mix. Maybe I could hang them at the room at my dad's house. Something about that tugged at me, like it was giving in to something I'd been fighting for a long time. It didn't make sense. The conflict with Dad had always been my mom's battle, not mine.

At least I'd thought so.

I hopped off the curved pine tree and wandered over to the driveway. I leaned against the car—my car—for a while. It still didn't seem real, having a car. Like I was pretending to be an adult or something. I fidgeted with the keys in my pocket for a minute before I unlocked the car and slid into the driver's seat. I put the key in the ignition. Just sat in the car listening to the radio. I flipped through several stations, found the one Mom listened to, and reclined as far back as I could in the seat. I felt antsy, like I had to get out. But driving without an adult would be breaking the law.

So was breaking and entering.

So was firing a pistol.

So what?

I turned the ignition, backed out of Dad's driveway, angled the car toward the curved road, and drove away.

❖

When I pulled onto his street, I dimmed the lights and turned off the radio. Instead of parking the car in his driveway, I pulled slightly off the road in front of an empty lot. I turned off the ignition and sat in the driver's seat for a long time listening to the tick of the engine before I decided to get out of the car. I was reaching for the door handle when my phone beeped. Sure enough, there was a message from Dad.

Where are you?

I typed back, *Needed to get out for a while.*

He wrote back, *Are you okay?*

I'm okay. I started to hit send, and then added, *Love you.* My thumb hesitated for a few seconds. Something inside me resigned itself to it, and I hit send.

I checked myself out in the mirror. The hand I ran across my head did little to tidy the mess up, but I got out of the car anyway. I strolled down the road at a steady pace, past the three houses that separated the open field from the house. I made my way around the back to Garrett's bedroom window. It made me think of Iggy, creeping through the woods around my dad's house and sauntering up to my window. I doubted Garrett had a gun. It took several rounds of raps to wake him up. When he didn't respond right away, I thought maybe they'd gone on vacation or something, but then I heard him.

"Who's out there?"

"It's me, Asher."

Then Garrett's grinning face appeared in the window. His hair stood up in awkward tufts. He was bare chested. He unlatched the window, slid it open, and leaned out.

"Merry Christmas," he said.

Relief surged through me. It was okay, my coming over.

"Is it still Christmas?" I asked.

"Are you my present?" When I stood stock-still and unable to respond, he laughed. "I'm kidding. Go around to the front door. I'll let you in."

I stuffed my hands into my pockets and walked around to the front of his house. The door didn't open immediately, so I had a few minutes to watch my breath puff out in clouds. The full moon appeared unnaturally huge in the sky. I stared at it and wondered if it always looked like that. Maybe I just never noticed. When the door opened, Garrett stood there in a T-shirt and pajama pants. He shivered.

"Oh my gosh, it's cold. Come inside."

Normally I would have done just that, but instead I said, "Look at the moon."

Garrett stepped outside onto the front step and pulled the front door mostly shut. He wrapped his arms around himself and stood right beside me. Where our shoulders touched, I felt warm. We gazed into the sky. I wondered if one of us should fill the space between us with words or descriptions, but we didn't. Instead we just stood there looking up at the moon, until I got distracted watching Garrett.

When I was little, I had a book about Peter Pan. On one of the pages in the book, there's a picture of Peter with the Lost Boys. They're going to sleep, but Peter's awake and filled with this wonder, standing on this mountaintop, watching over Neverland. In the blue light, I wouldn't have been surprised if a bright-light fairy landed on Garrett's shoulder.

Fairy. Gay.

Garrett caught me looking at him.

"Thanks," he said, and the mist his breath made in the air faded. "This is cool, but my feet are freezing."

I glanced down at his bare feet. "Oh, shoot. I'm sorry."

"Are you kidding?" he asked, his brown eyes pleading with me. "Don't apologize for this. Please don't."

We stepped inside his house, and Garrett quietly closed the door behind us. I followed him into the kitchen where he took two mugs out of the cabinet, filled them with water, and put them in the microwave.

"How was your Christmas?" he asked as he pushed the buttons.

I didn't know where to begin, so I said, "Different."

He nodded. "I thought you were going to Chicago."

"Yeah," I said. I watched him walk across the kitchen to the pantry and pull out hot chocolate mix. He tossed two packets beside the microwave, and then hoisted himself up onto the counter, facing me. It was stupid how just being in the same room with him made my pulse race. "But I had to come back a little early to spend Christmas with my dad."

"How's that going? Being with your dad? You guys didn't really talk for a long time, right?"

"Right. No, we didn't see him for over—" And I stopped. *We* meant Travis and me. I cleared my throat. "Almost a year. It's fine. That's where I'm supposed to be right now."

The microwave beeped. Garrett leapt off the counter and opened the door to stop the beeping. He took the two mugs out, set them on the counter, and poured the mix into each one. Then he got a spoon out and stirred them. "Oh!" he said, rushing over to the pantry. "We've got marshmallows. Those little ones. You want some?"

I smiled. "Sure."

He heaped a pile of them in the mug and carefully brought mine to me. Our hands brushed one another as I took it from him.

"How was your Christmas?" I asked.

He shrugged. "Typical family stuff. My grandparents came down from Orlando early yesterday, but they left this afternoon." Garrett took a sip from his mug. "It's hot."

I blew on the liquid, and the warmth of the mug heated my hands. I hadn't realized how cold I had been. I took a cautious sip. Perfect.

"Iggy was supposed to stop by, but he never showed up," Garrett said. "Typical."

Iggy. The last person I wanted to talk about was Iggy, but I said, "About Iggy. He's going through a tough time, Garrett."

"I know." He held the mug in his hands, steam rising up. His eyebrows wrinkled with worry. "Asher, he won't talk to me. I'm trying."

How could I explain that it wasn't his fault? Iggy was a lot like that feral cat I'd seen on Thanksgiving. It didn't matter who approached him; Iggy was skittish.

Garrett continued, "I know he got kicked out. And how do I know that? Because Rose asked me if he was staying here. I asked him point-blank, where are you living, and he told me not to worry about it. I invited him for Thanksgiving, for Christmas. My family expected him. He didn't even show up. No call. Nothing."

"He was at my house," I said.

"What?"

I hated this. I didn't want to help Iggy. I didn't want to repair the damage to his relationship with Garrett, but I owed him. "He must have found out we were out of town," I explained.

"I told him."

"He stayed in our house for a couple of days while we were gone."

"Wait. You invited him to stay…?"

"No."

Garrett hopped off the counter and started pacing. "So he *broke in* your house?"

"I don't think he had anywhere else to go."

Garrett motioned to his kitchen. "Why not *here*? Where he's *welcome*? Where he's *invited*?"

I didn't know what to say.

"Sorry. It's just, I don't know what else I can do, Asher. I'm done."

Done? As in, breaking up? I thought about Iggy walking all the way from my house to my dad's to deliver that message. I thought about what it cost him to reveal he was the one who broke into my house. "Garrett, he really likes you. Just give him time. I know he'll come around, it's just—"

"I thought you didn't like Iggy."

I chewed on my lip. He was right. I didn't like Iggy. "This isn't about how I feel about him," I said, but as soon as I said it, I realized I was lying. If Iggy hadn't given me the letter, I wouldn't defend him to Garrett. "Maybe it is. I don't know. He thinks you have feelings for me."

"What if I do?" Garrett said, all casual, like it wasn't a big deal. "He wasn't my first choice."

I felt myself growing angry. "You *told* him that?"

"No, but he isn't stupid."

I tried to picture that, being with someone and knowing they'd rather be with someone else. Was that how Dad felt when Mom slept with Levi's dad? Was that how Mom felt when Dad left? "Garrett, I'm *not*—"

"Yes, Asher, I know. You aren't gay." He ran a hand through his hair and then stopped midmotion. "Look, I'm glad you're here. Don't take this the wrong way, but why are you here?"

I considered telling him about Mom's suicide note and almost killing Iggy, but I settled on the truth. "I don't know."

He studied me for a minute, and then his face brightened. "I have something for you."

"What?"

"Come on."

We left our steaming mugs in the kitchen, and I followed Garrett to his dark room. He turned on the lamp beside his bed and quietly closed his bedroom door behind us. It cast a warm light. My throat constricted.

"You can sit down," he said, indicating his bed.

I hesitated. He rolled his eyes.

"I'm not going to seduce you. It's fine. Sit down." He moved to the foot of the bed, knelt down, and stretched underneath. When he emerged, he held a thick file folder. Garrett sat down on the bed next to me and peeked into it. What he was looking for was right on top. He slid the paper out and set it in my lap.

It was a drawing of me. Not really me, but one of those anime-looking versions of me. I'm wearing jeans and a hoodie. The Canon A-1 hangs around my neck. He'd gotten most of the details right on the camera. As for me, I'm looking off to the side, like something important has caught my eye. One of my hands is poised on the camera as if I'm just about to bring it up to my face and take a picture. And there's something sad about me. I can't place it, but it's the truth. I look cooler than I am in real life. Maybe that's how he sees me. I studied the picture. Maybe I could frame it and hang it in my room. "Garrett. This is really cool. Seriously."

"Drawing the camera was hard, because the angle you're at, see? It's hard to get the perspective."

"How do you do that? I mean, do you just draw from memory?" I asked.

He shook his head. "Not exactly. Well, sometimes. I did a rough sketch at the homecoming game. You were going around taking pictures. And it was like you blended with the crowd, but the way you looked at everything. I don't know. It was cool."

Garrett had been sitting with a crowd of people, including Iggy, at the football game. He'd sketched me out then? With all those people around him? I guess I wasn't the only one who spent time observing people. "Do you have anything I can put this in? So it doesn't get messed up?"

"Sure. My mom has tons of files." Garrett's leg bounced up and down. "So does that mean you like it?"

I gave him an *Are you kidding me?* look, and he laughed.

"I guess that's a yes," he said.

I nodded superfast, and the smile he gave me made it hard for me to breathe.

He nudged me with his shoulder. "I'll go see what I can find," he said as he stood up. "I'll be right back."

Garrett gently closed the door behind him. My eyes couldn't absorb enough of the drawing, but I would have plenty of time on my own to study it. I carefully set it down on his dresser. The last time I'd been in this room, Iggy took up too much space. I wondered if Garrett would care if I stretched out. Probably not. My shoes hung over the side of the bed; I didn't want to put them on top of his comforter. His pillow was soft, like the one Aunt Sharon had at her house. The sheets faintly smelled of coconut, and I wondered if he used some sort of scented bath wash. I imagined him staring up at the ceiling, trying to sleep at night. What did he think about? This would be his view. A fan hung from the ceiling. In the summer, did he watch the hypnotic blades turn? Did he stare at his drawings like I stared at my photographs? I closed my eyes. My body relaxed. I tried to see if I could recall the view from memory, the view Garrett had in the moments before he drifted off to sleep.

"Hey."

Bright light poured in through a window. I squinted and blinked, shielded my eyes, and jolted upright. Garrett kneeled beside the bed.

"Did you sleep okay?"

I stretched and shivered. Someone had draped a blanket over me. "I fell asleep."

Garrett grinned. "Yes, you did."

My feet felt heavy. I wiggled my toes. "I'm still wearing my shoes."

"I thought about taking them off, but I was afraid I'd wake you." The way he was studying me made me want to pull a blanket over my head. "You're cute when you wake up."

I grumbled and hid under the pillow. Garrett tugged on it.

"Hey. Asher."

I peeked out at him. "What time is it?" I asked.

"A little after nine."

I threw the cover off and said, "I've got to get home."

Garrett put a hand on my shoulder, and the heat of it stopped me. "It's okay. My mom called your dad last night. He knows where you are." When he saw my confused expression, Garrett added, "I woke my mom to tell her you were here. You fell asleep. I didn't want to wake you up, but I didn't want anyone worrying about you."

They'd talked to my dad. How much had he told them?

"Are you hungry? Mom's making pancakes."

I considered that a moment. Yes. I was hungry. I nodded.

"Good, because she made enough batter to feed an army." Garrett hopped up and headed for his bedroom door. "I'm really glad you came here last night." The door shut behind him.

He was glad I came to his house, but why Garrett's? My first thought was of course I'd come to Garrett's; I didn't have anywhere else to go. But that wasn't true. It wouldn't have been the first time I'd knocked on Levi's bedroom window. Levi understood. He knew my history. He would've gotten it. Even Kayla would have been a better choice. But I'd driven the car to Garrett's.

I sat on the edge of Garrett's bed. *This is what it's like, when Garrett wakes up in the morning. This is the light filtering into his room through the curtain. This is the way his room smells. When he first opens his eyes, this is what he sees.* I touched the pillow I'd rested my head on. That's where he put his head. I knew what his mattress felt like underneath him. I wanted to commit it to memory, but I was afraid it would occupy too much of my time, recalling this moment, these images. I could lose hours remembering this if I wasn't careful, so I steadied myself, stood up, and walked out of his room.

They were nice, Garrett's family. The pancakes were different. They did this gluten-free thing for Emily, so the pancakes tasted gritty. It wasn't too bad if you poured plenty of syrup on top. I'd never spent time with Asher's dad before, although I'd seen him plenty of times at church. Turns out he was clever and funny. They laughed a lot at his house. They liked each other. It was nice, but it made my heart hurt a little.

I thought about my mom.

I'd put off heading back to Dad's house for as long as I could, and I had a feeling Garrett's family might have plans but were putting them off because I was around, so I sent Dad a text with Garrett's address and the message: *Could you come get me?* I wouldn't risk driving illegally again. He wrote back that they were on their way.

I was watching for Dad and Helen, so as soon as they pulled up in the driveway, I thanked Garrett's folks and told Emily and Garrett I'd see them at school.

Garrett waved at me from his front door and called, "I hope everything's okay with your mom."

Mom? I nodded, like no big deal, and quickly got in the backseat of Dad's car.

So he knew. They all knew. Garrett's dad, mom, and sister. Dad told them when they called. I was a pity case. It was Travis dead all over again.

"We need to talk," Dad said when I got in the car. His voice sounded stern, but he was grinning and waving at Garrett like everything was great. I stared out the window and didn't say anything. He pulled the Land Rover to the side of the road next to my parked car. Maybe the talk would take place once we got back to the house.

"I'll see you at home," he told Helen, and he kissed her and motioned me out of the Land Rover.

Helen walked around to the driver's seat. The expression on her face was unreadable behind her black sunglasses. I hesitated by my car, waiting to see if Dad intended to let me drive. Grounded from the car seemed like a reasonable punishment to me, but he moved to the passenger's side. Okay. So I wasn't exiled from driving. Once we were settled, he rested a hand on my shoulder.

"You can't do this," he said.

So we were going to settle this now. Driving after curfew without a license definitely constituted breaking the law. I got it. It wasn't like I didn't know what I was doing. I'd chosen to do it anyway. "I know. It was stupid." I waited for it: the lecture. *If you'd been caught. Do you have any idea how much trouble. We were worried sick.* But it didn't come.

Instead Dad said, "I love you." He patted me on the head. "So much. You have no idea."

His eyes welled up and he bit his bottom lip, then sat back in the passenger seat. "Okay," he said, like it was all settled. "Let's go home."

CHAPTER TWENTY-THREE

Although my pass said restroom, I headed straight to my locker and pulled out the grocery bag. Rumor had it the school was loaded with cameras, but I didn't see anything that looked like a recording device. I doubted going to my locker would get me a referral, but I decided to grab a book out of it just in case. I could claim I needed something for class. I lingered in the next hallway until I was sure it was clear, then I casually dropped the bag in front of Iggy's locker.

During the passing period, I stopped by Kayla's locker as an excuse to check on the package. It was still there.

"Have you seen Iggy?" I asked.

"I don't think he's here today," Kayla said as she shoved a book in her locker. "Lucky bastard." She held the book in place, readied the door, and then slammed it shut to catch the book before it fell.

"You know that's just going to tumble out when you open the locker, right?" I asked.

"So?" She adjusted her book bag. "Any clue how long you're going to have to stay with your dad?"

"I don't know. I talk to my mom every day. She sounds better. Aunt Sharon's got her going to therapy there."

"What about your house?"

These were questions I wanted to ask, too. "My aunt says they've got it covered. The only thing that matters is getting Mom healthy."

Kayla whistled. "Your aunt must be loaded."

"No. She's a social worker. I think her partner is," I said as we rounded the corner.

"Partner?"

"Carol. She's a lawyer with some big firm in Chicago," I explained. Suddenly Josh Llowell's face appeared directly in front of me. I started to walk around him, but he blocked my path.

"Josh," Kayla warned, but he ignored her.

"The cops came to my house Christmas night," he said. "You need to get your facts straight, Price."

Kayla puffed up for a fight, but I held up a hand in front of her and faced Josh. I sort of expected to get punched, but at least this time I'd deserve it.

"You're right," I said to him. "I jumped to conclusions."

"Damn right you did."

"I'm sorry."

"Sorry?" His face inched closer to mine and he lowered his voice so only I could hear. "My dad was pissed. He didn't believe me."

Up close, I noticed the fading bruise on the side of Josh's face. I lost my grip on my book and dropped it to the floor. The way Josh's jaw jutted out, like he was barely holding it together, told me everything I needed to know.

Kayla interjected, "You didn't seem too worried about pissing off your dad when you broke into *my* house."

I expected him to fly into a rage or at least make a sarcastic comment, but instead he bit his lip and shook his head in utter disbelief. He lowered his voice. "Kayla, I got this crazy idea that you'd get a kick out of it—a party at your house."

"You thought I'd *like* that?"

"Having everyone at your house? Being cool?" he sort of scoffed. "Yeah, I thought you might. Don't worry. I get it now." Josh sauntered off, but halfway down the hall he turned back toward her and yelled, "You know what, Kayla? Whatever I did, I'm sorry! You hear that?"

Heads turned toward Josh, then back to Kayla. I waited for Josh's punch line, a crushing comment, but he vanished into the crowd. I gathered my books up off the floor.

Kayla bent down to help me retrieve the last few papers and whispered, "Did Josh Llowell just apologize to me?"

"I think he did," I said. Once a kid in elementary school put gum in this girl's hair. Everyone knew he liked her, but it sealed the deal on her utter hatred toward him. Some guys behaved like jerks to get attention, but we weren't in elementary school. Before I could stop myself, I asked, "Is it possible Josh *likes* you?"

She shrugged. "He asked me to homecoming, but I thought he was joking."

"Wait," I said, and sat up. No doubt Josh was a jerk, but she never mentioned he'd asked her to homecoming. Kayla had told me I was the only one who knew about the abortion, aside from her mom and doctor. It hadn't occurred to me that maybe Josh should have had a shot at stepping up.

She reminded me, "He broke into my house. You think he did that because he *liked* me?" She made a face like she smelled something foul.

❖

I was in the middle of a pretest in geography when Mr. Spivik's phone rang on his desk.

"Yes, he is," he said. "I'll send him down." He hung up the phone. "Mr. Price, you're wanted in the office."

The office?

Mom. Panic itched under my skin. "Should I take my stuff?" I asked, but Mr. Spivik just shrugged at me.

I turned in my unfinished pretest and scooped up my book and folder. What if she'd actually done it? A shiver rushed through me and I picked up my pace. By the time I got to the office, I'd run through the scenarios. I expected to see Dad standing there, a grim expression on his face. But waiting for me in the office was none other than Pearl. Instead of a robe, she wore a pair of beige pants and a red sweater. On her feet, however, were slippers. That comforted me.

As soon as she saw me, she demanded, "Where have you been?"

The office secretary busied herself on the computer. I wondered if she'd intervene if Pearl hit me.

"I've been with my dad," I explained. "My mom's in Chicago."

"Why the hell didn't anyone tell me?"

My eyes shifted to the secretary. I knew she'd heard Pearl say *hell*, but she ignored it. Would Pearl get in trouble for using profanity? There were benefits to being old and retired.

I lowered my voice. "Mom's staying with my aunt for a while," I explained. I didn't want to give her too much information.

Pearl said, "It's hell losing a child. You never get over that."

It was the first time since Travis died that Pearl had mentioned him, and something about the way Pearl said it made me wonder if she had any kids of her own.

"Is that why you came here?" I asked. "To find out where we were?"

Pearl blinked at me. "I don't give a rat's ass where you are. But if you'd keep in touch with me, I wouldn't have to drag myself all the way to school to deliver a message."

Didn't she have a phone?

She reached a shaky hand inside a brown paper bag—her version of a purse, I guess—and handed me an envelope.

What was with me and envelopes?

"Go on," she said. "Read it."

It wasn't sealed. "You opened it."

"Of course I did. I wanted to know what it said."

What was with me and people reading my letters? I glared at Pearl, but then I looked at the return address: the *Photographer's Lens* student photo contest.

"You're a finalist," Pearl said before I could open the letter.

"A finalist? I didn't enter anything."

"I know. I did."

Was she deranged? I wanted to be irked with her for entering me in a contest without asking for permission, but I was too excited. I fumbled with the letter, pulling it out of the envelope. "I'm a finalist!" I announced.

The secretary glanced up from her computer and hurried around the corner to see what all the fuss was about.

"Don't get too excited," Pearl said. "You didn't win. You're a finalist."

I scanned the letter while the secretary huddled up next to me. She looked over my shoulder, and then called into the other room, "Mr. Boatwright! Come see this."

Mr. Boatwright moseyed out of his office and joined us over by the glass window. "What's this?" he asked.

The secretary read directly from the letter. "'We are pleased to announce that your photo submission, *Strays*, has been selected as a finalist in the *Photographer's Lens* student photo contest.'"

"*Strays*?" I asked. "What photo did you enter?"

"The photograph you took with the drug addict and the cat," Pearl said. "Not those with the girl. Those were crap."

She'd developed the picture and sent it in without even consulting me. I pictured it in my head. Iggy and the cat, slumped over, eating scraps. She'd picked out the name: *Strays*. It was perfect. And awful.

"Finalist?" Mr. Boatwright asked. "What does that mean?"

Pearl lifted her chin. "It means Asher's photographs aren't crap."

Usually, I'm invisible. I walk through the hallways, go to class, do my homework, and avoid making an idiot of myself. It works for me. When teachers call in me in class, I'll answer the question, but I can't breathe right until the attention focuses somewhere else. Some students like being acknowledged for what they do. I fly under the radar. I maintain my grades, but I don't want an A+. I can't handle that pressure.

Teachers don't get that.

Apparently principals don't either.

I didn't think anything of it when Mrs. O'Flaherty, the art teacher, scanned the lunchroom. I figured she was looking for one of her art students. She talked to the lunch lady for a minute, and when her gaze landed on me, I knew I was in trouble. Kids turned as she hurried past them and buddied up to me at the lunch table like a lifelong friend. She smelled like what I imagined an exotic spice from the Orient would smell.

"I just got off the phone with a reporter," she said.

Reporter?

"Don't worry. I told him anything you did, you did on your own," she said, her thick black hair piled up on top of her head. "But how exciting!"

Apparently while I had headed back to class, dazed, between elated and horrified, Mr. Boatwright had contacted our local newspaper about doing a cover story to acknowledge my achievement. Even though I'd never taken one of her classes, the reporter asked to interview Mrs. O'Flaherty. I was pretty sure she hadn't known I'd existed until the call.

"I organize a student exhibit at the local library every year. It's short notice, but we'd like to feature your photograph in the show as well." She kept talking about displays and locations, but I couldn't concentrate on anything but the photograph of Iggy being made public.

"Good, then it's all settled," Mrs. O'Flaherty finally said. She squealed. "*Photographer's Lens*! Oh, I can't wait to see this photograph!"

You and everyone else.

"Your parents must be so proud," she said, her hands clutched in front of her.

I thought of Mom and the photograph of her on Travis's bed with the grief book on her chest. What if Pearl had sent that one in? What would the world do with it?

"Can you get me a copy of the photograph tomorrow?" Mrs. O'Flaherty said.

"I don't know. I'm not sure…"

"Sometime this week, then. The sooner the better. I'll see you then." She strolled across the lunchroom, pausing to talk to a few art students along the way. Kayla bit into a chocolate chip cookie and smirked at me.

"What?" I asked.

"Asher's famous," she said, a few crumbs spewing from her mouth.

I didn't crack a smile.

Kayla put the cookie down on her plate. "Hey. This is what you want, right? Why the face?" She punched me gently on the arm. "Smile. Jesus, Asher, let yourself be happy."

"Happy about what?" Garrett asked as he set his lunch tray on the table.

"Asher's famous," Kayla announced.

"How's that?" he asked me.

When I didn't respond, Kayla launched into a detailed account. I attempted to tune her out—I wanted the subject dropped—but I couldn't resist correcting her as she talked. "*I* didn't enter it."

"Well then, who did?" she asked.

"My neighbor, Pearl, and she had no right—"

"Okay," Kayla said. "Pearl entered his photo in a contest with *Photographer's Lens* and he won—"

"I didn't *win*. I'm a finalist."

Garrett's eyes widened. "*Photographer's Lens?*"

"It's for high school students," I clarified. "It's not like—"

"It's still a big deal," he said. "Wow. I mean, you can put that on a resume. You're a sophomore, and you've already landed *Photographer's Lens*? Who does that?"

I hated the way his reaction sparked something inside me. His response made me wish I could enjoy it. "Yeah, well, I don't think I'm going to do it."

"What?" Garrett asked. "Why?"

In the fine print of the letter from *Photographer's Lens*, there'd been a section on rules. Turned out, Iggy was right. You couldn't use people's images on film without their consent. No way would I put Iggy's photo out there for the whole world to see. Not even with his consent. Not after he'd given me the letter from my mom.

Damn Pearl. Maybe I wouldn't be a photographer after all.

"I just don't want to," I muttered. "I've got to go."

❖

All day I'd thought about what I wanted to say in the session with my therapist. I played through scenarios in my head, trying to prioritize, but there was just too much. So when I settled onto the sofa and she asked, "So how was your holiday? Did you have fun in Chicago?" I blinked at her. There was no way I was going to get her up to speed in fifty minutes. I sighed. Her eyebrows scrunched together. "Bad?"

"Uh…"

She waited.

I didn't know where to start. I was so bad at this.

Finally, she asked, "Did you go to Chicago?"

Chicago. Okay. "Yeah."

"Last time you said your dad was upset about that."

That felt like ages ago. Since we only met every other week, missing one session really screwed things up. "They worked it out. I came back early to spend Christmas with him."

Her eyebrows shot up. "Your parents compromised?" I nodded. She smiled and scribbled something on her yellow pad of paper. Yeah, that was good. Considering they'd gone a year without speaking, this was serious progress. I hadn't thought about that. "And Chicago? How was it?"

"Great." I started to tell her about Aunt Sharon's place, but I glanced at the clock and realized we only had forty-five minutes left. I stopped midsentence. She waited for me to continue.

"How did they like your gifts?" she asked. That had been a big part of the last session—what to give people.

"Yeah, everyone loved the photos." I scratched this place on my ankle where my sock rubbed funny. "My dad, he got me a car."

"Wow! Do you like it?"

I nodded. "It's weird though. Levi said I'd get a car if I played my cards right. And I got a car."

"Hmm. How do you feel about that?"

If Travis had been alive, would I have a car? Did that even matter? Instead I started to tell her how my mom gave me a phone and Dad got angry, but that sort of negated the whole idea that they were getting along, which they kind of were now that Mom was getting help. I shut my mouth. Anything I said seemed like it *meant* something, so I had to think about it first. People do stuff with what you say. She continued to stare at me, like she was trying to understand. I wasn't making sense, and I knew it. This was so hard.

"It's okay, Asher. We have plenty of time." She was trying to comfort me, as if we had all the time in the world to work through everything.

"We only have forty minutes," I said, my voice cracking on the *forty*.

She glanced up at the clock. "You're worried about having enough time?" she asked.

I rubbed my hands together "Yeah."

She leaned forward. "Okay, ignore the clock," she said. Ignore the clock? I looked back at the ticking second hand. My leg started bouncing. "Asher." She put her legal pad down on the table next to her.

I picked up the throw pillow next to me and gripped it.

"Let's try something, okay? Can we try something?" When I didn't answer, she said, "Close your eyes."

"Wait. Are you going to try to hypnotize me?" I asked.

She smiled and said, "No," but not in a condescending way. "Just trying to remove some of the distractions in the room. Do you want to try?" I took a few breaths, and I cautiously shut my lids. Almost immediately, I felt myself grow calmer. I sat like that for a while, squeezing the pillow. "That's better. Now I'm going to ask you a few questions, and I want you to say whatever comes into your mind, okay?" I listened to myself breathing. "What are you worried about?"

I don't know how the pillow survived the session. It took a while to get the swing of it, all these stops and starts, but with my eyes squeezed closed, I managed to tell her about the break-in and giving the police Josh's name and getting Earl's gun and almost shooting Iggy. I told her about the photographs in the Art Institute and Pearl entering me in the stupid contest and how I'd never be a photographer. I almost cried when I told her how hard I'd tried to protect Mom by hiding the truth and how she wanted to kill herself anyway and how much I hated her and loved her. When I finally blink-opened my eyes, I thought for sure we had gone overtime, but we still had a few minutes left. How was that even possible?

"You okay?" she asked.

I ran my hands over my face. "Exhausted." But it was more than that.

"So where is the gun now?" Of course she was worried about the gun. I almost shot someone.

"My dad has it," I said. "I told him to take it."

I expected her to offer up some kind of sage advice, maybe even extend the time so we could work through all of this, but instead she said, "I think this may be a good place to pause." Seriously? I put it all out there, and she thinks it's a good place to *pause*? I tossed the pillow back into the corner. "You were really brave today, Asher." She said it like I'd done something noble, and I suppose I should have felt good about it, but I just felt drained.

"So what am I supposed to do?"

"What do you want to do?" She was good at throwing things back at me like that. It didn't normally bother me, but right then it irritated the crap out of me. "It might be useful to consider what you have the power to change," she said, and I started to answer, but she stood to signal the end of the session.

Apparently I was supposed to let that gnaw at me for the next two weeks.

Chapter Twenty-four

That Sunday, Dad dropped me off early at church for youth group. He and Helen planned to join me at the contemporary service later, which suited my plans. I held the paper bag in my left hand and waved to Dad with my right as he pulled away from the curb, and then I stepped just inside the building until I saw his Land Rover turn left out of the parking lot. I was all set to exit when I heard a voice behind me.

"Good morning, Asher," said John, extending a warm hand. "Happy New Year!"

I glanced around for his girlfriend, Sara.

"So you're joining us for youth group today?" he asked.

My brain raced for something to say, but rather than flat-out lie, I said a vague truth. "I've got something else I have to do. I'll definitely be there next week."

He nodded. "Excellent. I'll look forward to that. How's your mom? Is she parking the car?"

He didn't know. I cleared my throat. "She's staying with my aunt in Chicago for a while."

"Ah. That explains it. I've been trying to call her. Left messages. I knew you were out of town, but I thought she'd be back by now."

My hand got sweaty from where I was holding the paper bag, so I switched it into the other one. Did John know that Mom had been interested in him? Did he know how hurt she had been when she found out that he was seeing someone? Well, maybe he should. I decided to push the issue. "How's that lady?" I asked pointedly. "What's her name…Sara?"

"Sara." John's eyes dodged mine and he took a deep breath. "Yeah. That was a mistake. Nice lady, though."

I rocked back and forth on my feet, anxious to get away.

"I don't know what I was thinking," he admitted. "I spent the last ten years tending to Meredith. It's hard to know what to do with myself."

I didn't know how that fit into the Sara thing, but whatever.

"I'd like to talk to your mom."

I wasn't sure if that was a good idea. I couldn't predict how she'd react to things these days. "I'll tell her you asked about her," I said.

"I'd appreciate that." He looked like he wanted to say something else, but I had things to do. "So, I'll see you next week."

I headed over to the bathroom to hide out until the service started. Then I pushed through the church doors. I strolled across the parking lot and turned down a side street, retracing the steps I'd made only once before—the day Travis died. Unlike that blistering summer day at the pool, this one was crisp and cool. Now I wore jeans and a long-sleeved shirt with a hoodie, instead of swimming trunks. My bare feet were tucked inside my new black Converse as I trudged along the side of the road. This time I didn't run, and I knew exactly where I was headed.

Something heavy filled my chest as I walked past the community swimming pool. The ambulance had been right there, sirens and lights. I avoided looking up the concrete path to the entrance. Instead I made my way over to the food pantry and aimed for the abandoned building behind the Dumpster. A beat-up car was parked behind it, but I didn't see anyone. I spotted the cat first. It had dropped a few pounds since Thanksgiving, so I wasn't sure it was the same cat until I saw its dangling back paw. It slinked from the Dumpster over to a shadow of the building and disappeared from my view. As I got closer, I heard voices. It's not like I hadn't anticipated running into someone, but I had counted on Iggy being there alone. Maybe the building was a gathering place for gang members. What if they robbed me? All I had was Pop-Tarts. While I stood there debating, a couple of people rounded a corner of the building. I jolted with adrenaline, ready to run, or stop, drop, and roll, or something. The result was my body sort of twitching with my feet latched to the ground.

"Asher?" one of them called suspiciously. Iggy had always

been thin, but he appeared emaciated, like those photos of Holocaust survivors. He was with two other people, a guy wearing jeans and flannel and a girl with black boots. They looked older than high school, and I didn't recognize them. They appraised me, so I tried to play it cool.

"Hey, Iggy," I said.

Iggy fist-bumped the guy, and the couple wandered off toward the car half-hidden by the Dumpster. Iggy narrowed the distance between us. He seemed off-kilter, like the landscape shifted underneath him, maybe because his shoes were missing laces. Iggy glanced at the paper bag. "What are you doing here?"

I handed him the bag. He opened it. I'd put two packages of Pop-Tarts in there. I thought he might hand it back to me, but he didn't.

"You weren't at school," I said. I expected him to ask me how I'd found him, but he didn't.

"I'm dropping out." His eyes looked all red and droopy, but not like Mom's from crying. He was definitely on something. "I'm short credits. Unexcused absences," he said. "Screw that. I'll just get my GED or something."

The patchy grass around the brick wall had turned a golden brown. Gray sand mounds of abandoned fire-ant hills littered the ground. I wondered what the building looked like inside. "Thanks for getting that letter to me," I said.

"Letter?" he asked.

"From my mom."

"Oh, right." He shuffled his feet in the sand. "Well, you didn't turn me in to the cops."

"I didn't know it was you at first," I admitted. "I told the police Josh Llowell broke in."

Iggy said, "That's funny," but he didn't smile.

It wasn't funny since I was pretty sure Josh's dad beat him up over it, but I didn't mention that. I tried to imagine what it must be like for Iggy, trying to figure out where to sleep and what to eat. "Is this where you stay?" I asked.

"Sometimes."

I softened my voice. "Look, Iggy. Why don't you let me take you home?"

He snorted.

"Or go to Garrett's? His parents would let you—"

"God, you sound just like him."

Iggy swayed a bit, and then he maneuvered over to the brick wall where I'd taken the picture of him and the cat. I followed him. He dug the Pop-Tarts out, opened the package, and offered me one. I declined. He broke off a piece and nibbled on it. Like a rodent, I thought, and then I felt bad. I didn't want to hate him anymore.

"I see how you look at him," Iggy said. "Garrett."

Okay, maybe it was okay to hate him. "I don't know what your hang-up is with that," I said. "I'm not—"

"Right."

My foot twitched on the end of my leg. I couldn't help but wonder who else might have noticed my reactions to Garrett. Iggy took another bite of the Pop-Tart. I shook my head to clear it, to remind myself why I'd left church to find Iggy.

"Look, I know Garrett cares about you," I said. "He's just trying to help."

His words slurred a little as he responded. "Oh, he wants to help, but he has conditions. Like, if I do smack or even smoke weed, it's a deal breaker. It's like he's my mom."

"Is that so terrible?" I asked. "Wanting you to be okay? Garrett's a good guy."

"Yeah. What's a good guy like him doing with a guy like me? Huh?" Iggy laughed, all hollow. "You ever wonder about that?"

I did wonder about that. I wondered about that a lot. "You're pushing him away," I said. "Why can't you just—"

"Don't pretend like you're here because you care. It kills you, doesn't it? When he touches me," he said. "At first I thought maybe it was a religious thing with you."

I wanted to say it didn't bother me, the two of them, but that was a lie. It did. More than it should.

"But that's not it," he continued. "You know when I figured it out? That night you came to his house to study, when I was playing the guitar, it clicked."

"I have no idea what you're talking about," I said.

"Asher doesn't hate gays," Iggy spoke slowly. "He *is* gay."

The words *I'm not* swirled in my mouth, but I didn't say anything. I thought about Earl, who said everything he thought, no matter who it hurt. I clenched my teeth. "Garrett's too good for you," I said. "He deserves better."

"Like you?"

I felt like pounding him, but there was no point. I didn't come here to argue. His plan involved staying homeless, breaking up with Garrett, and getting his GED. Who can argue with that? "I'm going," I said as I stood up.

"Don't act like you're better than me," he said.

"I never said I was."

Iggy held the bag up. "Thanks for the Pop-Tarts. Seriously good deed. You should feel good about it."

Screw you.

❖

I arrived back at church just before the first service ended. I wanted to disappear somewhere, but the second I walked into the vestibule I saw John and my dad talking.

Crap.

Garrett sidled up next to me as I resigned myself to moving toward Dad and John. Garrett scanned my face, like my conversation with Iggy might be visible to him.

"Someone saw you walk off," he explained. "They called your dad. Are you okay?"

"Yeah."

"Where were you?" he pressed.

I kept my eyes forward. I didn't want Garrett reading my expression. He was far too good at that. "With Iggy."

Mixed emotions flickered across Garrett's face. "Okay," he said, and I wanted to tell him how lost Iggy was, how it was worse than we thought, but it was too late. Dad spotted me. His mouth formed a straight disapproving line. I scrambled for a story.

"We need to talk," Dad said, and he glanced at Garrett. "In private."

Garrett gave me a slight nod and backed away to give us space, but Dad didn't intend to talk in public. I followed him to this small side room that served as a library. A tall bookshelf filled two walls, and it only had space for a small table and two chairs.

He closed the door behind us. "You lied," he said wearily.

I sank down into the chair and folded my hands together in front of me. I'd asked Dad to take me to church. I'd told John I had something to do. Technically, I didn't lie.

"Where were you?"

"I was checking on someone," I said.

"Someone?"

I weighed my options. Should I tell him about Iggy? How much? I felt like I was in way over my head. Nothing felt clear in this. Dad's steady hands rested at his sides. He always seemed so certain. Sometimes when you tell adults things, they try to fix it without even asking if that's what you want, but I just felt tired. "There's a guy from school who's been missing, and I had a hunch where he'd be. I wanted to check it out."

"And the Pop-Tarts?" he asked.

"I wasn't sure if he was eating."

Dad rubbed his hand against his face. "I thought you were bringing them to share at youth group."

"I never said that."

"You never say anything," he said wearily. "That's the problem." Dad sat down in the chair across from me. He leaned on the table. "If you wanted to check on someone, why didn't you just tell me that?"

I shrugged.

"Did you think I'd say no? That I wouldn't help you?"

There was too much wrapped up in it. The photograph, Iggy's break-in, his relationship with Garrett…how could Dad help me with any of it?

He reached across the table and took my hand. "If you're worried about a friend from school and want to help him, we can help you do that." His grip felt warm and solid.

"I never said he was a friend," I said, but I didn't pull my hand away from Dad.

"Not a friend?"

"No. We sort of hate each other, but I owe him."

Dad processed that. I expected him to ask why we hated each

other, why I owed him. I was all set to shut Dad out, but he nodded like he understood. There was no way he could possibly understand. "Did you find him?" he asked.

I hesitated a second before nodding.

"And is he okay?"

I considered Iggy's slurred speech and haggard appearance. He didn't seem okay at all. I'd kept his hiding spot a secret, but now I wasn't sure I'd done the right thing. "I don't think so."

Dad squeezed my hand. "Does he have someplace to stay? Is he safe? That's the most important thing."

"He has places he can go, but I don't think he wants to."

Then Dad leaned back in his chair and clasped his hands together. He was silent for a bit and closed his eyes. I couldn't tell if he was thinking or praying. I'm not sure there's a difference. Finally, he said, "Asher, I don't want to tell you what to do, but if this kid isn't safe, we have to do something about it."

We.

I knew he was right.

Dad asked me to join him in the contemporary service, but I told him I needed some time alone to think. I stayed in the library, resting my head on the table until the sounds of people mingling died down. I wasn't ready to face John. I didn't know how to explain myself. Maybe Dad would do it for me, but I didn't trust him to say the right thing. I thought about Mom and how, if she were here, I'd be home already, sitting in my room. I pulled out my phone and sent a text message to her. *I love you.*

I did. And I missed her, too.

She wrote back. *I love you, too. Are you okay?*

Yeah. Not the same without you, but okay.

A knock sounded at the door, and I tucked my phone into my pocket. Garrett peeked in. "Can we talk?" he asked.

"Sure."

Garrett closed the door behind him and restlessly patted his stomach a few times. His shirt read, *No Jesus, No Peace.* It fit snug, showing off his build. He waited for me to say something, but I didn't, so he scanned the titles of the books. He pulled one off the shelf, flipped through it, and put it back. Finally he took a seat. "So," he said. "You were with Iggy." Garrett's brown eyes searched my face. He looked so concerned, sitting across from me. Something cold ran through my veins, seeing Garrett worried about Iggy, desperate for news.

"I was going to bring him something to eat and try to get him to go home, but he wouldn't listen."

"You know where he is?"

"Yeah."

Garrett held his hands open toward me, like he was physically pleading for more information. I relented.

"He's been hiding out in this abandoned building over by the food pantry," I said.

He shook his head, an expression of disbelief on his face. "How long? I mean, was this last week or what?"

"Thanksgiving."

"Thanksgiving?" Garrett covered his face with his hands. "And you knew about this?"

I nodded.

"Why didn't you just tell me?"

I'd convinced myself I was keeping Iggy's secret, that I was doing him a favor. Maybe I'd hoped Iggy would disappear. Whatever the reason, it hadn't stopped me from taking his picture. I thought about Rose and how worried Iggy's family must be. Of course Garrett would be furious with me. I decided to tell him everything. "He's planning on dropping out of school, Garrett. He's using drugs, too."

Garrett crossed his arms in front of him. "And you're okay with that?"

"No, I'm not *okay* with that. I told my dad. We've got to figure out what to do. He won't go home. I tried to convince him to talk to you—"

"Really? Convincing him to talk to me? Well, that's nice, Asher." The sarcasm in his voice was completely foreign to what I'd grown to expect from Garrett. "Don't you think he'd rather talk to you?"

I was at a complete loss. He waited for me to respond, but all I could manage was a stupid sounding, "Uh?"

"I thought you hated each other," Garrett accused me, and then the sarcastic front fell. His eyes pleaded with me. "You know, when you said he wasn't my type, I never thought you meant he was yours."

Whoa.

"You said you weren't..." he whispered. His eyes filled up with tears. "You said you weren't gay."

I was too astounded to say anything. He wiped his eyes with the hem of his shirt, revealing his stomach. I smiled, but my eyes burned, too.

"You think this is funny?" he demanded.

"No," I said because I felt like crying, too. "You think I like Iggy?"

"Don't you?"

"No," I choked out. "I can't stand him. But I owe him." And suddenly, it felt like the floodgates inside me burst open. In a torrent, I found myself explaining it all: the photo from Thanksgiving, how Iggy found the suicide letter my mom left for me, and how he trekked to my dad's house to deliver it to me, even though he hated me. Garrett listened while I explained why I couldn't release the photograph and why I felt like I needed to help Iggy.

"So you and Iggy aren't...?"

I'd never seen him so vulnerable. I got up from my chair and walked around to where he was sitting. "No."

Garrett hid his face. "I feel so stupid," he said through his fingers.

I knelt down beside him, wrapped my hands around his wrist, and gently pulled his hands away from his face. I'd meant to comfort him, but the moment our skin met, my heart started thudding. I shook my head slightly from side to side, a feeble effort to clear it, but our hands touched, and our fingers entwined. My face shifted closer to his until our mouths were only inches apart. I could feel his breath against my face. Every cell in my body ached for him.

I could tell he wanted me, too, but Garrett didn't move a muscle. "I won't kiss you," he whispered.

I hovered, suspended next to him.

"It's up to you, Asher."

I swallowed at the effort of controlling myself.

He won't kiss me.

It's up to me.

All I had to do was lean forward and I could feel his lips against mine. He'd let me, but it was up to me. His lips were so close. My body shivered. And then I pressed my lips against his. A tremor rippled through my body at the feel of my mouth against his, but just as quickly as it started, Garrett pulled away.

I staggered back. I struggled to catch my breath.

Garrett mirrored me, his eyes wide and searching, his breath coming fast. "Tell me you feel that with Kayla," he demanded.

"No."

"Jennifer?"

I shook my head. "No."

It was everything I could do not to lunge back to him, but I reminded myself he had pulled away from me. "What about you?" I asked. "Is that how it is with Iggy?"

He ran a shaky hand through his hair. "No. Never."

I struggled to get a grip. I was still quivering. Was this how Levi felt about Jennifer? "You pulled away," I said.

"Trust me. I didn't want to," he said. "I need for you to be sure, Asher. I can't go through this again."

Again? "What about Iggy?" I asked.

He shook his head. "I haven't even seen him since before Christmas," he said. "He pushed me away a while ago."

My brain raced. I couldn't wrap my head around our conversation. My nerves were too close to the surface. Garrett said I had to be sure, but I wasn't sure of anything.

He added, "This doesn't mean I don't care about what happens to Iggy."

I bit my lip. Guilt started creeping up in me when I thought about how far my mind was from Iggy just a minute before. "What are we doing?" I cried, covering my face with my hands. Images of Iggy overdosing in the abandoned brick building surfaced in my mind. Travis died while I was kissing Garrett. Who was to say this wasn't the same?

"Don't," Garrett said. He scrambled over to me and took my hand. I thought I might hyperventilate, my breath was coming so fast.

"Please. Asher."

My hand felt warm in his.

"Don't do this," he whispered, then he cradled my head against his chest. "Shh. It's okay."

The pace of my pulse slowly decreased. How was it that being close to him could affect me in so many different ways? I hesitated only a moment, and then blurted, "I say I'm worried about Iggy, but look at me."

"Yes, look at you," he said, and he was so sincere it made my heart hurt. "The guy who always tries to do the right thing."

I wished I could see me like he did, but I was pretty sure kissing in the church library didn't rate among the right things to do. It would be so easy to just ignore it all since Iggy didn't want help anyway. It didn't ease my conscience.

"Asher," he said. "It's not your fault that Iggy refused help. You aren't the first person to try to help him."

I pulled away from Garrett so I could see his face. "Should I call his parents?" I asked.

He considered that for a moment. "I'm pretty sure they know."

"Why don't they *do* anything?" If Iggy refused to get help, what were our options? Call the police? Iggy had just thanked me for not calling the cops on him for breaking into my house, and now I'd kissed his boyfriend. Was I supposed to call the police now? "I can't turn him in," I said. He'd know I was the one who called. He'd think it was tied up with my feelings for Garrett. He'd tell everyone, and he'd be right.

"What if he dies from an overdose or something?" Garrett said, mirroring my own fears. "I can't live with that on me."

But I already knew what it felt like to be responsible for someone's death, and whether you want to or not, you live.

CHAPTER TWENTY-FIVE

Iggy's house didn't smell like I thought it would. I'd assumed he lived in squalor, sort of like how he looked, but I was wrong. His house smelled like fresh-baked cookies.

I tried to find traces of Rose's fairylike grace or maybe Iggy's saunter in Iggy's mom, but aside from the shape of all of their mouths—thin—no resemblance existed. Iggy's mom was thick and solid, like a hefty tree trunk. While Rose's pixie cut fit her face, this woman's short hair made her look like she might work in a prison, but she smelled like vanilla. Iggy's mom sat across the table from Dad and me, her eyes big like she lived in perpetual surprise. Or maybe like nothing surprised her at all anymore.

"The doctor prescribed meds for depression, but he didn't like how they made him feel," she said. "He was better on the pills."

I thought of Mom and her pills. Was she better? I wasn't sure.

"When he took that money from his job, I wanted them to press charges. Maybe he'd finally understand. But they didn't." She said it like his stealing was common knowledge, but it was the first I'd heard of it. Iggy had worked at the local grocery store, but I thought he had quit that job. It made me think of how Dad assumed everyone knew Travis wasn't his. Maybe they didn't. Maybe people were too concerned about their own stories to pay attention to anyone else's.

A picture of Iggy and Rose hung on the wall right above the mom's head. Iggy's hair was short, his brown eyes wide like his mom's. You didn't see much of Iggy's eyes these days with his hair hanging like a curtain.

Dad squeezed my shoulder. "Asher says he's been living on his own," he said.

"I told him if he ever brought drugs into the house, he was out. That's not as easy as it sounds. Money started disappearing from my purse. The ring my mom left for Rose went missing. And when I confronted Iggy"—the way his name sounded from her mouth made me realize how much she loved him—"Rose begged to let him stay. They say the addiction takes over. I try to remind myself of that. It helps."

We heard the front door open and slam. "Mom?" Rose raced into the room and stopped when she saw us.

"Is he okay?" she asked her mom.

"He's not dead," Iggy's mom said, her voice tired.

Rose reminded me of a bird, poised on a branch, all set to take flight. Her mom motioned her over to the empty seat beside her. I wondered what it would feel like, waiting weeks for the news that your brother had died, instead of minutes. What if someone could have told me how to save Travis?

"I know where he is and I know what he's doing," I said.

"Is he still at Wild Bill's?" Rose asked. "He was sleeping on the floor there for a while."

Wild Bill's? I imagined the run-down house across from the post office, the sagging, leaking roof and the porch covered with vines. Bill was certified crazy and an alcoholic.

"Bill had to tell him to leave," the mom said. "He was shooting up."

Shooting up?

"He's over at that abandoned brick building by the homeless shelter," I said. "I'm pretty sure he was on something when I saw him. I thought maybe you would want to go get him or something."

Rose made a small squeaking noise, and her mom reached over and clutched her hand, like they were holding each other together. "Asher, we've tried. He can't come home. He'll tear us apart. I can't tell you how hard this is," Iggy's mom said, "but if you think he has drugs on him, you should call the police."

❖

I loaded the film into the camera while Levi sat on the kitchen counter, chowing down on Doritos.

"He didn't resist or anything," Levi said, spewing crumbs. "No one's bailed him out either. Man, that would suck, sitting in a jail cell."

"Make sure you wash your hands before you touch the reflector."

Levi licked his fingers and took a swig of Gatorade. I clipped the bag and stored it in the cupboard.

"I wasn't done." Levi protested.

I ignored him. Pearl would have my ass if he got cheese marks on her equipment. We had work to do.

"Later," I said. "Come on."

Pearl must have been watching for us, because her front door swung open before I had a chance to knock. "School gets out at three. Where the hell have you been?" she asked.

I glanced at my phone. It wasn't even four yet.

"We had to stop and kick a few puppies on the way over," Levi said. "You know, because we're bad kids."

Great job, Levi.

Pearl pointed a bony finger at him. "Look here, smart-ass, I—"

"He's an idiot. No one listens to him."

Levi's jaw dropped. "Excuse me?"

"The photos," I said with clenched teeth.

"Hey, I'm here doing you a favor," Levi ranted, standing stubbornly on the front step of Pearl's house. "You think I want to spend my afternoon playing your assistant? I've got—"

Pearl reached over and smacked his cheek. It wasn't a hard smack, but it was enough to startle Levi into silence. "Okay," Pearl said. "That's better. Come on in."

Levi followed me inside. He was sort of dazed. "She hit me," he whispered, his palm resting against the side of his face.

"I know."

"You owe me," he grumbled.

Pearl led us over to the coffee table. The reflector and tripod leaned up against the sofa. Levi reluctantly headed over to gather the equipment. "I've got a lens here. It should do," Pearl said. "And I got another letter from *Photographer's Lens*." She held it up with a shaky hand. Of course, it was already opened. "They haven't received that signed form back yet," she said. "They can't officially reward you until—"

"I'm dropping out of the contest," I said.

Pearl blinked at me. Levi paused midmotion and turned to me. He rested the equipment back against the sofa and stood to his full height. "Wait, that photo thing?" he said. "You're not doing it?"

Pearl huffed and crossed her arms across her bathrobed chest.

"I never got permission to take the photo," I said. "I can't enter it. Maybe I can enter a different shot?"

I'd never seen Pearl look so angry. "The deadline's passed to enter," Pearl said. "The rest are crap."

"Thanks," I said, and then I went ahead, even though I knew it would make her angrier. "Why didn't you ask me first? You just entered a contest without even asking me about it."

She raised her voice. "We talked about it."

"No, we didn't. You said it was the best of the photos I took, but you didn't say anything about entering it in a contest."

Pearl put her hands on her hips and jutted her chin out toward me. "Well, don't worry. I won't waste my time on you again," Pearl said. "Take the damn equipment." She shuffled out of the room. "Lock the door behind you," she called.

Great. Something tugged at me, but I'd said the truth. She shouldn't have done it without talking to me about it. Levi rested the equipment back on the floor. "What?" I asked.

He motioned after Pearl, like I should go chase her down, which was ridiculous since she hadn't even gotten out of the room yet.

"I'm not going to apologize," I said.

Pearl dismissed me with a wave of her hand as she continued to waddle out of the room. "I don't want your damn apology!"

"She's old," Levi hissed.

"She hit you," I hissed back.

He scowled at me, like he was so disappointed. Then he plopped onto the couch like he wasn't moving until I fixed things. By that time, Pearl had rounded the corner. I followed her into the hallway. "Pearl?"

She ignored me and opened the door to the darkroom.

I glanced back over my shoulder. I didn't want Levi hearing. "About the photo," I said. "Can I talk to you?"

Her eyes narrowed suspiciously, but then she led me into the darkroom, turned on the light, and closed the door behind us.

"The guy in the picture doesn't know I took the photo. He doesn't know it was entered in the contest or anything. I can't ask him."

"Can't or won't?" she asked.

I thought about that. Iggy was in jail. It was my fault. Plus I still owed him from what happened to my mom. "Both," I said. "It's complicated."

"Why don't you just ask him?"

"I can't," I said, and I tried to think about why that was. "He hates me."

Pearl humphed. "You do something to him? What, you stealing again?"

Again? Jeez. "I never took—"

"You doing drugs? Is he your dealer?"

"What? No."

"What the hell is wrong with—"

"He knows I'm gay," I blurted.

Pearl stared at me for a long time. I didn't realize it was true until I'd said it out loud. I swallowed and blinked back the stupid tears that threatened to spring up in my eyes and waited for her to say something, anything. I searched the spaces in my brain and stood in the florescent overhead light of the darkroom, waiting for Pearl. Maybe she'd call me a pervert and tell me to leave. I wouldn't put it past her.

"Who the hell cares how you get your jollies?" she said curtly. "Now, go get the equipment. And try not to do a crappy job this time."

❖

Ms. Hughes offered extra credit to anyone who was going to the art exhibit. Of course, we had to do a write-up of one of the pieces and staple the program to it in order to prove we'd actually gone. It was only ten points, but I noticed Josh jotted the date down in his folder. With basketball starting, he needed to be eligible.

The bell rang.

As I tucked the art form into my folder, Garrett showed up next to my desk. I fumbled, and my pencil fell on the floor. He picked it up and handed it to me. The plaid shirt he wore would have looked goofy on anyone else, but he made it look effortlessly hip. Everything about him made me feel off balance.

"So you made a decision about Iggy," he said as we headed out into the hallway.

Even the sound of his voice made my nerves stand on end. I felt the distance between my arm and his as we moved through the crowd. "I met with his mom," I said. "She told me to make the call."

"I feel like I let him down," Garrett said. "Maybe I should have gone to him, you know? Talked him into going into rehab or something."

My internal organs twisted. Guilt. I understood that. The words Iggy had said about Garrett surged to the surface of my brain. I couldn't tell Garrett how I'd confirmed Iggy's doubts: *He's too good for you.* But maybe I was wrong. Who was I to make that call? What Iggy said had more to do with hurting me than Garrett.

"Levi thinks he'll end up in rehab anyway. I don't think Iggy wanted help," I said as I stopped at my locker.

"No." Garrett tilted his head. "Still, calling the police, it's a tough choice to make. You doing okay?"

I'd been thinking about Iggy a lot. According to Levi, no one had bailed him out. I couldn't imagine what that would be like. But then there are all sorts of prisons, I guess. Mom carried hers around with her. "I think so. I feel bad, but I don't know what else I could've done," I said as I twirled the combination lock.

"You could have done nothing," he said, and the way he said it made me think he wasn't really talking about me.

I yanked up on the handle, but it didn't open. Must have dialed incorrectly. I tried again. "I've known he was in trouble a long time," I said, thinking about Thanksgiving. "I didn't do anything." Finally the locker opened.

"Neither did I. So what does that make me?"

I placed my folder in my book bag and pulled out my thick biology textbook. When I closed the metal door, I turned to look at Garrett. He leaned against the locker next to mine, an arm hanging loosely at his side, his notebook tucked under his chin. He raised his eyes to me. "His guitar is still at my house. It just sits there against my wall," he said. "I didn't want him to hate me, so I didn't do anything. I told myself he was okay."

People told themselves all sorts of lies. Sometimes lies were easier than the truth.

"Do you think they let people visit him?" Garrett added.

Visit him? "You want to go see him? In jail?" I kept my voice measured, steady.

Garrett leaned his head back against the locker. "I don't know. Maybe? I just feel so bad about it all. Can you imagine how awful it is to be locked up like that?"

I'd been thinking about it, too, but I hadn't considered visiting him. Just because I didn't want him dead didn't mean I wanted to be his new best friend. "He hates me. This sealed it. You know that, right?" I said.

Garrett lowered his voice. "Yes, but can you imagine?"

Imagine what? How Iggy felt?

"I want to do this right," he said.

"This?" I asked.

He lowered his voice. "Us."

I wasn't sure there was an *us*. I hadn't figured that out. Okay, so I was pretty sure I was gay, but I didn't know what that meant. I wasn't ready for a relationship. What would that do to my mom? Two sons: one dies and the other turns out to be gay. She'd hidden Aunt Sharon's sexuality from me my whole life. What did that mean? "Garrett, I need time to think this through," I said.

"Me, too," he said. "We'll take things slow. And we can help each other now, right?"

Take things slow…it reminded me of how John described his relationship with Sara to my mom. Could you take things slowly? One time Dad claimed Helen encouraged him to do the right thing. She had tried to help him, but they had that attraction. Was it just an excuse to be together? Wasn't the result the same?

Garrett stepped out into the stream of people in the hallway. "I'm really glad we talked. You always understand."

People justified their actions. I couldn't figure out if Garrett and I were doing the same thing.

CHAPTER TWENTY-SIX

Slick sweat collected under my arms even though I'd applied plenty of deodorant. The temperature in the library seemed cool enough, so it must have been my nerves. I'd kept my coat jacket on so no one would see how drenched I was. I cautiously sniffed at my armpit. At least I didn't stink.

The reporter was due to arrive any minute. I couldn't figure out why the newspaper was interested anyway, but whatever. Mrs. O'Flaherty fussed over the display, inching the photographs miniscule amounts to the left and right. My stomach rolled and grumbled. I started for the bathroom, but the art teacher stopped me.

"Where are you going?" she asked.

"Bathroom."

She glanced at the clock on the wall and grimaced. "Okay," she said. "But hurry."

I rolled my eyes. I didn't need her permission. We weren't at school. And even if we were, I had no intention of making headlines for crapping my pants. When I returned, Mrs. O'Flaherty was chatting with a guy wearing jeans and a polo. He had a digital camera swinging around his neck. I hoped he didn't plan to take my picture.

"This is Asher," Mrs. O'Flaherty said, nudging my arm.

I extended my sweaty hand.

"Hey, I'm Tom," the reporter said. He smelled like hot dogs, and he had what I guessed was a ketchup stain on his shirt. "So, these are your photos?"

"Yeah."

"Nice."

I'd consulted Pearl first. She recommended that I opt out of the exhibit altogether since everything except the Iggy shot was crap. After that, I asked Mrs. O'Flaherty. She suggested I divide the display into three sections—one highlighting favorites from my early black-and-white photographs, the second including color, candid shots, and the last section inspired by my visit to the Art Institute.

The reporter looked over the display for a few minutes, and then he took out a pad of paper. "Mind if we sit down somewhere?" he asked.

The library renovation had included these nooks where people could huddle up with a book. We settled into one of those, two chairs facing a window overlooking a playground. I unbuttoned my jacket.

"Okay," Tom said. "So tell me how you got started with photography."

I cleared my throat and told him about my aunt sending me a Minolta, and how I picked the last roll of black-and-white film off the shelf at the grocery store. He scribbled notes.

"You don't do digital at all?" he asked.

"No."

"Why?"

"I don't know. Maybe because people change the images," I said. "With film, it just is what it is."

He nodded, and then asked, "Now, are all those taken with a Minolta?"

"No." I didn't mention tossing the camera into the pool. "My neighbor used to be a photographer, kind of a big deal, actually. Anyway, she let me borrow her Canon A-1 and taught me some things. She lets me use her equipment."

"Lucky you!"

I thought about Pearl's rancid turkey and said, "Yeah."

"Tell me about the color photos, the candid shots."

I thought about the first candid—of Dad and Helen—and how I'd chucked the camera into the pool. But that was black and white. My first color candid was of mom, sleeping.

"Yeah, uh…really that was my mom. She'd been pushing me to try color."

He wrote a few more things down, and then he took a deep breath. "You know I'm going to ask," he said.

I yanked on the sleeves of my jacket. I still didn't know how to answer the question he was going to ask me.

"Why did you turn down *Photographer's Lens*?"

I thought about Iggy. "I didn't enter the photo. Someone else entered it for me," I explained. "So yeah. That was it."

"I see. But you"—he reviewed his notes—"you were a finalist, right? That's a big deal. Most people would be pretty excited about that."

My knee bounced. I shrugged.

"Is it a shot you wouldn't have chosen? Is it something embarrassing?" He pressed for details.

I admitted, "I took the picture without getting permission."

"So the person in the photograph wouldn't sign off? They didn't want everyone to see them?"

"The person in the photograph doesn't know I took the picture."

Tom tapped his pencil against his notepad and chewed a bit on his lip before he asked, "And when you found out you won, you didn't ask if you could use it?"

"No."

He raised his eyebrows. "And it's not out there on display?"

"No."

Tom looked off into the distance for a moment, and then he asked, "What's in the picture?"

I just sat there. I wasn't going to tell him.

He chuckled. "Okay. Then can you tell me why?" When I didn't answer after a lengthy pause, he coaxed, "Was it because you didn't want the person to know you took the picture?"

"No."

"Was it because of who it was?"

"Uh, not really."

"Or maybe what they were doing?"

Jeez.

"Because most people wouldn't turn down an opportunity to receive that type of recognition. *I* wouldn't turn it down." He opened his arms wide. "I'm just trying to understand."

I shifted in my seat. I remembered the feel of my finger pressing the button on the Canon A-1, the feel of my finger on the trigger, and said, "It's just, sometimes when you take a shot, you don't stop to think if you should."

He smiled at me and jotted something else down on the notepad. "Okay," he said. "Now how about we get a photo of you for the paper."

Great.

❖

Dad, Helen, and her folks arrived first. I saw them enter through the front, but apparently they didn't want all the other kids to think they'd just come to see me because they visited every exhibit. Earl ignored them and used his walker to nudge people out of his way.

"Photography?" he asked, looking at my display. He waved his hand dismissively at the pictures. "You like this kind of thing?"

I nodded.

"Sort of a sissy thing to do, don't you think?" Earl said, then he tilted his head toward the center section. "She's cute."

He meant Jennifer.

"Did she let you kiss her? Bet they'll let you kiss 'em if you take their picture. She your girlfriend?"

"Just a friend," I said.

He leaned heavily against the walker. "Your dad says you don't want the Python." His face was lined with disappointment. "When my daddy gave it to me, it was one of the proudest days of my life. I love my girls, don't get me wrong, but I'm no good to my daughters. Now, a son. Got a lot of stuff to offer a boy, you know?" His eyes got kind of wistful.

I clutched my hands in front of me. "I didn't know what I was doing with it," I admitted. "It sort of scared me."

"If it didn't, I'd think you were an idiot," he said, and then he eyed my photographs. "How'd that picture of me turn out? I'm an ugly bastard, right?"

I laughed. "I've got it at home. I'll bring it to Dad's on Sunday and show you," I said.

He nodded thoughtfully. "You still want to learn how to shoot a gun? Every boy should know how to shoot a gun."

"Can I bring my friend Levi with me? I think you'd like him."

Dad, Helen, and Penny wandered up.

"You think it's okay if we take Levi and Asher to the range sometime?" Earl asked.

Dad wrapped a protective arm around Helen while he tried to read my expression. I nodded. "I think we can arrange that."

"There are some really talented students at your school," Helen noted. "I'm impressed. Did you see the anime drawings?"

Pride welled up in me. Of course I had seen them. "That's Garrett," I said.

"Right, your friend," Dad said. "Nice family."

They quietly took in the photographs, starting with the early black and whites. Even though it wasn't my best work, I'd included the curved pine tree. If Dad remembered the day I took the photo, he didn't show it. They talked about the candid shots, the perspective. But when they got to the last section, Helen grabbed Dad's hand tightly. His face contorted with the effort to restrain emotion.

"Nice job, sport," Dad said, but he wouldn't meet my eyes.

"We're going to go, okay?" Helen said. "Call us if you need anything. I heard there was some nasty weather up north."

Jennifer dragged Levi to the exhibit, but rather than check out the other artists, they came straight to me. "There I am!" Jennifer said, pointing to the candid shots from the homecoming game. "And my head shot."

Pearl thought they were crap. She preferred the photo I'd taken of Kayla—the one where I thought she was staring at Jennifer. Turns out she hadn't been looking at Jennifer at all. It wasn't until the photo was developed that I realized the focus of Kayla's attention was actually Josh. He's barely visible, blurred, but I'd decided to include the photo in the Jennifer shots. Since the others contained Jennifer, the viewer's eye focused on finding her in the image. You couldn't tell what was really going on unless you studied the photo separate from the others.

Jennifer handed Levi her phone and told him to take her picture in front of the display. She feigned a surprised expression, like *Oh my gosh, pictures of me!* She positioned her hands on either side of her face because apparently that's what people do when they're surprised. She tried to convince me to pose in a picture with her, but I refused.

Levi evaluated the photos by whether or not he'd been present for them.

"I was there for that one," he said, pointing, "and this one, and—"

"Don't touch them," I said.

He paused at the photo of the Budweiser sign. "I forgot to tell you that Mom let me put the sign up."

"Cool."

Jennifer tugged at his hand. She was already looking at the pictures in the last section. They studied the photographs together, Jennifer's eyebrows scrunched together. Levi sniffed and wiped his nose on his sleeve.

"It's beautiful," Jennifer said, blinking. "It really is."

"Thanks."

Levi had his bulldog face on. He sideways hugged me, patted me on the shoulder, and said, "They turned out good."

A few people I didn't know stopped and looked at the photos. Some of them asked me questions about inspiration and details in the photos themselves. It was easy to talk about the black-and-white photos now, what I'd tried to capture and why. Talking about Jennifer and techniques was easy, too. One guy once worked for a photographer up in Georgia. We chatted for a while, but my eyes kept shifting to the door.

Josh only came to the exhibit for a few minutes. He grabbed one of the programs and did a quick walk-through. I knew he'd have to review one of the pieces to get extra credit, and I was wondering if anyone had nudes on display anywhere since that might interest him. He stopped by my display and stared at the photos for a long time. I hesitated to talk to him but decided this might be my only shot. "Did you decide what you're going to write about yet?" I asked.

"Probably this one," he said.

It was one of the pictures from the homecoming game. It figured he'd pick that one since he was visible in the background.

"My rock-star brother was in town," he said. "Evan."

Like I didn't know who Evan Llowell was.

"See that? I wasn't in the homecoming court. Just standing off to the side. They've got this wall in our house with pictures of Evan. Awards, newspaper clippings."

If it was tough for Josh, I could only imagine what it was like for

Vince to live in the shadow of both his brothers. Still, it sucked. Maybe it was easier when you were like Vince and no one even bothered to compare. I thought about apologizing for Christmas again, but something told me that would be a mistake. Instead I pointed out Kayla in the foreground of the photo.

He squinted at it. "Is she looking at me?" he asked. "I don't get her. You know, I've been nothing but nice to her. Why does she hate me?"

Nice to her? I guess to him it must seem that way. I tried to find the truth of it.

"I don't think it's about you," I said.

Kayla would kill me if she found out I'd said that to Josh, but it seemed like the truth.

"What do you mean?" he asked.

There was no way I was answering that.

Josh lowered his voice. "Is there something between you guys? I can't figure it out."

"We're just friends," I said.

"There's something about her," he said, rubbing his hand along the back of his thick neck. "Even with all the creepy Satan-worship stuff."

"Uh, I'm pretty sure she doesn't worship Satan."

"It's weird. I like her, you know? But she makes me feel like an idiot." He stared at the photograph. "Maybe you could put a good word in for me."

Was he kidding? He'd made my life hell through middle school. He treated his little brother, Vince, like a lethal virus. He was the *reason* Kayla had an abortion. Still, I found myself feeling sort of sorry for him. "I'll do what I can," I said, "but I can't make any promises. Kayla thinks for herself."

He grinned. Obviously he liked that about her. "Thanks. Seriously, it means a lot," he said and wandered off into the crowd.

Only twenty minutes of the exhibit remained. I was beginning to think I was going to have to call Dad and have him pick me up, but then the door opened. When Aunt Sharon, Carol, and Mom walked in, the full impact of how much I'd missed her hit me. She'd put on some weight, and she'd gotten her hair cut into a stylish bob. I ignored what Mrs. O'Flaherty told me about staying by my display and nudged my way through the crowd to where they stood, searching for me. "Mom," I said.

Her eyes lit up when she saw me, and she threw her arms around me. Normally I would rather have a sharp stick poked in my eye than hug my mom in public, but now I didn't care. She pulled back and put her hands on both sides of my face. "Look at you!" she said, wiping tears from her eyes. "I swore I wouldn't do this. But, Asher, you're taller."

I grinned at her. I didn't care if she was crying. "You look amazing, Mom."

Mom turned and grabbed Carol's and Aunt Sharon's hands. "These girls have been taking good care of me."

"I can tell," I hugged each of them. "How was the flight?"

"We had a delay," Aunt Sharon said. "Good thing I booked a morning flight. We actually came here straight from the airport."

"Wow."

"I came to see these photographs," Carol said. "Where is your exhibit?"

"It's in the back," I said. "But first, Mom, there's a section that was inspired by our trip to the Art Institute. Did you see the section on childhood?"

She nodded.

"Yeah," I said. "I just wanted to let you know."

"Okay."

Aunt Sharon squeezed her.

"I'm okay!" she assured us.

My eyes met Garrett's as I led them through the crowd. I motioned toward my mom and he gave me a thumbs-up as I moved to where the photographs were located. Aunt Sharon and Carol looked at all the photos, but Mom stared at the section I called *What is Left*. One photo captured the stack of dirty clothes in Travis's closet. The bulb from above had been too bright, but Levi used Pearl's reflector and a sheet to diffuse it so I could take the picture. I called that one *Clean*. There's a photo of Travis's stuffed dog, Og. The light from the bedroom window illuminated his faded fur and the wide stitches where Mom had repaired him when he'd burst at the seams. I titled it *Saved*.

I watched Mom closely as she looked at the one of his book bag, his baseball glove, and his toothbrush. She nodded with understanding, a pained expression on her face, but not like it used to be. A different pain. She still cried. I wrapped an arm around her, and she leaned into me. "It's perfect," she whispered, and patted my arm.

It wasn't perfect.

I saw the flaws in lighting and perspective.

It wasn't my best work, and it would never be featured in a real gallery or earn an award, but I didn't take photos to impress anyone. I'd captured the truth.

About the Author

Elizabeth Wheeler's passion for writing, directing, and teaching is driven by a quest to unleash the authentic human experience in literature, on the stage, and in life. As a teacher, she is touched and inspired by the real-world examples of how students, facing adversity, assimilate the lessons learned from those experiences to persevere and transform into triumphant adults. A former Chicago model and actor, Elizabeth now teaches English in rural Illinois. She is a graduate of the University of Florida and the inaugural novel writing program at the University of Chicago's Graham School. As an advocate for student storytelling in the print and digital world, she has spoken internationally as well as at educational conferences in Illinois. Elizabeth is co-founder of a professional theater company, Heart and Soul Productions, and director of her school's drama program. A fifth generation Floridian, Elizabeth now lives in Illinois with her husband and two sons.

Soliloquy Titles From Bold Strokes Books

Driving Lessons by Annameekee Hesik. Dive into Abbey Brooks's sophomore year as she attempts to figure out the amazing, but sometimes complicated, life of a you-know-who girl at Gila High School. (978-1-62639-228-1)

Asher's Shot by Elizabeth Wheeler. Asher Price's candid photographs capture the truth, but when his success requires exposing an enemy, Asher discovers his only shot at happiness involves revealing secrets of his own. (978-1-62639-229-8)

The Melody of Light by M.L. Rice. After surviving abuse and loss, will Riley Gordon be able to navigate her first year of college and accept true love and family? (78-1-62639-219-9)

Maxine Wore Black by Nora Olsen. Jayla will do anything for Maxine, the girl of her dreams, but after becoming ensnared in Maxine's dark secrets, she'll have to choose between love and her own life. (978-1-62639-208-3)

Bottled Up Secret by Brian McNamara. When Brendan Madden befriends his gorgeous, athletic classmate, Mark, it doesn't take long for Brendan to fall head over heels for him—but will Mark reciprocate the feelings? (978-1-62639-209-0)

Searching for Grace by Juliann Rich. First it's a rumor. Then it's a fact. And then it's on. (978-1-62639-196-3)

Dark Tide by Greg Herren. A summer working as a lifeguard at a hotel on the Gulf Coast seems like a dream job...until Ricky Hackworth realizes the town is shielding some very dark—and deadly—secrets. (978-1-62639-197-0)

Everything Changes by Samantha Hale. Raven Walker's world is turned upside down the moment Morgan O'Shea walks into her life. (978-1-62639-303-5)

Fifty Yards and Holding by David Matthew-Barnes. The discovery of a secret relationship between Riley Brewer, the star of the high school baseball team, and Victor Alvarez, the leader of a violent street gang, escalates into a preventable tragedy. (978-1-62639-081-2)

Tristant and Elijah by Jennifer Lavoie. After Elijah finds a scandalous letter belonging to Tristant's great-uncle, the boys set out to discover the secret Uncle Glenn kept hidden his entire life and end up discovering who they are in the process. (978-1-62639-075-1)

Caught in the Crossfire by Juliann Rich. Two boys at Bible camp; one forbidden love. (978-1-62639-070-6)

Frenemy of the People by Nora Olsen. Clarissa and Lexie have despised each other for as long as they can remember, but when they both find themselves helping an unlikely contender for homecoming queen, they are catapulted into an unexpected romance. (978-1-62639-063-8)

The Balance by Neal Wooten. Love and survival come together in the distant future as Piri and Niko face off against the worst factions of mankind's evolution. (978-1-62639-055-3)

The Unwanted by Jeffrey Ricker. Jamie Thomas is plunged into danger when he discovers his mother is an Amazon who needs his help to save the tribe from a vengeful god. (978-1-62639-048-5)

Because of Her by KE Payne. When Tabby Morton is forced to move to London, she's convinced her life will never be the same again. But the beautiful and intriguing Eden Palmer is about to show her that this time, change is most definitely for the better. (978-1-62639-049-2)

The Seventh Pleiade by Andrew J. Peters. When Atlantis is besieged by violent storms, tremors, and a barbarian army, it will be up to a young gay prince to find a way for the kingdom's survival. (978-1-60282-960-2)

Asher's Fault by Elizabeth Wheeler. Fourteen-year-old Asher Price sees the world in black and white, much like the photos he takes, but when his little brother drowns at the same moment Asher experiences his first same-sex kiss, he can no longer hide behind the lens of his camera and eventually discovers he isn't the only one with a secret. (978-1-60282-982-4)

Meeting Chance by Jennifer Lavoie. When man's best friend turns on Aaron Cassidy, the teen keeps his distance until fate puts Chance in his hands. (978-1-60282-952-7)

Lake Thirteen by Greg Herren. A visit to an old cemetery seems like fun to a group of five teenagers, who soon learn that sometimes it's best to leave old ghosts alone. (978-1-60282-894-0)

The Road to Her by KE Payne. Sparks fly when actress Holly Croft, star of UK soap *Portobello Road*, meets her new on-screen love interest, the enigmatic and sexy Elise Manford. (978-1-60282-887-2)

Swans and Clons by Nora Olsen. In a future world where there are no males, sixteen-year-old Rubric and her girlfriend Salmon Jo must fight to survive when everything they believed in turns out to be a lie. (978-1-60282-874-2)

Kings of Ruin by Sam Cameron. High school student Danny Kelly and loner Kevin Clark must team up to defeat a top-secret alien intelligence that likes to wreak havoc with fiery car, truck, and train accidents. (978-1-60282-864-3)

Wonderland by David-Matthew Barnes. After her mother's sudden death, Destiny Moore is sent to live with her two gay uncles on Avalon Cove, a mysterious island on which she uncovers a secret place called Wonderland, where love and magic prove to be real. (978-1-60282-788-2)